Ian Macpherson is UK Edi[t]
Agency, and he lives and wor[k]
Orient. He is married with two children. He enjoys the
sea, the grape and practicing philosophy. *Invisibility* is
his first novel.

Ian Macpherson

Invisibility

Matador
9 De Montfort Mews
Leicester LE1 7FW, UK
Tel: (+44) 116 255 9311 / 9312
Email: books@troubador.co.uk
Web: www.troubador.co.uk/matador

ISBN 1 905237 49 9

Cover photograph and design © Andrew Farrar

Typeset in 11pt Stempel Garamond by Troubador Publishing Ltd, Leicester, UK
Printed in the UK by The Cromwell Press Ltd

Matador is an imprint of Troubador Publishing Ltd

"poor Gill, I don't know how she puts up with it..."

1

The fit young sportsman from Amnesty International's Tokyo office assumed his favourite position. Reclining the chair as far as he could, leaning back he propped his stockinged feet up on the desk. Heels together, he made a vee shape with his feet and lined his eyes up with the gap between the ankles to make an aiming sight. Settled now, very deliberately he unbent the red size six paperclip and stretched the Double Strength Mura 20mm rubber band between the tips of his left thumb and first finger. Breathing in slowly, he pulled back on the catapult until lungs full and band extended, he released his breath and grip and waited the split second for the tell tale sound of success: the hollow ring of paperclip on metal, barrelling down the waste paper basket.

Of course as this was the Zen version of paperclip archery he could not actually see the target hidden behind the desk and filing cabinet; and the ceremonial aspect of the preparation was to still his wandering mind until it was also in the waste paper basket, and everywhere in between. These variations on the Western version, the common or garden way sitting upright with target in sight, which he had mastered so well that he consistently scored 20/20, had kept him sane through all the weeks of tedium, in fact he would claim that this had been his main direct experience of Japanese culture.

When even more and more devious versions of this paled his standby diversion was internet golf. The internet was too new and golf too old to belong to any one place, but the Japanese website he favoured, golf-winsome.jp, was, unsurprisingly, the best he had found. His favoured partner, Bill van Lente III, a US Navy meteorology officer stationed in the Philippines, and he both worked from a decreasing handicap, now standing at seven. They played several times a week taking it in turns to choose the links, both being in nearby time zones and both having a lot of time on their hands. When Bill was on leave or family duty Bo had found that the citizens of Japan played courteously and were a comfortable local point of contact.

These and other amusements took him through the morning, until his favourite time of day when his Philippina girlfriend, Timi Loha, came down two storeys to collect him for lunch. Sometimes they went out to snack; sometimes they just locked the door, stayed in and snacked on each other. When she could, Timi stayed until mid-afternoon, chatting and playing and playing and chatting, and when she couldn't she would join him at internet backgammon from her PC upstairs; they would still chat, but now screen to screen.

The worse time of day was around 5.00 in the afternoon. Timi had to go home to her "'orrible, 'orrible" arranged husband, but worse the phone could ring; not everyday, but often enough to discourage an early exit. That would be London calling, usually either his fiancée Kelly Cuss, his formidable mother Miriam, or once in a while his nominal boss from Amnesty whose name could be difficult to remember; mercifully he always re-introduced himself first.

But whoever called from London left him with a knot of dread. The wedding was looming in three months, two months three weeks and three days to be precise, and that date had been tied in with the end of his Amnesty stint in Tokyo. All those relations to satisfy, all those roles to play, more mother-prodded studying for the legal career and now a wife-in-waiting whom he had seen only once—for a long and not entirely successful weekend in Hong Kong—in eight months. "Ah well, has to be done," he had said wistfully to himself more than once after a long distance chivvying phone call from Miriam or her new *aide de camp* and co-conspirator Kelly.

Evenings were by contrast some relief. Walking and walking for miles around the streets of the city, a kind of maze with straight lines, admiring the decorum and good manners, the mixture of deference to the old and embracing of the new. He had often thought of living here for longer, doing something else of course, finding an unattached Timi and living by the rules of his own discrimination and eccentricity; but somehow a sense of duty always pulled him elsewhere, to where he was expected, although he had to admit the pull was showing signs of wear and tear just lately.

2

Colonel Krop Mo Do of the State Safety & Security Agency of the Democratic Peoples Republic of Korea is not bored at all; in fact he is thoroughly enjoying himself. He enjoys his lunch in the second floor canteen. He enjoys the daylight; his recent promotion has meant he no longer has to work at night, the best time for interrogations, but even now his office is in the basement, next to the very same confessionals. No, a bit of daylight does his mood swings no harm at all.

And another perk of the officers' canteen is the beer, sometimes even imported beer. As he clunks the bottle down, empty, a brainwave from an anecdote puts an even broader smile on his pockmarked face. He springs up from the table, wipes his mouth with a soft paper towel, yet another perk, and heads burping jauntily back downstairs.

A young man is standing to attention waiting for him in his office. Colonel Krop remembers that just before lunch his superior General Mung had told him about a young Patriotic Duty conscript who had just joined Krop's department, a certain Sung Pak Dong. Sung's father is the recently arrested US spy he may have heard about. Colonel Krop had. His sister is troublesome too, a counterrevolutionary lecturer under snitch surveillance. Young comrade and Officer Cadet Sung was enthusiastic about the Agency and he may be helpful, Mung mused, perhaps more so if he were shown what was in store for his treacherous relatives. Colonel Krop could not disagree.

"Stand easy," orders Colonel Krop. The young conscript relaxes imperceptibly. "Do you know why you are here?"

"No, sir."

"It's because you have impressed those above you, and they in turn have told those above me to instruct you personally in the craft of confession and the art of persuasion. Have you heard of me?"

"Yes, sir."

"Good. Walk down the corridor, and look through the

peephole to room sixteen, and come and tell me what you see." Krop sits at his desk smiling, waiting to see if the memory from the anecdote holds true. Less than a minute later officer Cadet Sung Pak Dong returns.

"There is a young woman kneeling, sir. That's all."

"Why is she kneeling, Sung?"

"Is she Christian, sir?"

"Very good. She is kneeling for two reasons. Firstly, she is indeed Christian, and worse than that Falun Gong, a new Chinese strain of the reactionary disease, and that is one reason she is in here. She is also kneeling because just before lunch I told her to kneel. And to stay kneeling until I returned. And why did I do that?"

"To show her you are her superior, sir."

"Again you have half the answer correct. Yes, I am her superior. After three weeks in here she will do what she is told," he laughs at some memory kept to himself. "But there's another reason. She is in pain, kneeling for an hour is most uncomfortable, even for a Christian. But she is the cause of the pain, not I. She has undoubtedly been beaten and shocked repeatedly, probably molested by the sergeant's men too, all to no avail. No confessions, and from a Christian. That is even more insulting. And so I was called in to encourage her. But this time the cause of her pain is self inflicted, and to remove the cause is easier than to ignore the effect. That is a good first lesson for you, officer Cadet Sung."

"Yes, sir."

Colonel Krop waves him to follow, and together they enter the cell. The young woman, maybe mid-twenties but hard to tell, filthy and determined, somehow other worldly, does not look up. Krop walks up to her, and lifts her chin and face to him.

"The discomfort shows on your face. We can sit more comfortably in my office. You know by now what we want. You know by now how much we want it. We are not asking for much. The name of the worshipper with whom you were observed. We only want the name. Let's put an end to this unnecessary behaviour."

The girl looks up, clearly now in agony once her still forbearance has been broken. She shakes her head wearily, despairingly, defiantly.

Krop walks over in front of her. Her face is just in front of his fly. He unzips his fly and points his penis at her face. With a small grunt he starts to urinate in her face. She looks away. He grabs her hair fiercely and turns her head back to face his stream of urine. She tries to squirm away but his hand holds her head towards him like a vice. The room fills with the smells of the urine, the beer in the urine. After a minute he stops. She falls to the ground and sobs uncontrollably.

"The name of that worshipper!", roars Krop, standing over her, his penis still out.

"Kang Chol Han," she whimpers.

"Again!"

"Kang Chol Han," she cries, louder and louder until she is screaming "Kang Chol Han, Kang Chol Han!" Krop kicks his boot into her side, then with his sole almost gently pushes her over into a bundle lying in his urine.

Back in his office Krop laughs out loud. "I knew it, I knew it! I remembered the old story from Camp 18. Almost identical. Some religious running bitch refused to yield to pain, terrible pain, but a piss in her face, a piss in her face, and out it comes!"

"And now sir, what do we do with her?"

"Anything you like. Have some fun. You look like a virgin, clean her up and enjoy her. Then we will order her to a labour camp, she will be worked to death or near it. But this Kang Chol Han, now he is not such a lucky man. He will be encouraged to reveal his fellow religious zealots, and he will, and so on, until all the anti-statists are eliminated."

"And will he be sent to a hard labour camp too?"

"That depends if he is Redeemable or Irredeemable. You see if he just went to one prayer meeting out of curiousity, or friendship, found it all opiatic and never went back, he is Redeemable. It would have been better for him if he had snitched immediately, but even so he could just be re-educated in a minor camp with the works of the Great Leader and Dear Leader, the Great Leader's chapter on Dealing with Cancerous Influences Of Presumed External Divinity, for example, or the Dear Leader's recent article entitled Away From The Mind Impure From Prayer. He would learn these by rote, be set a snitch quota and entered into a snitch cell network. Then he would resume his previous work, but probably without a chance of promotion or access to privileges."

"But if he were Irredeemable, like the Christian bitch here, if he were like her, then we could send him to the labour camps?"

"After confessing more names, yes. He will have no purpose for the collective except his labour, and so he will be laboured until he dies. But first he will be beaten heartedly. For the others, you see."

"Yes, sir."

3

Two months, two weeks and one day before the end of his current life, Amnesty International's representative in Tokyo had returned from lunch feeling on the edge of ease. Timi had not been seen for three days; he did not like to—or even know how to—call her at home, and did not know in exactly which of the offices upstairs she worked. A long afternoon beckoned, and he thought he would start with the latest round in the Zen paperclip world grand prix championship and allcomers pro-am challenge cup. Well, not quite all comers because he was the only one, but the score of 17/20 was there to be beaten. But then again, he thought, no, you can have too much of a good thing. He remembered a conversation in the Foreign Correspondents Club the night before about internet cricket. Bo had been intrigued, as an ex-varsity opening batsman, to find out how unplayable Glenn McGrath and Shane Warne really were. He found the website, downloaded the goodies, took out his flight simulator console from the bottom drawer, asked the umpire for middle-and-leg, sat upright and prepared himself to face the music. He adjusted McGrath down to 80 m.p.h. and played forward defensive until his eye was in. Five dots and a maiden beckoning, he tried to glance Glenn for the single down to long leg to keep the bowling but was promptly fielded by Jason Gillespie.

In front of him the awesome Warne was prepping them both up, tossing the spinning ball menacingly from hand to hand without taking his eyes off his opponent, when the batsman heard the door knock, lots of urgent taps. Surprised, he said "Come in" to his first ever visitor who did not rejoice in the name of Timi Loha. He twisted sideways and over his shoulder saw the extremely pretty young oriental girl who was just about to change his life.

"Beaumont Lloyd Saint John Flowerdew Pett?" she asked with a fluster.

"Sinnjon," he replied, putting the console towards silly mid-on and standing up to greet this most welcome interruption.

"Sorry?" she gasped.

"Sinnjon. It's pronounced Sinnjon. Spelt Saint John, but you say Sinnjon. Look, never mind all that, take a seat, well take my seat, I'll put the kettle on. Tea? Coffee? Something cold from the fridge?"

"Alright, tea, but I won't sit. You see Mr...Mr...which is it?"

"Oh, don't worry about that sort of thing, just say Bo, everyone says Bo."

"OK Mr. Bo, listen..."

"No, not Mr. Bo, just Bo, as in...Bo."

"Right, Bo," she said, becoming more breathless and agitated. "I need your help. My father has been imprisoned, he is innocent. In North Korea, I have just arrived from North Korea."

"Well, I'm sorry of course, but what has he done?"

"Nothing, he's done nothing, I mean he has not done anything."

"You speak very good English."

"I'm a translator, look forget that, he has been falsely accused and..."

"Sorry to interrupt. Please sit down, you're making me get all het up now. Start again. Deep breath. What's he done? How can I help? Oh, and what's your name?"

She sat down, slowed down, sipped some tea and took a long breath. "Sorry. You're right. Start again. My name is Sung Lo Hi, I'm an English Language Senior Instructor at the Pyongyang People's University and a translator for the Ministry of Repatriation, Unification and External Affairs. My father, his name is Sung Pi Jam, he is a nuclear physicist who has been working on our uranium enrichment programme, and they suspect he has been selling some secrets to the CIA. But he would never do that. Right now he's in prison awaiting trial, a show trial, and once convicted as an Irredeemable he faces a life of hard labour in one of the camps. As his daughter I will have to go with him there too."

"Why, what have you done?"

"No-one has done anything. Because I am his daughter. It's the Confucian way."

"I thought it was communist, Stalinist?"

"It's a bit of everything, Confucian communist."

"I'm sorry to hear that, sounds rotten. But how come you are so sure he has not been selling secrets to the Americans?"

"I know him, he hates American values. No, it's my fault, I have been to some underground meetings, samizdat meetings, there is a small intelligentsia starting to uprise. Only a few of us, but there must have been a snitch, the whole system is built on snitches."

"But that doesn't make any sense, surely they would rather have him enriching their uranium and aren't too bothered about a few eggheads doing whatever it is you do."

"You don't understand their mentality. They are governed by paranoia. Three people criticising is more damaging to them than three million suffering in silence. No, they put him in there to make me confess with whom I am meeting."

"I'm sorry to be so slow, but why don't they just arrest you? Torture you? God forbid!"

"They tried. I hid. Now I'm here." For the first time she looked more comfortable.

"Sorry for all the questions, but it's not everyday, you know….Lovely to see you and all that, but how come you are here? I mean, presumably you didn't swim."

No, she had borrowed from Kimiko Sato, her new best friend and passageway neighbour in the Morning Calm block of central Pyongyang, Kimiko's Japanese passport and some clothes to get out of North Korea to Tokyo for a few days. She showed him the passport: they looked alike, especially now, she pointed out, that she had cut her hair spiky like Kimiko's. Getting in and out via China was no problem on a Japanese diplomatic passport, having money here was a problem, and Kimiko had helped here there too.

"This Kimiko seems like a good friend."

"She's my best friend now. Bo, I'm sure you know her. You don't have to pretend to me. I know what she is."

"What's that?"

"She is the Amnesty International spy in North Korea. Not a spy of course, an observer. But illegal. Half legal. Undercover. Her official job is at Japan North Korea Trade Authority."

"Ah," said Bo, trying to sound like he knew all along.

"Yes, and she said go and see," she said looking down and reading from the same slip of paper still in her hand, "go and see Beaumont Lloyd Saint John, sorry Sinnjon, Flowerdew Pett. That's you," she laughed. "Bo. What happened to the rest?"

"The rest?"

"The rest of your name."

Bo was looking at her properly for the first time. Now the whirlwind had stopped whirling and stopped agitating, he saw a mighty attractive young woman, early twenties, higher cheekbones than he was used to admiring in Japan, and all the better for it he thought. She had one of those black spot things women sometimes have on her cheek and a fully measured mouth and curved upper lip. But it was her eyes that entranced him most. Somehow rounder than they needed to be, and a mysterious light brown colour. Her hair was unusual, jagged and fluffy. Even sitting down she looked taller than usual, thin and rather languid. She wore dark clothes and her black hair made her face paler and her eyes even more interesting. He was thinking all this was tremendously good news. He started to explain his name conundrum for the one hundredth time, but this time took care to make it sound more interesting than he thought it was. "It's my father fault. He was a mad keen sportsman, player and spectator. Beaumont was a rugby player, Lloyd a cricketer and St.John a footballer. Flowerdew was my great grandmother's name and Pett her husband's. They joined them up because she had all the dosh. Double barrelled name, double barrelled dosh by all accounts."

"What is this double barrel Dosh?"

"Money, she had all the money. Mostly blown now, or so they say. So I dropped the mont, Lloyd, St. John and Flowerdew early on in my school career for obvious reasons of self preservation. So now it's Bo Pett. Pett-san around here. Listen, shall we have dinner on Saturday?"

She stood up sharply. "Saturday! You don't understand Bo. It's now, I need you to help me now. My father could be dead by Saturday. Tonight. Or you are busy?" she asked, with a hint of flirtation.

If only, Bo thought. "I can juggle things around, tonight is fine." They made the arrangements.

Bo saw her out, came back into the office with a spring in his step, rubbed his hands, relishing the excitement, and relishing the thought of Sung Lo Hi. What does he call her? Sung? Low? High? Either way, he felt chipper than he had for weeks.

The telephone rang. He stopped in his tracks, looked at it, said to it "Not tonight Josephine", wondered abstractly why he had said that then and never before and shut the door behind him, telephone still ringing.

4

Bo skipped into the cupboard he called home, took a beer from the tiny fridge, pulled down the single bed from the wall and looked out at the concrete block opposite. "Your starter for ten," he said aloud, before drifting into thought. The name of this beautiful North Korean temptress, is it Sung Hi Lo. Or is it Sung Lo Hi? Better get that right. And what about this Kimiko, and her working for Amnesty behind the scenes. He supposed it was one of those need to know jobbies. Fair enough, he thought, the less known the better in that world. And how about him going to North Korea, springing the old boy from jail? God knows how, he supposed she had some sort of plan. Pretty plucky girl, smuggling herself out of North Korea like that, and some kind of underground freedom fighter too. As he reflected on Sung Lo Hi his first thoughts were, regrettably he acknowledged, of her in bed rather than her father in prison.

Bo concluded that this little episode, this minor distraction, was just what his sanity needed. Let's face it this whole Amnesty job had been a bit of a mistake. Nothing ever happened. He was constantly amazed that anyone needed any sort of activist office in Tokyo at all. It all seemed so civilised. In fact being too civilised and driving everyone mad was the main problem. Bo took hours worth of satisfaction if a train was a minute late; he liked to kick the one scrap of litter he found every week into the middle of the road for all to see, and of course pretend not to see.

The fact is he was only here to kill time, to wait for Kelly to finish some exams and for him to get some experience for his CV, to lift him above the thousands of other new lawyers scrapping around the job market. His mother Miriam had hit on the idea of Amnesty International, or AI as she always called it. His mother was not just a lawyer, but an academic litigator, and involved with all the usual causes of London, North.

He had feared the worse from his interview. A rather tiresome girl with a crew cut had kept him sitting there while she studied his file. Eventually she asked, with a sneer barely concealed, "Beaumont, where to you want to go, what do you want to do?"

Bo hadn't actually thought out any details. "Well, something far away and adventurous. Somewhere exotic and dangerous."

She seemed surprised. "Have you ever done anything like that, you know something brave?"

"Hmm. Bungee jumps, three or four. Four. Parachute jumps, quite a few. I opened the batting against Oxford when Charlie Golding was their fast bowler. Not a lot of fun at the time."

"So you went to Cambridge?"

"Yes. Three years. Law. Very boring."

"It's not on your CV," she said turning the page "ah yes, here it is hidden away."

"Well, one does not like to mention it. Anyway, counts against one these days. Charterhouse and Cambridge, asking for trouble."

"I wouldn't have minded the opportunity."

"That's life though isn't it? You wanted the opportunity and I wanted a bit of P&Q."

"P&Q?"

"Peace and quiet, sorry."

"No worries. So why now this activism?"

"Oh, I'm not your die hard activist at all, but of course I'm interested, human rights, that sort of thing, can't do any harm can they?"

They carried on in that vein for a while, Bo half trying to talk himself out of it, she amazed that people like him still existed. And she knew his mother, well her mother knew his mother. Weird. Afterwards she had discussed Bo's case with management. The consensus was that if he had been any good they would have him put somewhere useful, if only to keep his mother on board, but as he's a mere sportsman....they felt they had to have him anyway, send him somewhere out of harms' way. Ankara has a vacancy. Could be problematical. How about Tokyo, that's free next month? Really, didn't even know we had one there. Perfect.

So eight month's ago he had found himself with not much to do except tolerate the present and dread the future. He had come to Tokyo and absence had not made the heart grow fonder. "It's been so long we'll almost be like virgins on our wedding night"

Kelly had enthused in Hong Kong in July. Now it was only three months away, in mid December—so she could combine their honeymoon with her university schedule.

Bo swung his feet off the bed, walked into the wardrobe that was his bathroom and looked into the mirror. "You want to do it, don't you? Be a hero, push yourself, do a bit of good in this world. But you can't, can you? Haven't got the strength, don't know where to start. It's all mapped out. London and law. Kelly, he could love her again. Nice friends. Some people are meant to be adventurers, others dutiful. Bo, my friend in the mirror, duty calls." He pulled another beer from the fridge, lay down again and felt heavy as he dozed.

5

Sung Pak Dong is becoming worried. They should have been at Camp 18 two hours ago, and now the end of the day is soon to be upon them. He is the passenger, the leader of the detail, and the officer in charge. The driver, about his same young age but from the peasant class, is, he had decided, unforgivably stupid. Sung Pak Dong may have taken over navigation duties, but that was unofficial and only to relieve the boredom on the long drive. The driver is responsible, and they are lost. Sung Pak Dong looks over his shoulder at the Christian woman, now called 18-31909. She is in exactly the same position as she was, with exactly the same faraway look, making him exactly as bad tempered with her as he has been for the whole journey.

They arrive at a village on the edge of a forest. Camp 18 is in a forest. Sung Pak Dong becomes optimistic. "Stop here you idiotic moron!" The driver stops the jeep and passively awaits orders. "Ask a peasant where is Camp 18!" The driver leaves the truck and heads for the first shelter. He leaves there shaking his head and tries the shack next door.

From the back a clear, a calm and quiet voice says "They cannot tell him where it is because it does not exist. Although they all know where it is, they cannot admit to its existence. They are not authorised to tell you. You might be a spy for US gangsterism."

Sung Pak Dong thinks he hears a note of disrespect in her tone, and turns round to hit her firmly but she is just out of reach. He also realises that she is right, that it is getting dark and his first mission as an SSSA officer is not looking promising. A sense of fear attacks his stomach. He opens the door, jumps out, slams it shut and storms straight up to the first hut, kicks the door in and shouts "Camp 18, you fucking hicks. Where is Camp 18? And now!"

Inside are two or three families living together in the full onslaught of poverty. The glass has been broken and it is already cold, even now. The floor is dirt, there is one table and one stove.

No-one has shoes. Twenty four eyes look back at him with naked fear. He picks up the nearest relative, a young boy of about ten to fifteen, hard to tell, and shakes him. "Camp 18, you revolting piece of shit?!"

There is a knock on the planks of a door. It is the driver. "I have found out where it is, sir. We are nearly there." With a kick to send the table upside down into the air, Sung and the driver trot back to the car. "Remember who told you, we'll deal with them on the way back."

Back at the jeep, 18-31909 is looking impassively at them as they jump back into the jeep. The driver is about to start, when he jumps out again, opens up the back flap and throws six punches at her body and legs. "What are you looking at?" he shouts at her, but she does not reply. He hits her again. "I said, what…"

"Never mind that now, hit her later, let's go!" says Sung Pak Dong, suddenly feeling more secure in his mission.

They drive along in near darkness a narrow concreted strip with dense forest beside and above them, and arrive at the camp ten minutes later. It is a clearing in the forest which uses the trees around it as fencing from which to hang the razor wire. It is lighter in the clearing but the day is becoming darker. There is no watch-tower, but an armed sentry box. They spring to attention as the jeep arrives. Sung Pak Dong hands over the paperwork. The sentry relays the information into a walkie talkie. The barrier comes up and they drive through. The camp is empty. They head for the only solid looking building. Above it is a sign "Our Socialism Centred on the Masses Shall Not Perish". An elderly officer walks out to meet them.

"I am Camp Commandant Guk. Welcome to our camp. What have we here?" he asks looking in the back.

"Some Christian whore, sir. Falun Gong too. Ten years hard labour. You'll get to know her," he smiled. "Excuse me, sir, but where is everyone?" asks Sung Pak Dong.

"This is your first camp visit, I see."

"Yes, sir," replies Sung Pak Dong uncertainly, not knowing how he should take the statement.

"Working. They work all daylight hours, every day except of course the Dear Leader's birthday. It's a logging quota we work here. One hundred and eighty tonnes of hardwood a year. Hardwood, hard labour. They'll be back soon. You can spend the night in my house. The driver can muck in with the guards. There'll be a public punishment later."

"Thank you, sir" said Sung Pak Dong. "What is the punishment?"

"Well we were planning to flog a radio seller for slackness in the work detail. But now you have brought a newcomer we will flog her. We always flog newcomers on their first night with all the prisoners on parade. Not too much though as they have to work tomorrow. A dozen hard lashes are about right, maybe fewer if they are weak already. She can take a dozen easily enough. We use hoses now so they bruise beautifully but don't bleed. No infection. Nothing stops the work here. You must be thirsty, let's relax a little first with imported beer."

"Yes, sir, thank you sir."

6

They meet later at La Carpaggio, an Italian bistro near Kimiko Sato's apartment for dinner. He hoped she would appreciate a change from North Asian. She did. He ordered two glasses of Champagne as *aperativi*, and some rather rare Montefalco Sagrantino; the Champagne was poured and he raised his glass to her.

"To Sung Lo Hi and her mission."

"To Sung Pi Jam."

Bo looked at her quizzically.

"My father," she emphasised, "the reason I am here."

"Of course. To Sung Pi Jam. Now tell me all about your underground movement. Are you some sort of freedom fighter?"

"That's not important really. I'm here to help my father escape, and if it does not hinder his escape, to escape myself too."

"OK, so tell me about him."

He was born in Seoul, South Korea in 1949, but when the Korean War finished in 1952 his family found itself on the wrong side of the border. His father, Lo Hi's grandfather, was an architect, trained in Japan, and they were comfortably off, in the middle of the emerging middle class. He was also an idealist, and after 1952 he was happy to work for the good of all in the new North. Of course he was an intellectual, which meant privileges, living in Pyongyang, an apartment, good school for his children.

"I thought intellectuals were despised," said Bo.

"That was in the cultural revolution in China. In North Korea there are three official classes, still today. Everyone is a peasant, a worker or an intellectual, you have to belong to one of these three classes. Intellectual is best. My father was always clever, and at this good school he excelled at science, physics in particular."

But her mother had died from a weakness brought on by pneumonia when Lo Hi was only six, and she had grown up caring as best she could for her father and her younger brother Pak Dong. Pak Dong and she did not see much of each other right now; he had had to join the army to do his Patriotic Duty, his conscription.

Bo told her of his similar experience: his father had died in a motorcycle accident when he was only five, his elder brother was a civil servant with whom he had nothing in common. She asked, possibly hopefully, if he had been in military service. Hardly, he had replied. Bo and Lo Hi were starting to feel relaxed with each other.

"But back to my father. At university in Pyongyang he graduated with honours and in 1979 was sent to Moscow to study nuclear energy, and he worked there until the late eighties when he was brought back to be one of the senior scientific managers on our nuclear power programme. Of course most of his co-workers had studied in Russia or China, and knew each other, and the Russians and Chinese were paying for it all, and it was in those early days totally peaceful in its intention, no doubt about that."

"And now it's not so peaceful?"

"Yes and no. It's hard for outsiders to understand the state's central philosophy of Juche, and its advanced degree of paranoia. Juche means man succeeding over his enemy nature by self reliance. This leads to extremes of pride and poverty. The paranoia comes about because inevitably they have started to believe their own propaganda, that we are in constant danger of a US invasion to finally settle the unfinished Korean War. Put them together, and you have an overwhelming desire to have nuclear weapons without the money—dosh—to do so."

"So how come they think he's selling secrets to the Americans, it doesn't sound like there's anything to sell?"

"On one level there isn't, the technology is about USA 1965, but no-one in the West knows if that means 1963 or 1967, and there's a big difference. It is on that level that what he knows is valuable."

"So your father knows what they haven't got?"

"Exactly."

The first course arrived, prosciutto from Zibello itself, and for *secondi* she ordered arragosta while he settled for steak *a la brace* and they talked of other things: Bo's ideas on Amnesty; he had nothing against it, but thought the reason he was being sent to Japan would be to save whales, but that was Greenpeace, and she thought he was joking, but he knew he wasn't; Kimiko and the AI undercover operation in Pyongyang, how hard they made it to be friends with the Japanese, and why they hated each other so much, how she assumed Kimiko reported to him, an impression he didn't entirely contradict; of her dreams of escape, how in spite of all her qualifications and fluency this was her first trip abroad, and that had to be in disguise and was highly illegal—not to mention downright dangerous.

After dinner, and refreshed by the Barolo, Bo asked the question that had been nagging at him since she first mentioned the word "escape". "Tell me, have you any ideas of how we—you that is—are going to spring him from jail? I mean, I presume they are pretty good at the lock and key scenario."

"Yes, Bo, I have a wonderful idea of how WE are going to spring him from jail. My only problem is that you are going to find it so fantastical that you will not believe it."

"Well, now I've got to know, come on."

"You've heard of the Invisible Man?"

"Not for a while, is he still around?"

"Oh yes, he's still around."

"Remind me who wrote it."

"Another Englishman. H.G.W..."

"H.G.Wells of course. I haven't read it since prep school fifteen years or so ago. Good read, but what's the connection?"

"Right, here goes. As a very young student scientist my father's great idol was H.G.Wells, especially the story *The Invisible Man*. By the time he was admitted to university at seventeen he had taken the theory of invisibility, clearly a work of fiction, and constructed a model around which it might work in reality. At university he had the facilities to move it forward, and he became even more convinced it would work. He began experimenting, but the surer he was that it would work in theory, the less able he was to prove it in practise because he had no facilities to test it.

"Then he went to Moscow, and all that changed. Not only were there all the machineries and laboratories he could wish for, as a foreigner he could work on anything in his spare time and no-one asked too many questions. By the time he came back to live at home he had become invisible many times. Not only that but he had overcome H.G.Wells's great problem."

"Remind me."

"He could return back to visibility. He also managed to bring back from Moscow the equipment, he calls it his apparatus, disguised as lab equipment. I myself have done it many times. It's fun, and safe."

Bo expressed mild amazement, what else could he do? He didn't know whether to take it seriously or not. On the one hand it seemed completely absurd, really beyond belief, on the other here she was, clearly risking life and limb, and apart from the Invisible Man the whole story made perfect sense. And he did find her more and more attractive as the story unfolded. It was without doubt the most amusing evening he had had in Tokyo for months, and with a bit of luck might get even more amusing yet. But at just this early stage of his imaginary seduction she revealed her plot.

"Basically, what you have to do is enter North Korea from China, become invisible in my apartment, walk into the prison unseen, and smuggle him out."

Bo leant forward. "Doesn't sound too much of a problem."

"You are joking?" she asked uncertainly.

It was true that by now he was thinking she was bonkers, cute but bonkers, but he had become attached to the short term possibilities which may have led her to feel he was less unequivocal about her medium term objective.

At the end of the meal she offered to show him something that will prove to him without any doubt that invisibility can be done, back at Kimiko's room, and that particular part of her crazy scheme Bo was not going to dispute.

7

Kimiko Sato's cupboard was not much bigger than Bo's, but done in the Japanese way. Bo noticed hopefully a futon ready to unroll. Some papers were laid out on the table already, as if she had expected him to come back with her.

First, she showed him some photographs of someone not being there. In the first photograph sat a middle aged man, boffinish, presumably her father, then in the second photograph the same scene but nobody there. Then there was another pair of pictures: one with the man standing in front of a window, and then just a window with a city scape in the background.

"I took these photos myself," she said excitedly. "Look, in this one," she said showing him a third now-you-see-him-now-you-don't shot "on the table you can see the apparatus." Bo took the photograph and for the first time their hands touched, a touch he released slowly as he looked at her and smiled.

She brought his attention back to the photograph.

"You see those two boxes on the table. You sit or stand between them. In three minutes you are gone. I have seen it work dozens of times. It's fun to go outside in the summer, but too cold in the winter because only the skin is invisible."

Bo had to admit he had become as intrigued by all this as he had by Lo Hi, and letting his arm brush against hers with what she thought was an unexpected degree of nonchalance, asked about the rest of her plan.

She reached over for the briefcase on the table, opened it and took out some blank pages.

"All the plans are here," she said, "but written in invisible ink in case I was stopped. Here is the complete plan of what we have to do."

"Invisibility is quite the thing with you," he said, "but how do we get to read it?"

"You don't. Not until I'm certain you will be part of the team."

"Team?" he asked "How many people are in on this?"

22

"Just Kimiko and I so far. She is expecting you to be with us."

"And you, what are you expecting?"

"Nothing, but I'm hoping."

Bo sat up, turned sideways and looked directly at her. "This is actually quite serious, isn't it? You really plan to do it."

"Yes, and it will not be easy. There are many problems. First we have to get you into North Korea. You cannot go from Japan because there are no connections, so you have to go to Shanghai. Then you need a reason to visit. Then you need a visa."

"Well I can do all that easily enough."

"Yes, but it gets worse. We have to break you up from your tour group, get you into the prison, you have to find him, and then you have to make him escape."

"Yes, I see what you mean, not that easy really."

"And then we have to somehow get you both, both highly wanted men, out of the country."

"Well, it is sounding pretty drastic."

"Are you still ready for it?"

"I have to say it's not without its challenge; it sounds like mission practically impossible."

"And I have not mentioned the worst part yet."

Bo laughed cautiously. "Go on, I hate to think what that could be."

"Cold. Freezing cold like you cannot imagine. You see you have to be naked to remain invisible. Only the body is invisible, you cannot wear any clothes because they will show."

Bo stood up; all this talk of cold had somehow made the fire go out of him, but he managed to say "if David Blaine can do it, so can I."

"Who is he?"

"You don't know? Lucky you, he's some kind of crazed self publicist, but I seem to remember he did manage to freeze himself for weeks on end. There must be a knack. I'll ask him." He picked up his coat and dressed for outside. "Lo Hi, it's as intriguing as you are but I better be going; but please come round to the office tomorrow and we'll start again, see what can be done."

"Bo, thank you for a lovely night, my first in a country of freedom."

"I've enjoyed it a lot too. My first fun night since I've been here. Tomorrow." He kissed her on both cheeks and let himself out.

Bo walked casually back home. A strange night, a very strange night, he reflected, but later, falling asleep, his last thoughts were of Lo Hi herself rather than her rather desperate rescue mission.

8

Colonel Krop, takes the Sung family files from his desk, puts them in his lap, leans back in his chair, props his feet up on the table and opens them in turn. The father, Sung Pi Jam, had a clean life up till three months ago. A good family, intellectual class, university, top grades, studied nuclear physics in Moscow, no known contact with the US aggressors there, back home into fine job, important job. A note from Moscow times that he had been approached by the KGB, doubling as British intelligence to test him, he had refused outright but had not reported it. Not ideal, but some intellectuals are like that. An early widower, but we cannot blame him for that, never re-married, slightly unpatriotic on his part, but not decisive. Two children, the daughter Lo Hi and the son Pak Dong. Then this recent trouble. Two denunciations, one under torture so unreliable, but another from a working snitch in his department, usually sound. Under surveillance since, nothing significant. Arrested a month ago after snitch repeated the denunciation, apparently first hand observation of an English language telephone call on a smuggled cellphone. Denies everything, but not questioned under duress yet so not broken.

Colonel Krop puts down the file and picks up the next one. Sung Lo Hi, 25 years old, intellectual class, brought up by aunts after mother died and father worked in USSR. Studied languages, English and Japanese, works as translator for Ministry of External Affairs. Still sees university crowd, mostly English speakers. Unobservable potential for slandering Leadership. Snitch in the circle reports enthusiasm for democracy but just debates and no activity. Snitch himself now under suspicion of under reporting, but all debates in English so not easy to find snitches. Clever, thought Krop, as he made a note about English Language recruitment on a separate pad. Engaged, but seldom seen with one particular male. Father's surveillance revealed her friendship with Kimiko Sato, a new and unverified potential spy from the Japan North Korea Trade Authority. Krop looks up at the ceiling and blows out. He is sure this so-called Trade Authority is just a hot bed of espionage, but so far they have had no snitch feedback and no successful surveillance. Krop adds to his note to increase observation of the daughter, maybe offer her illegal influences, a radio, cell phone, magazines and work backwards.

Colonel Krop then reaches for the file on the son, the SSSA's young recruit Sung Pak Dong. When Colonel Mung first mentioned that they had a son of a traitor, well probable traitor, in the team, Krop's first thought was to suspect the son of being influenced by imperialist propaganda and enrolling for the CIA. But reading the boy's file Krop relaxes. Everything in his upbringing suggests a clean thinking youth. From the intellectual class, he excelled at sports, political knowledge and especially chemistry throughout his school days, and at university joined, voluntarily, the Future Officer Corps. His degree, with Utmost Accolade, was in Chemistry and Chemical Science. Krop noted his research on artificial germs, and thought that later he might be seconded usefully to the Patriotic Biological Defence Force. Recruited as a snitch, he denounced two lecturers for unenthusiastic interpretation of the Great Leader's early speeches. He was graded as Second Division material at the Future Officers, but only because he did not plan a military career. He requested to join the SSSA on graduating. No, this young Sung Pak Dong is a good boy, worth developing, and worth developing personally.

The knocking on the door stirs Krop from his thoughts. "Open!" he shouts, and Sung Pak Dong marches in, salutes and stands to attention in front of him.

"And so, how was your journey to Camp 31?"

"Fine, sir, thank you."

"You did not have any problems?"

"No problems, sir."

"Funny, because one of our snitches in the village reported to his intermediary, who in turn reported to Captain Yon here, that our snitch was severely attacked without warning by your detail on the way back from the camp. Do you remember the incident, Officer Cadet Sung Pak Dong?"

Sung Pak Dong looked uneasily at the far wall, his discomfort broken by sudden screaming from a nearby room, cut short in turn by the sound of a large crash. "Sir, we punished him for revealing the existence of the Camp to a stranger."

"But your journey was without problems. Why did he have to reveal these directions to you?"

"We were temporarily misplaced, sir."

"So you beat up a helpful snitch. It will at least reinforce his cover, but that is not the point. The point is also not that you lied to me, Sung Pak Dong. The point is that you lied to a representative of the Democratic People's Republic of Korea, the Korean People's collective. You have cut us, in the same way that your Christian bitch cut us. Your loyalty is what is temporarily misplaced."

"Sir, my most utter apologies to yourself and the Service." Sung Pak Dong was standing totally stiff to attention, eyes focused on a particular brick in the opposite wall, fear and tension blocking out the distraction of the distant screaming which had started again. "I can promise you my loyalty. I would die for The Great Leader and for the Dear Leader. I did not want to cause disappointment on my first assignment. It will never happen again."

The screaming has stopped again. The vacuum had its own tension. Krop gestured to Sung Pak Dong to sit down in front of him.

"You're a young man, but sincere, and young men make mistakes from good intentions. You have had many advantages in your life. Your family, tell me about your family."

Sung Pak Dong relaxes a few degrees. He knows that Krop knows about his father, and so a certain wariness remains. "My family is from the intellectual class, sir. My mother died when I was young, and my father spent a lot of time studying in Moscow. My sister and I were brought up by my grandmother, and we lived with her and two aunts and an uncle."

"A large and happy family. A united family, would you say?

"Yes, sir. A happy and united family."

"As were mine," said Krop, now walking around the room, slowly circling Officer Cadet. "But I had no parents. The American imperialist bombers killed them when I was a baby. There were many like me, killed by their bombs and tanks and bullets, by their ceaseless desire for world hegemony."

"I am sorry, sir."

"No, don't be sorry, Sung Pak Dong. My family was bigger than yours, and more united, our parents were all the families of Korea, represented by the Great Leader. He came to our orphanage once. The greatest day of all our lives. We vowed then to dedicate our lives to his service, and thereby to the service of the collective. Without his vision and protection we would all have perished. Instead we became his protectors, and the protectors of his Juche Principle, as will soon be embraced by all free people of the world. My loyalty is more easily placed than yours. You have two families, your blood family, your Confucian family, and your motherland family, your Communist family. Sometimes there are choices, uncomfortable choices." Sung Pak Dong was uneasy again, his mind racing ahead. "The lesser good, or the greater good, we might say."

"Yes, sir"

"And you must in your own time do what is best for both families. The protection of the large family sometimes calls for the sacrifice of the small family. I think you know to what I am alluding?"

"My family father's circumstance, sir."

"Indeed. And your sister's circumstance too."

Sung Pak Dong looks across sharply. "My sister, sir? But she is a lecturer at the university, and a translator for our Trade Ministry."

"By day she might well be as you describe, and by night a counterrevolutionary as my files reveal. You are an Officer Cadet with a promising future. You could have a military career, or continue as a scientist. Maybe a combination of these worthy goals. But you must be careful that your closest relations do not hinder your progress. On the other hand, they might enable you to make greater progress. But enough of that for now, Sung Pak Dong." Krop is standing right behind him with a friendly hand on each shoulder. Close by the screaming disconcertedly starts again. "You should have a reward for completing your mission and understanding the bigger perspective." He walked over to a drawer and pulled out an envelope. He handed over six five Euro bank notes. He then tears a chit out off a book and fills in some lines and signs it. He hands both to Sung Pak Dong. "These are for the Tourist and Wellwishers Store. Buy yourself something smart to wear. Gain respect from the masses."

Sung Pak Dong steps forward and salutes, a cheeky smirk now on his face.

9

Officially the Amnesty International, Tokyo Branch, opening hours are 9.00 a.m to 6.00 p.m., with lunch from 1.00 p.m. to 2.00 p.m. Bo, never the greatest riser, had fallen into the habit of arriving at about 11.00 a.m. and leaving after any UK phone calls, nine hours behind, around 5.00 p.m.; lunch was flexible, to meet the demands of Philippino diplomacy. But on this beautiful early October autumn day Bo found himself there early, before 10.00 a.m. He had come, guiltily, to look up some files about North Korea.

There had been quite a few over the last eight months, but he had not paid much attention to them. In fact he had not paid any attention to them, telling himself he was only being copied for information. As part of the East Asia area he received copies of reports on all local countries, overwhelmingly China, and although at the beginning he read them copiously, more recently he had filed them on arrival, but not without a slight sense of guilt. He read the Japanese English language papers from cover to cover every day, looking for any hint of constitutional deprivation, but had yet to find anything too upsetting. The office subscribed to a couple of weekly political newssheets, but Bo hardly bothered with what he considered to be their infantile left wing posturing and appalling layout and design.

He pulled open the filing cabinet, found the North Korea divider and took out a pile of papers. Feeling rather sheepish he quickly realised he had not even filed them in date order, just shoved the latest report on amongst the others.

He sifted through them, marking lines in the margins:

Systemic food shortages continued; more than 40 per cent of children were reported to suffer from chronic malnutrition. Concerns about the nuclear capability of the Democratic People's Republic of Korea (North Korea) continued to prevail in the international arena. The North Korean government continued to deny its people fundamental human rights, including freedom of movement and expression. Hundreds of people fled to China, and those forcibly returned were at risk of detention, prolonged interrogation and imprisonment in poor conditions. Independent human rights monitors were not allowed access to the country.

Since 2002, defectors among the flood of refugees from North Korea have detailed firsthand accounts of systematic starvation, torture and murder. Enemies of the state are used in experiments to develop new generations of chemical and biological weapons. A microcosm of these horrors is Camp 22, one of 12 concentration camps housing an estimated 200,000 political prisoners facing torture or execution for such crimes as being a Christian or a relative of someone suspected of deviation from "official ideology of the state."

Relations between Japan and North Korea continued to be tense. This was attributed in large part to the abduction of Japanese nationals by North Korean government agents in the 1970s and 1980s and reports that a substantial part of North Korea's nuclear program was built using materials from Japan. Normalization talks have still not taken place.

More than ten political prisons and work camps now hold an estimated 200,000 North Koreans. As a result of the brutal conditions, punishing labour demands, severe nutritional deficiencies, and frequent arbitrary executions, the Centre for the Advancement of North Korean Human Rights estimates that some 400,000 prisoners have died in these camps since they were established by Kim Il Sung in 1972.

A combination of insufficient domestic production, the narrow and inadequate diet of much of the population and growing disparities in access to food as the purchasing power of many households declines meant that about 6.5 million vulnerable North Koreans out of a total population of 23 million were estimated to be dependent on international food aid. The situation remained particularly precarious for vulnerable sections of the population, including young children, pregnant and nursing women and elderly people.

Relief agencies said that while they sought US$225 million for aid in 2003, they received pledges for only 57 per cent of that amount. Some countries appeared to have cut off aid to North Korea after a worsening of relations over the country's nuclear weapons program.

Political opposition of any kind was not tolerated. Any person who expressed an opinion contrary to the position of the ruling Korean Workers' Party reportedly faced severe punishment, as did their family in many cases. The domestic news media continues to be severely censored and access to international media broadcasts was restricted. Religious freedom, although guaranteed by the Constitution, was in practice sharply curtailed. There were reports of severe repression—including imprisonment, torture and execution—of people involved in public and private religious activities. Many Christians were reportedly being held in labour camps, where they faced torture and were denied food because of their religious belief.

Thousands of North Koreans were reportedly apprehended in China and forcibly returned to North Korea. A number of sources reported that on their return they often faced prolonged detention, interrogation and torture. Some were reportedly sent to prison or labour camps, where conditions were cruel, inhuman or degrading.

Public executions continue. Executions are by firing squad or hanging. In April, the UN Commission on Human Rights passed a resolution on North Korea expressing concern at public executions and imposition of the death penalty for political reasons. Reports suggest that extrajudicial executions and secret executions are taking place in detention facilities.

There were reports indicating that women detainees were subjected to degrading prison conditions. For example North Korean women detained after being forcibly returned from China were reportedly compelled to remove all clothes and subjected to intimate body searches. Women stated that during pre-trial detention the male guards humiliated them and touched their sexual organs and breasts. Women who attempted to speak up about these conditions were reportedly beaten. All women, including those who were pregnant or elderly, were forced to work from early morning to late at night in fields or prison factories. Prisons lacked basic facilities for women's needs. There were unconfirmed reports that pregnant women were forced to undergo abortions after being forcibly returned from China.

For more than a decade, North Korea has suffered from a "silent famine" in which hundreds of thousands are reported to have died of starvation and related illness. One of the main reasons is that the North Korean government has imposed severe restrictions on independent monitors, food donors, international governmental organisations and NGOs.

Hundreds of thousands of people have died as a result of acute food shortages caused by the loss of support from the former Soviet Union and economic mismanagement. Several million children suffer from chronic malnutrition, impairing their physical and mental development.

Government policies are mostly to blame. The government appears to have distributed food unevenly, favouring those who are economically active and politically loyal. Government restrictions on freedom of movement prevents North Koreans searching for food or moving to an area where food supplies are better, as they face punishment including detention if they leave their towns or villages without permission. They also hamper the movement, access and monitoring of international humanitarian agencies who have been involved in distributing food aid. This has contributed to donor fatigue and a fall in food aid commitments.

Widespread malnutrition has led to the movement of tens of thousands of people into China. Thousands have been forcibly repatriated by the Chinese authorities, and have then been detained by North Korean authorities in appalling conditions. Detainees are reported to have died of hunger. Many have reportedly been tortured during interrogations by the North Korean authorities.

Some North Koreans have been publicly executed because they have stolen food or goods to survive—school children have reportedly been taken to see the executions.

Children, women and the elderly are reported to be among the principle victims of North Korea's famine. Many women forced to go to China in search of food have been preyed on by trafficking gangs, which operate on both sides of the China-North Korea border.

Efforts by the international community to assist in the provision of food to North Korea have been undermined by the government's refusal to allow swift and equitable distribution of this food, and by the restrictions on freedom of information.

He put down the pile of papers, and looked at the four fifths still left to read. Should he have done something? All this time, sitting here, wasting day after day, while just 800 miles away people were living in appalling repression and poverty? But what could he have done?

He stood up, angry with himself, "You could at least have read the reports, taken some kind of interest!" he said aloud to his conscious, "instead of sitting around playing games here all day." Or been like this Kimiko Sato, presumably she was some kind of activist, risking torture and death and God knows what else. He could have at least asked to go there, undercover like she was. And Sung Lo Hi. If she was actually caught doing what she was doing? She really would be better off committing suicide. And her father already in prison? The hard labour penal camps, the most desperate places on earth, and she having to go there with him.

Bo paced the office, indignation in his thoughts, a sense of determination arising, an inkling of a cause stirring, all interrupted simultaneously by the telephone ringing, the fax machine whirring, and a knock on the door.

10

Lo Hi stretched and yawned, stretched again and swung her legs off the futon. Bit of a mess here, she thought unkindly, my friend Kimiko must be the only untidy Japanese woman in the world. But probably I am too tidy, she corrected herself. She boiled the kettle, made the tea, rummaged hopefully among the use-bys in Kimiko's fridge, sipped the tea and thought about yesterday and today.

Kimiko had been right about Bo in one respect, but rather wrong in another. He was gorgeous all right: sexy, blonde, tall. She loved his almost formal clothes and good manners, she liked the soft way he spoke, and with consideration. He was attracted to her, that much was clear too. But above all the liked the way he moved. At first she could not work out what he reminded her of, but the memories brought the answer: a tiger, the way he walked, long steps with a certain nonchalance in the bounce. She was attracted to him too, no doubt about that either. Kimiko had mentioned the Philippina girlfriend and English fiancée, a rich doctor apparently; although the way Kimiko said it sounded more like a witch doctor. She hoped he was not a serial flirter, that he was pulled towards her alone, but took the thoughts no further.

But Kimiko had been wrong about his sure-fire warrior status. "He would be perfect; strong and brave, longing for adventure," Kimiko had said in Lo Hi's apartment. True her information was not first hand, she had never actually met him, rather was told about him somehow—probably some secret Amnesty cell structure she assumed.

No, Bo was no Rambo that was for sure. He was athletic, a great sportsman Kimiko had mentioned, although Lo Hi's suspicion was that he probably had the peculiar English trait she had read about, where they would prefer to play the game gracefully rather than to win it. Then she thought that maybe she had been too strong on the cold part of the escape; but it would be cold, really very, very cold.

She finished her tea, and put the cup down with the thought that in spite of these doubts he was her best bet; in fact he was her only bet, apart from raising the ante dramatically at the US Embassy. She had come this far, taken these appalling risks on the faith of Kimiko's enthusiasm for him, and now she had to make it work. She looked at the map, counted her remaining money, and decided to walk around Tokyo, for North Koreans the Forbidden City, second only to Washington as a centre for thieves, gangsters and political opportunists.

Her work had shown her what the outside world was like, there were no shortage of magazines and even television programmes censored to show the horrors of decadent dog eat dog-ism; the opposite effect was predictably the result. But walking through the streets, live and in person, for the first time brought home to her not so much that of which she had been deprived, but that of which she was determined to enjoy and share. She did not know how and when, but only a strong conviction that one day she would walk these streets as an equal. She caught a glimpse of herself in a shop window, and froze. It's either this or the gulag, she thought, there is no middle ground, no way of going back to teaching lies or translating platitudes.

Her meanderings found her near to the US Embassy, and she walked closer to it and rehearsed what she might have to say if Bo did not perform. But whom could she trust there? What exactly would she say? To whom? Even if they believed her, why would they want to help a low level physicist? Would she make it worse for her father by escalating it? She knew none of the answers, only more and more questions.

She walked through the park and sat and watched. She must succeed, and with Bo. They could escape, escape from prison, escape from North Korea, escape to the West, to the USA. Escape together, be together, live together. A whole world of future happiness and fulfilment unfolded, and she stayed there lost in dreams, dreams all the stronger to escape the grimness of the reality. When that thought arose she stood up from the bench, determined a fixed look in the direction of the AI office and walked purposefully, and hopefully, to see her saviour, yes she thought, her saviour Bo Pett.

She arrived just before afternoon tea, and as she tapped on the door she heard the phone start ringing and Bo's voice "Oh hi Kelly, hang on a second. There's someone at the door." He walked over and opened it.

"Shabbu Sh'u!" she said.

"What's that?"

"An old Korean greeting, not used much these days, but I say it like a habit," she smiled, he noticed.

"How does it go?"

"Shabbu Sh'u!"

"A bit like What Ho!"

"What Ho! Yes, I read that in a book. P.G. Wooster."

"That's the one. Woops, I'm on the dog and bone, make yourself at home."

He walked over to the desk and picked up the phone. "Oh, just a courier," he said to the phone after a few seconds.

A long conversation started, and quickly Lo Hi deduced it was with his fiancée. She could only hear his side of it of course, but it was not encouraging, not in tune with her thoughts in the park.

"I know, but there's not long to go."

"Yes, I am too."

"Of course I don't mind. And have you invited the Tompkins too?"

"I don't know what to wear exactly, traditional but not the details. I'll ask Ben."

"Well put her next to Auntie Hazel."

"Ten minutes maximum."

Lo Hi stood up and wandered around, looked out of the window at the enormous expanse of Tokyo.

"Let's decide nearer the time, we'll play it by ear, last minute it."

Looking around the office her eyes fell on the fax machine. A fresh message had arrived. She looked over to Bo, and he was still looking the other way and talking to his fiancée. "I'm not sure, probably work here all day and catch a film tonight."

She looked at the fax. It was from Amnesty International in London, a fax copy of a letter sent to Mr. Beaumont Flowerdew-Pett.

Mr. B.L.S. Flowerdew-Pett
Regional Organiser
Amnesty International
Room 1818 Time-Life Building
3-6 Ohtemachi; 2-Chome
Chiyoda-Ku
Tokyo 2456-8789
Japan

Dear Bo,

I am sure it will come as no surprise to you that as a result of the financial cutbacks we have been forced to make, we are re-evaluating our resource structure.

Our Japanese operation has for some time been considered something of a luxury, and in view of the lack of activity to and from the AI branch in Tokyo, we regret to inform you that we are no longer able to justify it staying open.

I see from your contract that you have three months remaining. Our plan is to honour your salary until that time, but to save money by closing down the office forthwith.

I am sorry to be the bearer of bad tidings, but I am sure you will agree it is for greater good.

Yours sincerely,

Mrs. Camilla Sidebottom

Head of Worldwide Resources

Lo Hi looked over at Bo, still on the telephone. "Well, I can't do much more from here."

Lo Hi, with a depression in her stomach, felt exactly the same. No Amnesty International, no Kimiko, no Kimiko, no Bo, no Bo, no official British cover, the project suddenly doomed. She walked over to the door and opened it. He spun round, frantically waving her to stay. She looked back at him sadly, shook her head, and walked through the door. As she turned round a small, thin girl with "Timi" on her name badge walked past, gave her a look of curiosity and walked into Bo's office without knocking.

Lo Hi crept back to the door. "Who was that?" she overheard the girl say.

"Oh, just a courier," Bo replied, and Lo Hi, with heavy feet and heart, walked down the stairs and out into the vast nothingness of downtown Tokyo, the loneliest place in the world. She could walk to the US Embassy from here. That was the easy part. She approached the enquiries desk as the receptionist was preparing to close it.

"I'd like to speak to someone from Intelligence please."

"We don't necessarily have Intelligence here, ma'am. Can I help you in anyway?"

"No thank you. I have something very important to say. I am from North Korea. I am sure they will want to see me."

"Take a seat over there please, I'll see if anyone is available, but you may have to come back tomorrow." Lo Hi sat on the bench, casting her fate solemnly to the winds.

11

Madame Comrade Instructor General of the State Safety and Security Agency, Ni Joy Ping, stands in front of her class of Officer Cadets. "Sit down," she beckons and they do. "For our third week we have been joined by Sung Pak Dong. Stand up, Sung."

The class, neatly arranged in now asymmetrical rows, sits stiffly upright and listening, turns round as one to stare blankly at the newcomer. She continues instructing. No notes are taken, it is not that kind of class.

"Before proceeding with our investigation of the causes of treachery and deviancy, for the sake of our new Cadet, and to remind us all, I will read out again our instructions from the Democratic Protection Council of North Korea. "It says," she offers herself her reading glasses and looks over them at the elite students arranged below, and takes a deep and reverential deep breath before pronouncing: "The State Safety & Security Agency is to carry out a wide range of counterintelligence and internal security functions. The Agency will carry out duties to ensure the safety and maintenance of the system such as search for and management of anti-system criminals, immigration control, activities for searching out spies and impure and anti-social elements, collection of overseas information, and supervision over ideological tendencies of residents. It will search out anti-state criminals— a general category that includes those accused of anti-government and dissident activities, economic crimes, and slander of the political leadership. Camps for political prisoners will be under its jurisdiction. It will have counterintelligence responsibilities at home and abroad, and run overseas intelligence collection operations. It will monitor political attitudes and maintain surveillance of returnees. Agency personnel will escort high-ranking officials. The Agency will also guard national borders and monitor international entry points.

"Officer Cadet Sung, our syllabus this semester is taking each point of this in turn. You have missed two lessons and will be expected to learn the contents from your fellow students in your own time."

Sung Pak Dong feels proud of himself, proud to be here now with his year's elite. Whilst paying sincere attention to her lecture on the Causes of Deviancy and the Effects of Cynicism he manages to look discreetly at his fellow students, themselves picked from the elite of military families and graduates, future career officers, and his being swells with a sense of belonging.

Of what had brought him here so suddenly, with so much irregularity he is not so sure. He had resigned himself to being in the second division of the SSSA, as high as he could expect as a short termer; not a bad life at all, but now, suddenly access to the elite is his.

The hasty interview with the fearsome Colonel Krop, the trust of his detail to Camp 31 with the Christian traitor, his apparent forgiveness for lying and roughing up a snitch, and even more so his access to privileges all this had been so unexpected. There was his father to consider, and he still could not believe the theory about his sister, but if they said she was near to subversion she must be so. But surely, he reflects, all this should go against him?

"Sung."

He snaps out of his curiousity "Madame".

"Last week we learned the value of sleep, or rather the value to us of lack of sleep." Some tittering of relaxation in the class. "Would anyone care to summarise for Comrade Sung?"

Immediately from behind another student jumps to attention. "If I may explain?" he says and she nods approval. "The body needs no sleep, but the mind needs four hours a day, not necessarily consecutively. Without sleep the mind will fail after three days. The truth we are seeking comes from the mind and not the body, so interrogation of an unslept mind is most fruitful, if time consuming. The best solution is to torture the body first to soften up the mind, and if the correct answers are not forthcoming, we then deprive the mind of sleep, the same mind remembering the pain its body brought to it under torture. Speed and noise and light are important, as is night time activity."

"Good, and later we will show you live examples of prisoners being subjected to active sleep deprivation. Now we have physical exercise and training, this afternoon more studying of the Dear Leader's speeches, and this evening no doubt we owe Officer Cadet Sung Pak Dong a small initiation."

All eyes now turn to look at him, and their faces for the first time stretch into grins. Some hands are banging in anticipation on the desk. A horrible feeling of dread hits Sung Pak Dong, made worse by the leers and looks of glee from his fellow students. On her way out, General Ni says loudly above the excitement of what waits for Sung Pak Dong "and tomorrow morning, dawn, don't forget the firing squad, three committed homosexuals, without repentance...."

12

Bo had cut the call from Kelly as short as he could. Timi had replied suspiciously that "if she's just a courier, she's a very pretty one", but to her Bo had seemed half distracted—as if not listening properly to her. He walked casually over to the fax machine. "Don't get many of these" he commented, picking up the sheet. He read it, put it down by his side, raised an eyebrow, reread it, and said absently to Timi, "I have some work to do tonight, so see you tomorrow, if you don't mind."

He ran down onto the street, looked left and looked right in vain; in the few minutes since she had left Lo Hi had vanished into the nothingness of downtown Tokyo, the busiest place in the world. He walked the streets aimlessly, trying to think, couldn't, and headed for the park for some time to himself.

Wrapped up in a light raincoat against the first chill wind for months, he tried to think what had happened, and what to do. A horrible sense of crossroads was looming. Thinking had never come naturally, he never gone in for that sort of thing as such, good fortune somehow had usually managed to intervene before much thinking had been needed. Decisions, now he reflected on past events, seemed to have arisen on their own. He seemed to have been born with promise and providence, had never suffered, not really suffered, even this Amnesty interlude had not involved any hardship, absolutely nothing compared to the people he was supposed to be protecting.

Outside himself he looked up and saw a delightful Tokyo park scene, children and ducks, unaware of fate, playing on the grass or in the water. He smiled again, enjoyed the smarter air, but as quickly turned back inside himself.

No, life had all been simple enough until university; then it had all started to go wrong. Day to day had been fun enough, the great sportsman, the friends, the parties, and at first the girls. But girls had turned to girl, and ill consequence seemed to have been born there. The affair with Kelly seemed right at the time. An affair between two people, he to be a lawyer, she to be a doctor, their professions almost demanded it. Her family was richer, which he had abstractedly thought would not do any harm. His mother and her parents even liked each other, in retrospect he felt a sure warning sign of trouble. The fling turned into an affair into a commitment into an engagement and now into marriage. He wished he could now unscramble the whole lot, but a heavier part of him told him he couldn't. It wasn't Kelly, it was all the baggage: the families, the friends, the effort so far and the expectations to come. The institution. But it was worse even than that. The predictability of what was to come haunted him the most. He felt as if he could write the script for the next fifty years right now. Work, Kelly, babies, work, holidays, house moves, work, schools, duties, work, deaths and grandbabies, work, work, work. Then the lights go out. But that seemed to be it, the way the world worked: you had certain responsibilities to other people, and the decent thing was to sacrifice one's own life so others could have theirs by their expectation of yours. But what happened if everyone felt the same, if he and Kelly could think truthfully to each other, maybe she thought exactly the same, but for the same reasons of duty could not stop the show going onto the stage. "We're doomed, destined to each other and the dead hand of certainty and security," he said to the park at large.

Then now this crazy, weird delightful Sung Lo Hi arrives on the scene with some crackpot scheme. Not a whiff of certainty or security about her or anything she stands for. He doesn't know what to make of it, all this invisibility nonsense. And those files he had read in the office, the place is clearly the worst kind of shithole. And right next door to him too, definitely on his patch. About which he had done precisely nothing. In fact he had done worse than precisely nothing, he had practically encouraged it by his neglect. Her old man is certainly in prison, and quite probably innocent, and about to be despatched to some hell hole of a hard labour penal colony from which he is not expected to return. She'll have to go with him. Getting him out? Doesn't sound too good about the cold, but he can learn the tricks. And she's pretty, no doubt about that; but more, she's flightsome, and smiling again Bo knew he did like a girl, one in a million, who was flightsome.

Just when he felt a decision was needed, a decision between Kelly and Lo Hi, he stopped in his tracks, clicked his thumbs and he realised it wasn't. He needn't choose between Kelly Cuss and Sung Lo Hi, between certainty and insecurity, between duty and adventure, between love later and love now. No, he could have them both. The wedding was ten weeks away, so he had, say, two months in which to save the world in the shape of old man Sung, maybe save his beautiful daughter too, maybe even save himself. Maybe that's the answer. One big bad mad moment, as crazy as you could imagine, and then the dullest payback of forever. Maybe that's how it all works, how to keep everyone else happy.

Bo stopped and looked around. He had become as lost in the park as he had lost in his thoughts. He headed back towards the Tower. As he walked a nagging doubt arrived. He wasn't really going to have his cake and eat it, but he was going to try a different cake for a while. Yes, that's it. Feeling lighter again, now smiling he strode purposefully back to his cupboard, and then on to find Lo Hi.

13

Back home Bo laid out some clothes. He did not have much in the way of a James Bond Milk Tray outfit, but he found some well worn jeans and one of his old college rugby shirts, his best Nikes, and his smart dark brown leather jacket. That's about as tough guy as I'm going to manage, he thought to himself as he hurried into the shower. He ran through the scenario. He would arrive at Kimiko's space, and say to her "I really want to help your father; shall we discuss it in bed? Er, no, maybe not. I really want to help your father, and want to know all the plans. Let's start tomorrow, tonight, today, right now". Bo, scrubbed and dried and dressed, flew down the stairs two at a time into the late afternoon.

He reached Kimiko's block half an hour later, and rang the bell and looked into the camera. No reply, so he rang it again, and looked more squarely into the camera. Hell's bells, he had not thought that she could not have been there. He crossed the road, looked up hopefully at the block, and waited. He waited for twenty minutes, looked at his mobile phone and saw it had been only five minutes, and went for a walk around four blocks. A real twenty minutes later he was back, but again there was no reply to several times of asking.

Bo rang the porter's bell. "Mushi mushi" came the reply. Then he could not remember her name. Kimiko Sabo, Saso, Sako was it? So slowly he said "Kimiko Sa-o, is she in?" He replied something in Japanese that prompted Bo to remember Sato. "Sato, Kimiko Sato?" Another reply in Japanese. "Number 89". Right number; still no reply. Bo was about to leave when the buzzer sounded, and he pushed the door to see the porter side up to him. He signalled for Bo to wait on the chair in the lobby, and disappeared.

Half an hour later and no Lo Hi; an hour, two hours later and still no Lo Hi. The doubt was becoming the certainty which he could no longer shut out. What if she's gone, given up on him, gone back to Pyongyang? But she wouldn't give in, not her. Give up on him, maybe, but never give up on herself. He thought back to the last time they were together—in his office with this fiancée on the phone and the terminally bad news from work on the fax. Maybe she decided he was not up to it. Maybe she was right.

An hour later Bo could no longer sit there surrounded by inadequacy and disappointment. He signalled to the concierge for a pen and paper and he wrote a note for her. "Look no further, I'm your man, when do we start? Call my cellphone 6758 8981, Bo"

He walked back in the dark and closed the cupboard door gloomily. A quiet despair arose, an unrelieved sense of frustration. He opened a half full bottle of sake, realised it was half empty, and determined to drink the disappointment of losing her, and all she stood for, into the night, one of the last nights abroad on his own with the future in front of him and not behind him. In this, at least, he succeeded.

14

The Execution Yard is in fact just a wall between two barrack rooms, joining them at one end. The wall has six shoulder high concrete posts in front of it. Sergeant Ming lines up the thirteen Officer Cadets for their first firing squad duty. He is not happy about the odd numbers. Twelve is the correct number of rifles, four to kill each prisoner, and he flusters to find thirteen to accommodate with still only three prisoners to despatch.

"You are uneven," he shouts in their faces. They do not flinch or look towards him, but straight ahead at the empty wall. "When the six o'clock klaxon sounds the three perverts will be brought out here, and placed against the wall. When I give the order "Prepare for Execution" you will aim at their body parts as I will instruct. When I say "Steady yourself!" you will become tense and prepare to deliver the bullet. Then I give the final order "Liberate!" and you will shoot them cleanly. Are you all listening carefully?"

A murmur of assent arises from the oddly numbered and forward looking firing squad.

"Good. You will form as one line facing the wall. Do it now!" The students form a line immediately. Sergeant Ming stands in front of them. "You four on my right will shoot the degenerate on the left of the wall. You four in the middle will shoot the middle deviant. And you five on my left, yes five, will shoot the girl boy on your right. Understood?"

Before he could check himself Sung Pak Dong coughed for attention.

"Cadet!"

"Sergeant where do I shoot him?" he asks.

"*I* do not shoot anybody, we all shoot together. I am about to explain. The first officer in line shoots at the forehead, the second shoots at the throat, the third shoots at the chest and the fourth at the stomach. So you," shouts Sergeant Ming at the third Cadet along, "where do you shoot?"

"Prisoner on my left, in the chest, Sergeant."

"Good, now do we all understand our duties? When the dogs are dead we can see how accurate your shooting has been. But now we have a problem, the squad on my left has five members. Who is the additional one?"

Sung Pak Dong looks straight ahead. "It is I, Sergeant."

"Then you can shoot him where you like, but not in the forehead, throat, chest or stomach. Where shall it be, Officer Cadet?"

"Wherever you instruct Sergeant."

"A good answer. Shoot him in the balls. One bullet two balls. Can you do that?"

"I will try, Sergeant."

But Sung Pak Dong has his own doubts about hitting so fine a target; he has never felt more uncomfortable about his body in his life. The initiation had started a few seconds after the nine o'clock klaxon the night before. Sung Pak Dong knew it was going to happen by the furtive looks and unsubtle gestures in the dormitory. When he was still uninitiated by lights out, he knew his test would come soon.

The first he had heard was slight movements from other beds as his fellow cadets headed towards him. Then a curtain was pulled back, allowing some light into the room. Then he felt many hands, some pulling off his bedding, some pulling away his pillow and holding it over his face, some tearing off his night clothes. Then he felt hands on his genitals, not roughly at first, but quickly more painfully. Soon he was made to stand up, now naked, with hands around his arms and shoulders pushing him, other hands around his genitals feeling him, then an open door, a cold draught of air, now a feeling of real cold. Next he felt other hands on his legs and feet, so now he is swinging on his back by his arms and legs, with a hand now more aggressively pumping at this genitals, and a feeling of panic and helplessness gripping him as he was rushed along into the cold, stopped and swung once, twice, three times, then thrown with a mighty heave into darkness.

He landed and within an instant knew he was in the thorns and nettles, and felt more and more stinging even as he rushed to stand up, and flee back to the barracks. Running back on the way he felt his left foot tread on something sharp and hard, and knew as well he had cut himself badly. He stood in front of the dormitory, very cold, stinging all over and bleeding, and banged hard on the door to be let in.

"Officer Cadet Sung!" a voice from behind him shouted. The physical training instructor, with a torch in one hand and a ping pong bat in the other, shined the torch at him, and Sung Pak Dong knew he had been deliberately trapped. "You know it is against regulations to leave the barrack dormitory at night."

"Yes, instructor." He knew it was useless to explain, that this was all part of the plan.

"Then you shall be beaten roundly by your class."

In the room, they held Sung Pak Dong, still cold, naked, stinging and bleeding from his foot over a chair and one at a time, with shout of exertion, each beat him once with the bat on his buttocks. Sung Pak Dong knew what he had to do; at all costs, under any circumstances he must not cry out or squeal or beg. After each blow it became harder and harder, catching and holding his breath each time a fresh onslaught of stinging pain fell on him, and then with only the final three to take and the end in sight, a reserve of courage and resolution saw him through, still uncomplaining if shaking almost uncontrollably.

After they took him down, shamed and slumped on the floor, they crowded around him and first one and then the other began to congratulate and welcome him. Another cleaned his foot, and then bandaged it. As he eventually lay in his bed again, clothed and warm, but unable to move through itching all over his body and the stinging on his buttocks, he felt pleased and proud, and fell into a fitful sleep to the murmurs of approval from his new brothers in arms and security.

The six o'clock dawn klaxon snaps him back to the task at hand. Three filthy men, middle aged but hard to tell, are being shoved along and tied to three of the concrete posts before the wall. It all happens surprisingly quickly. Sung Pak Dong looks at the man in front of him, ignoring the other two. The prisoner is slumped already, already dead in his mind. He does not look up when Sergeant Ming orders "Prepare for Execution." Sung Pak Dong raises his rifle, and still feeling the itching and soreness in his genitals from the initiation nine hours ago, aims deliberately at those of the helpless figure propped up before him.

"Steady yourself!" Sergeant Ming is walking behind them. Sung Pak Dong breathes in, holds his breath and tenses his finger on the trigger. He hears, he thinks he hears, Sergeant Ming opens his mouth to bellow "Liberate", and pulls the trigger at the same moment as the first sound, and twelve other bullets fly into their appointed targets fractionally later.

All three prisoners collapse stone dead. Sergeant Ming walks over to inspect the accuracy of his charges. "Fine, good shooting, but one of you shot first, shot as my orders were being given and not just afterwards as is correct. One of you is keen. Who was it?"

The officer cadets stood to attention, none prepared to give Sung Pak Dong's name, although they all know it was him. Sergeant Ming knew too, and with some approval, and with a wry smile to himself Colonel Krop knew later that morning too.

15

Bo wandered into the British Embassy. "Can I help you?" the quasi blonde Japanese receptionist, looking flirtatiously up at him, asked in unusually seamless English.

"Jeremy Lister, please" Bo replied into her cleavage inadvertently, and handing over his business card. Jeremy Lister was the father of his school friend Simon Lister, and when Simon found out Bo was being sent to Tokyo gave him his old man's details "should you ever be in full on desperation, otherwise give him a wide berth." "Why, what does he do there?" Bo had asked. "Beats me, sells vacuum cleaners, thinks he's Carlton-Brown, says he's never actually been able to tell us". "Sounds like a spy," tried Bo hopefully. "Not sure he's that energetic, more like a visa applications clerk with a 007 fantasy," reassured Simon.

"Is he expecting you?" asked the seamless one with the cleavage.

"Not exactly, please tell him I'm a friend of Simon, Simon his son. Er, Simon said it would be alright to call by".

He sat and re-read, skimming through in less than a minute, a Sunday Times Review now ten days old. He looked at the people coming and going. Embassy staff with metaphorical clipboards under their arms, British tourists speaking softly, Japanese visitors looking lost and awed. Ten minutes later he noticed a tall, slightly portly middle aged man nodding to the seamless cleavage and now heading his way.

"Flowerdew-Pett from Amnesty?" he asked. Bo stood and nodded, Lister shook his hand. "Pleased to meet you, and a friend of Simon in Tokyo, shall we take coffee in the canteen?"

They went down to an open plan basement, queued with a tray each, helped themselves to two automatic cappuccinos; Lister paid with a swipe and they sat down opposite each other.

"Well, thanks for seeing me without an appointment," Bo began, "it is just that I'm about to disappear—well not ultimately I hope—but still disappear in a way in North Korea, and I thought I should tell someone in case it all goes pear shaped. Simon said I should contact you whenever the need arose so here I am."

"Yes, I know," replied Lister into his stirring froth.

"You know what?"

"I know that Simon told you, I just called him to check while you were waiting. Can't be too sloppy about these things nowadays, we need to check if the person who says he knows our sons, knows our sons. He does. He confirmed you are who you said you are, well actually he didn't, but he did say he knew someone called Beaumont Flowerdew-Pett. Don't we all," he chuckled to himself sardonically.

"But isn't it three in the morning, or thereabouts? A little early, surely?" Bo asked worried about Simon's famously late sleeping pattern.

"Then the lazy little bugger will just be going to bed, so no harm done." Bo cared for Lister *pere* less by the moment. "Anyway, don't worry about that, what is this disappearing act you do or don't have in mind in NK all about?"

Bo wondered about telling him any more. He had come to confide in a friend's father who was also Her Majesty's trusted servant in these parts, not some supercilious, patronising know-all. "I'm going to release a political prisoner. I might get caught, and I want someone here to know in case I don't come back." Bo wasn't sure if he sounded melodramatic or nonchalant, but that was the gist of why he was here.

Lister couldn't help himself. "So, a British subject swims over to the last totally paranoid Stalinist lunatic asylum-cum-shithouse on earth, takes off his wet suit, climbs down a frozen chimney, murders the guards, springs God knows who or why, blows up an inner tube and they both paddle back to Okinawa and live happily ever after. Am I more or less right?"

Bo rose to the moment. "Well, I'm not planning to murder anybody actually, but otherwise remarkably prescient. Look, I can tell you are not too keen on the whole mission, but all I ask is that if I am not back here by this time next month…"

"…we send a search party?"

"No, but you try to help. Somehow." Bo stood up to leave, Lister gestured him down again.

"Sorry, didn't mean to be so sarky as we used to say. But you must admit it does sound a little unlikely. I mean, whom and why?"

"His name is Sung Pi Jam." Lister's brow alerted itself, Bo kept going, too late to stop now. "He is some kind of nuclear expert. They think he has been selling secrets and he's locked up. I met his daughter, and, well, I don't know why but I have ended up offering to help."

"Never heard of him, but he must have a lovely daughter," Lister deadpanned. "Look, don't get involved in this, don't meddle, you'll be way out of your depth the moment you start and from there the drowning will come upon you very quickly. I must advise against it, you do see that, don't you?" He looked at Bo, shook his head and said, "If you are not back in four weeks we will start asking questions, missing tourist questions. I can't do more than that." He stood up. "I won't even say good luck. I will say think again."

Lister, somehow now more obsequious, walked Bo upstairs and out of the front door, wished him good bye and once more good luck, and walked back upstairs to his office. He sat and thought and doodled. He got up and looked out of the window. Bo was long gone, lost in the morass of Tokyo's millions. Sung Pi Jam, eh? Amnesty International on an active mission? Can't be; cannot be done. OK, he's flying solo, but still. Lister picked up the phone, heard the dialling tone, and put it down again, picked it up again and pressed some numbers.

"United States Embassy," the voice replied.

"Harry Snide please," asked Lister, looking for his opposite number from the CIA. "Harry, it's Jeremy. I think we might have picked up something curious on our radar screen, heading for NK. A certain Sung Pi Jam was mentioned"

"Sung's in NoKo already. In the slammer too."

"I know that Harry. Look, pop round, there's someone doing something somewhere that our friends in NK should keep an eye on. For elevenses at the Interconti coffee shop tomorrow, perhaps?"

"'Our friends in NK'. What friends in NK? We haven't got any, that's the whole problem. We've got local friends all over the world, but not in NK."

"Or the whole of Arabia?"

The CIA man chuckled. Friggin' Brits, never fail. "OK, that'll be ten fifty unless I'm very much mistaken old boy", Harry replied in his best mocklish accent.

Lister smiled too as he put down the phone. "Hook, line and sinker."

16

"Hey, Jeremy, great to see you, buddy. You're lookin' your usual Britannic Majesty's best."

"Hello Harry. We do our best. Nice quiet spot here." They looked around the busiest coffee shop in the busiest hotel in the busiest city in the world, and leant forward to talk to each other quietly.

"So, you got some NoKo action for us," said Snide.

"Yes, a funny one. You've heard of Amnesty International I presume?"

"if you mean Amnesty commie pain in the arse, yes."

"Well their guy over here is going over there to liberate your spook Sung Pi Jam. Now what's that all about?"

"Well, for a start he isn't our spook. We'd like him to be, because he's one of the few who knows what the hell's happenin'. Nuclear wise I mean. Here's our server," Snide leant back and raised his voice to audible: "American coffee and Danish for me, Jeremy?"

"Black tea with milk and digestive biscuits. McVities."

They resumed their huddle. "So Amnesty is going covert?"

"I can't believe that. No, this guy is flying solo. He's a family friend of sorts actually, Beaumont Flowerdew-Pett."

"Crazy name."

"It gets worse. He's fallen for this Sung Pi Jam's daughter. Unfortunately we'll have to keep an eye open for him now we know he's there. So who is this guy of yours anyway?"

"Jeremy, here's the deal. The CIA are worried about North Korea selling uranium hexafluoride to Iran. Now Libya has rejoined the human race, we found out the material for their nuclear bomb came from NoKo. You've heard of Abdul Qadeer Khan?"

"The Pakistani nuclear black marketer?"

"That's him. Well we suspect that he has been supplying NoKo with the wherewithal to go nuclear from a factory in Malaysia.

French backing of course. For that he gets paid with medium and long range Nodong missiles, which is just about the only thing the God forsaken country can make. He then sells them on to Iran, Yemen, Syria, places like that."

"So, it's all part of this famous Axis of Evil?"

"Jeremy, we are not stupid. A little impatient compared to everyone else, maybe. We have pretty overwhelming evidence about what the NoKos are up to, but after Iraq no one believes a word we say, especially about WMD. And we ourselves are not 100% convinced about it, that's true too. We just don't know where they are at, or to be more precise we know they are up to no good, but how bad is their no good, that we don't know. But this Sung Pi Jam, now he will know. Trained in Russia, at the centre of everything nuclear goin' on there."

"And you want him to defect?"

"No, that's not the plan. He's more use to us there if we can turn him. Which looks unlikely I have to say. But we had some good luck, a chance conversation came good. It turns out his neighbour in Pyongyang works for something called the Japan North Korea Trade Authority, which is pretty much as it sounds. Now we've persuaded our friends in the JCIA to call this guy back and put in an active agent, who can get to know our man the neighbour, see if we can get to him round the back."

"And is he any good, this new agent?"

"She. I've never met her, but they reckon she's red hot. Bright and ambitious. Tough too. Kimiko something or other. Well she's got friendly with the daughter who lives there too, I guess that'll be the same one your Flowerman has got the hots for."

"Flowerdew."

"Whatever. Now her JCIA masters are telling us her plan is to compromise the daughter and then blackmail the father. All we want is information. With inside information we can get the Chinese, Russians, SoKos, everyone to believe us and put some squeeze on the Dear Gangster."

"You sound like there's a 'but'."

"Well, the first 'but' is he's managed to get himself banged up, pretty much the same day this JCIA hotshot arrives, so she can forget about compromising the daughter to turn the father. And there's another 'but'. We don't trust the JCIA on this one. Japan and North Korea go back a long way, there's a bunch of old agendas out there, and priority number one isn't necessarily helping their good buddies the CIA. They're bitching at each other over all kinds of stuff, war reparations, abductions, comfort women in comfort camps, disputed islands, you name it, there's a beef. The Japanese think they're pond life, and don't go out of their way to hide it. The NoKos think they're nothing but proxy US imperialists' running dogs. In love with each other they are not, and the big picture for the Japanese has nothing to do with helping us define our Axis of Evil. No, we reckon if she's as good as they say she is, she'll be working on their other stuff at best, and at worst disinforming us to keep the NoKos distracted."

Jeremy Lister leant back. "A pretty picture. So are you going to tell the JCIA girl about our Boy Wonder?"

"If we don't, and they are going to meet in the corridor if nothing else, she'll think he works for MI6 and smell a rat. She'll probably smell a rat anyway if she's that good. Yes, we can just let her know some crackpot Brit is trying to screw her friend the daughter next door. Leave it at that."

"So, where do you go from here?"

"We're going to send someone in to keep an eye on this Kimiko woman, see if she really is shooting for us as well as the Japanese. If she's straight we'll pull some hurry up levers with the JCIA. If she's messing us about we'll land her in the shit. Over there. Big time. Plus our new man can try to turn the daughter anyway, that could be fruitful."

"'New man', so you've got someone in mind?"

"Yeah, he sounds perfect, can keep an eye on your boy Flowerson too."

"Flowerdew," Lister emphasised, then wondered why he'd bothered.

"That's the one. No, our new guy is Korean, South Korean, actually South Korean American, born in Seoul, grew up in Kansas. Parents own a drugstore, the whole thing come true. He looks like a gook, got the lingo down too."

Lister and Snide nodded to each other and rose. "Well, thank you very much for elevenses Harry, a very interesting conversation." On the way out Harry said "Let's hope Flowerpot doesn't end up in the slammer too."

This time Lister didn't bother. "See you around, Harry."

17

Madame Comrade Instructor Ni Joy Ping enters the classroom and tells her charges to sit down. They sit down but do not relax. She stands in front of them, clears her throat and starts the lesson. Her voice is matter of fact and measured metallic staccato.

"First, the results from the firing squad. 100% accuracy and 90% timing. One of you shot ahead of the order. This is unusual. If there is a timing discrepancy in a first time firing squad it is normally for someone, sometimes more than one, being a little late, shall we say hesitant.

"We are four weeks into your twelve week Security Officers' Induction course, and now is the time to order you to start your special assignment. Each one of you can choose any subject you like as long as it furthers the aims of the State Safety and Security Agency. You will each work in your own time, and bring the results for us all to see in eight weeks from now."

The class falls even quieter than before, as each Officer Cadet considers his treatise. Sung Pak Dong knows instantly, without a moment's thought, what he will do: more research into truth serums, his unfulfilled course from university, and then without a further moment's thought a tingle of excitement at having access to equipment and chemicals that were just not available at university.

"Today's lesson is about using pain to extract information. Until now we have studied so-called passive methods to confession, mainly through sleep deprivation, our most powerful weapon, especially when combined with excessive light and noise, we called it Disturbed and Deprived Sleep. We looked at confessions through persuasion using loyalty, using rewards, using family honour, using reasonableness, using recruiting and using bargaining. We studied the effectiveness of passive menace, the sounds of screaming and shooting nearby, and other sorts of distraction. We emphasised that irrespective of a particular sleep deprivation scheme, it is beneficial to hold interrogation sessions at night, from midnight until dawn. Then last week you observed the effects of humiliation, especially potent with female prisoners.

"Most prisoners will be co-operative after some passive methodology, but some, especially Irredeemables, will need further persuasion through pain. If we suspect that the prisoner is ultimately Redeemable it is important that we leave no marks, but if we consider him or her to be Irredeemable it does not matter. Each interrogator has his or her favourite system of inducing pain, and the purpose of this course is not to rank them, or prioritise them, or officially to recommend or condemn method this over method that. Practiced interrogators usually stick to one method, as they become familiar with the resistance required and the medical risks involved. Although there will always be a prison doctor on hand who will advise on how much more pain can be taken in consciousness, nevertheless with greater experience of a particular method, the interrogator can then judge the breaking point himself, almost scientifically.

"Then you have to consider the facilities available. Here we have all the amenities of course, but in a small village police station you may be reduced to just using thorough beatings and they may not even be with the benefit of the suspect strung upside down. That will work, but can be hard work even with rubber truncheons and it is sometimes difficult to judge progress. Generally, short periods of pain are bearable, but longer periods of prolonged pain, especially when added to by peaks of repeatable intensity, are much harder to bear.

"Here we have a water dungeon in the basement. We will show you. It is totally dark and filled up to neck height with human sewage, all waste has been plumbed to go into it. We place prisoners there during the day, but they think it is overnight after sleep deprivation. We take them out and they talk. No-one will ever return, it is as simple as that. And not such hard work for us, other prisoners throw them in or fish them out and hose them down.

"If you cannot wait that long, for example with a detainee's connection who may be about to disappear, sexual treatment works well, and we will show you some experiments in this. For a man, hold him on the floor naked, legs apart, an Officer sitting on each knee and slowly increase the pressure as you tread his testicles onto the ground. Practically no-one can take this pain. But don't bother trying it on eunuchs! For a woman, a wire brush, or old toilet brush, or rat is good, into the vagina. But we have strict orders about children, introduced by the Dear Leader himself. No physical harm must come to any child under 16. But on their 16th birthday we can treat them like their parents. It gives them something to look forward to as they approach their 16th birthday, the prospect of a good gang rape to lose their virginity or loosen their tongues. This works of course with the protecting parents too. Maybe the Dear Leader was acting out of efficiency and not compassion." A nervous movement overtakes the class.

But now Sung Pak Dong was thinking back to the Christian woman he had taken to Camp 18. Presumably she had been passively persuaded by every psychological means, and when that did not work she had been beaten, shocked, molested and probably raped with some vengeance, but had withstood it all. She had finally been broken by an act of total humiliation, but he thought that was a lucky break for Colonel Krop, and although he was sure the Colonel deserved his luck, he could not help think there was a better, more efficient way. Under pain people will say anything to stop the pain. Under medication he was sure they would not be able to help themselves. His work at university with mice and rabbits had shown that beings could be made to be docile and communicative at the same time. But he always had to give the animals back alive so they could be used for other experiments; now they would be more freely available. Now, working on his special assisgment he might be able to experiment on a monkey, and then a real prisoner. Efficiency and confessions, he muses, could help each other and the State.

"So this evening you start work on your own projects," Madame Comrade Instructor Ni Joy Ping announces, as she closes the class, "and tonight we will see a live torture of a prisoner who has failed in his duty to reveal his treacherous connections by passive means."

18

While MI6 were entertaining the CIA for elevenses, Bo left the cupboard he called home in Shinjuku, downtown Tokyo. Actually, compared to most wardrobes where he visited his friends, his cupboard felt like a palace. He folded up the bed against the wall again, and put the computer screen away in its stowaway space. Bo had had a brainwave on the way back from the Embassy, and had spent a most fruitful evening investigating all the David Blaine activity in Tokyo.

On the internet Bo found out all he could about the Tokyo Blaine gang. There was not a website, but a few press references and a copious message board. His Japanese acolytes were certainly enthusiastic. David buries himself alive for a week; a Blainey in Tokyo does exactly the same, to the day of the week and the hour. They even had a voting system to pick the volunteer, all archived on the message boards. David stands on a pole for a couple of days, then jumps off it, ditto here. David freezes himself in ice, next thing someone tries it in Tokyo but this one went wrong, and the poor chap emerged severely frost bitten and suitably humiliated after only fifteen hours. Undeterred another follower picks up the cause three months later and this time succeeds.

They had a leader, Saba-san, who was featured in the press cuttings and ran the bulletin board. As far as Bo could tell there had been no physical contact between the group and their hero, and all the messages to David on the messages boards had gone unanswered. The group met every Tuesday, that very day, at 12.30p.m. in the Reduchi Park.

They were not hard to find in the park, denoted by the words David Blaine Fan Club East across the backs of eleven orange ski jackets, sitting and centred around an older man reading some text. He recognised Saba-san from the internet as the reader, and leader. Bo approached to hear, and even though they read in Japanese he understood enough to know the readings were from the David Blaine Magic book. No-one turned around to look at him, another unusual sign, Bo noticed, as he joined in the circle. Funny, here I am a westerner, a blonde westerner, at whom everybody stares all the time, and no-one is paying me any attention. Maybe I'm invisible already, Bo hoped without much conviction. The readings over, another member produced some drawings and a model of a glass box. From the drawings and the box, and from what he understood, Bo saw that they were planning to emulate the David-in-hanging-box-over-the-River-Thames stunt.

Eventually the meeting broke up with a ceremony involving the circling becoming complete, everyone lying down and overlapping legs to form an unbroken chain. After they had left he approached the leader. "I'm interested in ice, surviving in ice." Bo thought it better not to say anything about North Korean winters. The leader replied in perfect American.

"Hi, my name is Saba, Saba-san. Our group may look like we are only interested in the physical side of David' feats, but that is only the beginning. Only what you see. There is a spiritual dimension to it, in fact it is the only dimension that matters. We meet to explore the limits of physicality, and so often we meet the very spirits of the daring, of the frontiersmen who have touched death and failed to return. The void. These men are involved in acts of unspeakable bravery. Why do you want to know about ice death?"

"Um, well actually I don't. Want to die that is. No, no, I'm going on holiday, you see, mountain climbing, and remembered David Blaine and ice blocks, and thought you might be able to help me prepare. Staying warm I mean, you know when it's cold. I want to travel sparsely."

"I don't think you understand. We are not talking light-heartedly about going on holiday. We are exploring the tiny fractions of the evolving interface between danger, near death and death itself. Our masters are Houdini and Blaine and from them we find courage, we can share their first hand dangerous exploits and near death experiences. These experiences also bring us into contact with the spirits of those who have gone before, and from their mediums in that parallel world we can learn from those who have crossed the shallow divide between death and danger. This is not about going on holiday Mr., er Mr?"

"Pett. Mr. Pett, Pett-san if you prefer. No I just wondered, you know, how David prepared for living in ice for so long. I mean, what did he do?"

"We know what you mean Mr. Pett, but this is not a journey for mere initiates like yourself to undertake without any awareness of the far deeper aspects of its preparation. You can say he took cold baths, ice baths for preparation, or that he slept outside in Artic nights, but his and our work is not on the physical level. We suffer his physical torments, we replicate them, but like him we cross over to near death and back, Mr. Pett. I urge you not to go down this route unprepared. "

"So you can't tell me how to prepare to be cold?"

"I can tell you how to prepare Mr. Pett, but to say the truth— that to prepare the body you must prepare the mind—is worthless to someone like yourself who only dabbles on the fringes of spaces we have been to and returned from many times. But only we know how to go beyond preparation, and that is where you will need to be. Sayonara Mr. Pett."

"My mind or my body?"

"Your mind is always with your body, the perception of differentiation is the route cause of many of our societal grievances today. But you must take the body somewhere cold, much colder than here."

"Where to, to Russia?"

"I hear Russia is cold, but North Korea is colder. Prepare there. Goodbye Mr. Pett, maybe one day we will both know the meaning of touching the void, but first we must return from the void."

Bo walked away, his mind on Lo Hi again, an involuntary smile on his face and a small ache in his heart.

"Mr. Pett!"

Bo turned round to see Saba-san walking back towards him. "Very well, maybe I was too hasty. I can tell you are sincere, and after all our mission is to extend awareness of Blaine consciousness. If you would join our group I can take you to our baths, the baths where we prepared for the freezing void experience. But first, you must try to prepare for them, as they in themselves will be far more severe, physically severe, than anything you have undertaken, but maybe not as severe as to where your ultimate mission may take you. Meet me at the Ankara Baths, Guido-chome, on Friday after work. Once more, sayonara Mr. Pett."

"Sayonara Saba-san."

19

The Officer Cadets are uneasy. It is past ten at night, and past their normal bedtime. Every day started with the five o'clock klaxon, and followed by a swift routine thereafter: shower, breakfast, firing squad if needed, classes, exercise, lunch, class, sport, singing and studying, so that by nine at night they had no disappointment with the lights-out klaxon; in fact many were already dozing or asleep, in spite of the always-on radio carrying a news item:

The 60-year long history of the Workers' Party of Korea and the country is shining and the Korean nation has an immensely rosy future thanks to the Socialist revolutionary leadership exploits of Kim Jong Il. It is necessary to eternally glorify these exploits as an eternal foundation of the Workers Party of Korea. The last one decade occupies a most brilliant page in the glorious 40-odd year-long revolutionary history of his socialist leadership. Never has there been such a period in which astonishing victories and changes have taken place in all fields of the revolution and construction as the last one decade. Under the banner of glorious Kim Il Song-ism the DPRK has consolidated the single-minded unity of the revolutionary ranks in every way and firmly built up its military deterrent while providing a solid material foundation for building a great prosperous powerful nation. Modern production bases have been built in different parts of the country to meet requirements of the new century. The land of the country has been realigned as befitting the land of socialist Korea, a signal turn has taken place in the seed improvement and potato farming and many monumental edifices of eternal value have appeared. The Great Leader and now the Dear Leader have firmly protected the destiny of the country, the nation and socialism despite the most diffi-cult situation and the grimmest trial and brought about epoch-making changes unprecedented in the history of the nation spanning thousands of years, thereby providing a solid foundation for eternal prosperity of Kim Il Sung's Korea and happiness for all generations to come. The Korean people will never forget these immortal exploits no matter how much water may flow under the bridge.

Included in his benevolent revolutionary leadership exploits are all the ideological, theoretical, strategic and tactical guidelines that should be held fast to in the revolution and construction and the tradition of heroic struggle and a wealth of experience in which he has brought about epoch-making miracles and changes by turning adversity into a favourable situation, misfortune into a blessing.

The above-said exploits serve as an eternal lifeline of the country and revolution and treasure that the Korean nation should hand over to posterity and make them shine for all ages.

But tonight is the first live torture night, and none of them knows when it would start, only that like all deep interrogations it will be in the early hours. Some of them doze, or try to doze, or read, or just stay awake fully clothed and waiting.

It is Sergeant Ming himself who opens their door at one o'clock and orders them to follow. They climb into an old coach and are driven through empty dark streets, still near the city centre, to a building new to all of them. The coach parks, they enter an anonymous dank concrete five storey building by a side door, they follow Sergeant Ming downstairs, through brightly lit corridors and into a large empty room with only one bare light on a wire from the ceiling. As they enter their boot steps echo around the room as they had down the corridor. Sergeant Ming orders them to sit against one of the side walls, and cross legged they form a line accordingly.

"The prisoner is Hung Cho Kin, from the peasant class, accused of slandering the Leadership. He was arrested last month. The fellow slanderer confessed immediately, gave us another unconnected slanderer's name, was beaten quite leniently, recruited as a snitch, given a reporting quota and released. But this one, Hung Cho Kin, refuses to acknowledge another slanderer. But one thing is certain, there are always three in any conspiracy, that is human nature. His co-accused gave us his third name; and so must Hung Cho Kin.

Now this Hung Cho Kin has overhead hearing that the Dear Leader had one billion dollars hiding in a bank in Swaziland, an obvious slur because there is not one billion dollars in the world. His co-locutor has confessed as I said, but this one has not revealed to whom he passed on the slur, or from whom he also heard it."

Sergeant Ming takes the gun from his holster and places it on the table, pointing at the door. He turns on two study lamps and directs the shine at the door too.

"This is my cattle prod, I call it my persuader. It is not as powerful as a fixed electric installation, that is true, but for me it has the advantage of portability. It is a new model from France, but as there are no cattle in France they sell them to the Chinese. I cannot vary its voltage, so I control its effect by time. After sixteen seconds on a sensitive point most prisoners will talk. After nineteen seconds they will loose control of their functions and become messy, so I stop after seventeen or eighteen, depending on their strength. It is a primitive yet technically efficient persuader.

"Wait," he says and leaves, then comes back. "I nearly forgot. We do not always bother with passive menace first time under pain, but tonight for your benefit we will create extra pressure from outside. We will make another suspect scream, really scream until he, no make that she, begs then screams some more from just outside. Then we will fire a blank as if to terminate her, and so our Hung Cho Kin is in total shock." Then he leaves again, and the students fall still with some apprehension, and yes, Sung Pak Dong senses for some of them, some excitement.

The thought crosses Sung Pak Dong's mind that it would be exciting, even useful, to have a lie detector to help with this peasant Hung. He remembers the simple one they had made at university and tested on each other. Even that was 85% successful on average over many questions, and the students rephrased the questions each time to eke out any variations. They had all longed to build a proper polygraph. In his mid-thought the doors fly open and Hung is thrown into the room, pushed by the boot of Sergeant

Ming. Hung stumbles, is picked up and stood on a spot by the door. He screws his face up against the bright glare from the lights. He looks exhausted. The students note sleep deprivation objectively. Sergeant Ming walks back to behind his desk on the far side of the long room.

"Hung Cho Kin, you are a lucky slanderer. You have the opportunity to help instruct these future interrogators. Lucky is it not?"

Hung mumbles something that cannot be heard.

"Speak up, peasant, we cannot hear you!"

He tries again, but still cannot make himself heard across the long open space.

"Stand up straight. Look at me." It is plain to them all that the peasant Hung can only see light. "Now answer more clearly, more loudly, are you a lucky slanderer, or not?"

Hung collect himself, pulls some dignity from within amongst the fear and agrees that, yes, he is a lucky peasant, and a lucky slanderer.

From the corridor they all now hear the sound of struggle and raised voices, then blows being struck and a woman screeching. Then silence for a few seconds, then out of the blue more screaming, louder this time, then sobbing and pleading but the words are unclear. Then more silence. Then a piecing, ear piercing scream, a scream from total raw and acute intense pain. Then silence. Then a loud male shout, and order. Then a pistol shot. Then a more profound silence.

"Unfortunate that, Hung Cho Kin, some people will not learn to share their information for the greater good of the collective. I have just acquired this new electric stick, a new and untried model, and I hope you do not mind if I see if it is working efficiently."

Sergeant Ming strides across the room towards Hung, his red cattle stick held out before him. On instinct, Hung moves away, circling the room, until still looking at the approaching Sergeant Ming, he stumbles on the first cross legged student, who grabs his feet. Hung falls across them, landing with his head on the floor just in front of Sung Pak Dong. Sung Pak Dong can now see that he has some bruising around his face.

Sergeant Ming pokes him in the nape of his neck with his prod.

Within seven seconds, Hung is crying out. Sergeant Ming tries again on his inside thigh, this time for a little longer, and Hung starts to shake and doubles up around his thigh. Sergeant Ming reaches down, pulls him up by his collar and drags him to the spot by the door, and heaves him upright.

"Good, that seems to work, now the formalities are over I would like to ask you some questions, if you don't mind, peasant and slanderer Hung Cho Kin."

The only lights in the room were the two desk spotlights that are shining directly at Hung Cho Kin. He is standing in their full glare, mesmerised by the light. Sung Pak Dong, still sitting cross legged on the floor looks up at the prisoner. The shadows thrown by the lights from underneath make Hung Cho Kin look even more tired and terrified than he obviously is. He looks wearily, otherworldly as Sergeant Ming walks behind him. He is probably only about thirty, but now looks much older, hard to tell.

"Your friend Im Jung Son told us about another denigrator, the worker Jo Myong Chat. Do you know him?"

"No, we have never met. I have said so many times."

"Curious, because he says he knows you."

"It is impossible. I swear. We never met, I don't even know him."

"Yet you know the peasant Im Jung Son."

"Yes, you know that."

"And apart from Jo Myong Chat, how many other workers do you know?"

"I don't know any other workers, only peasants."

"What do you mean other workers? Other than whom?"

"I didn't mean other, it was in your question."

"And in your answer. Now we know you know another worker apart from Jo Myong Chat. You just said so. We seem to be making some pro..."

With no warning and in total surprise the lights go out. Sung Pak Dong glances to his left in the darkness and notices the passage lights have gone too, the whole basement is totally black. Another power cut, they all know immediately.

Sung Pak Dong stays on the floor and hears the sound of stumbling and a chair and table moving. Then Sergeant Ming cursing, then Hung Cho Kin yelping, then Sergeant Ming shouting "You filthy degenerate scum. Biting the hand that feeds you while the masses all pull their weight!", then Hung Cho Kin crying out, this time rising and falling, warbling in his pleas as the prod feels over his body in the blackout. "Bastard!" shouts Sergeant Ming again, followed by a crescendo screech, and then loud open sobbing from Hung Cho Kin.

The door squeaks open and the bellowing voice of Sergeant Ming echoes down the corridor demanding light. Without a reply, Sung Pak Dong assumes they are alone in the building. Then a dim light is seen, growing stronger, a torch in the passage, and a young voice saying "Power cut!"

"Idiot, we know there's a power cut!" shouts Sergeant Ming. "What about the generator?"

"We are firing it up now sir. But I came to say there is very little fuel left, maybe fifteen minutes, enough for you to clear the building."

At once they hear an engine start and see the ceiling bulb and two desks lights flickering back on unsteadily. Hung Cho Kin is now kneeling, doubled up on the floor, crying softly.

"Dog!" Sergeant Ming is in full voice inches from his left ear. He still has the prod in his right hand and places it deliberately between the kneeling Hung Cho Kin's buttocks. Hung Cho Kin cries out again, shakes all over, and falls reeling onto his side.

"We don't have long," announces Sergeant Ming reaching into the desk drawer and throwing the Officer Cadet nearest to him a coarse blood stained rope. "Tie him up."

The Officer Cadet loops the rope around Hung Cho Kin's wrist and is about to throw the other end over the beam when Sergeant Ming notices and hisses "Not that way, other way up." and undoes the rope, ties it tightly again around Hung Cho Kin's ankles and pulls him off the ground upside down.

"Now listen to me you peasant dog. We only have ten minutes. You were about to tell me about the other worker you smeared the Dear Leader to."

Hung Cho Kin can no longer talk coherently, his brain and body racked by lack of sleep and nourishment, and excesses of unknown horrors and deep pain.

"Who!?"

A burble of low moans is all that Sung Pak Dong and the others can hear.

Sergeant Ming turns to the Officer Cadets, and tells them in a calm matter of fact way about pressure points, areas of the body where his cattle prod is at its most effective. Then he walks over to Hung Cho Kin, still swinging upside down, and places the prod around his body.

"We already know about the nape of the neck and between the eyes, and you have seen the inside thigh and the rectum. But let me show you some others." With his left hand he pulls Hung Cho Kin's arm straight and feels for his funny bone. Hung Cho Kin is already crying out and shaking, but suddenly is shaking violently and crying desperately.

"Aha! Not so funny now is it?!" shouts Sergeant Ming and roars to himself with laughter.

"Then we have our old friend the testicles, and even better the upside down testicles." Even at the thought of this Hung Cho Kin starts shuddering and pleading, and so when Sergeant Ming applies his prod it seems impossible for Hung Cho Kin to take any more, but somehow he does.

"Name of worker?!"

Very quietly, and with a voice unrecognisable from the one of even an hour ago, Hung Cho Kin just mutters "No-one. I know no-one. Please."

Sergeant Ming walks back to him, and side foots him in the head. He reaches for the rope and releases it. Hung Cho Kin drops to the floor as a dead weight. Sung Pak Dong suspects for the first time that Hung Cho Kin might be telling the truth.

"Tomorrow. We resume tomorrow. And tomorrow after that. And then tomorrow after that. We have hardly started. It will stop when you stop lying."

Sergeant Ming turned to the Officer Cadets." We better go. We can lock him in here until tomorrow."

Sung Pak Dong would not normally have dared to ask so boldly above his station, but the last hours have blunted his sophistication. "Sergeant Ming, may I have him for my special assignment?"

Sergeant Ming looks surprised. "What do you mean, Sung?"

"I need someone to experiment on, Sergeant, for my project."

"You can do what you like with him between now and this time tomorrow. But I want him kept alive. He will confess or I will be the one to kill him."

"Thank you Sergeant," said Sung Pak Dong standing up. The others look at him with curiousity, and from the floor Hung Cho Kin looks up at him piteously. Sergeant Ming kicks him in the stomach on his way out, locks the door, and they walk in file down the passage as the lights go out.

20

Bo went back to his cave, and considered—with some initial enthusiasm—how to be a good Blaine acolyte and practice being cold before the rendezvous with Saba-san on Friday evening. In London he would have run a cold bath, ordered ice from Tesco on the internet and slowly lowered the temperature with each new block of ice. But here? There were no baths in most cupboards, and as far as he knew, even in Japan, they had yet to invent an ice shower, so Bo ran a cold shower as best he could. He tentatively offered it his hand, withdrew the offer, told himself to get on with it, kept his hand in, then his elbow and for a minute stood shivering under the mildly cold torrent. He stepped out, dried and dressed and observed that, come to think of it, that that was not even cold.

He happened to live around the corner from the Dynasty Inn, which had a Best Western sign outside. Bo had walked past it a hundred times without thinking about it too much, but now it became the obvious source for a bath.

"Hello, sir, you live near here", said the receptionist in hopeful English, half a question, half a statement.

"Yes, that's right," said Bo, slightly taken aback. "Um, do your rooms have baths?"

"All rooms have baths, same bath, same room. You want big bath, better public baths."

"No, you see I want a cold bath, one where I can control the cold. Adding ice for example. You have ice, no?"

"Yes, have ice. You want ice bath?" she asked with curiousity.

"Yes, but I'll take a room too, spend the night, but maybe half in the ice bath and half in the hot bed," Bo explained.

"OK. You follow."

They went upstairs to a long row of identical rooms, each with a high volume television blaring from inside. She opened a quieter door, flicked on a switch, turned sideways to squeeze into the room, and then opened another door, the bathroom door.

Bo peered inside and said "That's not really what I had in mind. That's really a seat which floods..."

"You don't like flooding seat? Is bath too. Room with bath only $310, take water often for price too."

"Er, no thanks," said Bo, and retreated back to his cupboard to regroup. Clearly a proper bath was going to be $500 plus a night, and he had planned on a few days worth of ice baths as even a token effort at Blaineism, which he felt was probably inadequate anyway. He looked out of the window and the word Ankara suddenly overtook him. "Of course," he said to himself standing up, "solution staring you in the face. Go to the very same Ankara, must be Turkish baths, before meeting the Blainies there."

Bo packed his towel and swimming trunks, uncertain if either would be encouraged or even allowed, and set off in search of the coldest available experience he could imagine. He had to walk up and down Guido-chome twice before finding it, but there above a doorway and a staircase he saw a sign "The Original and Authentic Old & New Ankara Turkish and Ottoman Baths". The word Ankara was emboldened and he recognised the Japanese characters for the sound below it. No doubt this was the place, and entering into a green lit passageway he followed an orange arrow taking him down to the basement. Bo opened the door and inside was greeted by extraordinary ornate mock Turkish décor, and behind a carved marble desk a bald and portly, uncomfortable looking and heavily sweating, Japanese man with a turban and robe.

"Man or woman?" he asked, wiping his forehead with a folded white hand towel.

"What do you mean, man or woman? I'm man, what woman?" replied Bo.

"Men only."

"I know, but why did you ask about women?"

"No can take woman."

"So I see. One man one hour please."

"Three hours only. Man only, no woman."

"I see, in that case I'll have one man for three hours."

"Say so start."

Bo thanked him the best he could, found a locker and half undressed until he could judge the local form. Everyone was naked, so he fully undressed, and went looking for the extremes of hot and cold that he told himself would make a man of him, or at least prepare him for the peer group Blainality of Friday evening.

Two and a half hours later, stark naked in the steam room, having worked his way up from the warm room, via the dry room and the sauna, unable to see a half a metre in front of him, scalding hot on the breath and sweating himself like a waterfall, Bo knew he could put it off no longer. The coldness beckoned, the call that had to be answered. He stood up, felt his way out of the steam room, and in the main hall could see a pool with surrounding pillars and no steam. Next to it were a series of showers permanently flowing. He could tell they were cold too. He walked over to the showers, aware of some eyes following him, put out his hand and withdrew it immediately. As nonchalantly as he could he sauntered back into the safety of the steam room, sat back down on a bench and wished he were anywhere else.

"For heavens sake man get a grip," he said to the steam. He knew the only way was to jump directly into the bath and take the shock, but also knew that the strict etiquette would require him to rinse off under the cold showers first. Logic told him the showers would be a good half way house too, preparation for the big dip. A horrible thought arose. This would be no small dip like he had in mind for now come Friday, but a prolonged soak. He also knew in true Japanese style it would be properly cold; oh! to be in Ankara now where he suspected they did things by less than the full measure.

He rose again and this time determined to go straight to the showers, without looking left or right, without holding out an exploratory hand, without flinching when the agony and shock hit him. After all, he had been to an English boarding school, he reminded himself. He found his way out into the main hall, took a deep breath, stared at the showers, and put his left foot forward for the short march.

"Mr. Pett, ah Mr. Pett". It was the ill-looking receptionist.

"Hello," said Bo, aware of his nakedness in front of the Turkishly robed inquisitor in front of him.

"Your three hours complete. Want more?"

"Oh no, that will be fine."

"No need pay now, pay leave."

"No, no, that will fine, enough's enough, ha ha."

"OK, I see now you go cold pool, have time."

"Oh, no, no that's alright, if the time is up the time is up, that will be fine."

The man turned and walked away, looking a little surprised and somewhat baffled. Bo skipped back to the changing room, feeling a little sheepish, and knowing that Friday's appointment, same time, same place, had just been cancelled.

Out in the street on the way home, Bo immediately noticed a chill in the air. Maybe the contrast to the humid heat of the Ankara, he thought, or maybe the onset of the dry chill of autumn evenings, but he wrapped his collar up as best he could after the first sneeze. He thought again of Lo Hi, and warming to the memory and the expectation, remembered how she had banged on about the cold. Well, he said to himself, you'll just have to wing it when you are over there. Make it up as you go along, as time has honoured. Smiling again, he sneezed, and sneezed again.

On first stretch the next morning Bo knew he was in trouble, that first sense of a tickle at the back of the throat. Maybe just a little sniffle later on, maybe full on flu he thought. Yesterday had been a bit of a dismal flop, all his efforts at practising cold had merely resulted in him catching a cold. But he must move on: today was the day for planning the journey to Pyongyang. "Lo Hi," he said aloud from his bed, "I'm on my way."

21

At exactly 8.30 a.m. Professor Ju Flo Mong of the Department of Biology faculty at the Great People's University in Pyongyang starts his day in his laboratory by refilling the water container for his white mice when the telephone rings. He hears coins entering the box at the other end of the line. He answers the phone.

"Sir, this is Sung Pak Dong from last year's course."

"Yes, Sung Pak Dong, I remember you well. And you are well?"

"I am well, sir, and now seconded to the SSSA for my Patriotic Duty. Sir, I have only a few coins and not much time. Directly I must ask: is it possible I can have some of the truth serum we were working on in semester six?"

"It is university property, I am not sure what would be the procedure. And why do you want it?"

"We all have special assignments and I have chosen a more scientific approach to finding truth. We are interrogating a potential slanderer. No more simulating on mice and rats, we can try it."

Professor Ju Flo Mong hears beeps and more coins. He is standing again now, and suddenly as excited as Sung Pak Dong. "I could bring some if you can arrange the permission. Where are you?"

"I am at the Freedom Flower Building on Donang Street. There is a side door on your right. Can we meet in an hour?"

Professor Ju Flo Mong hesitates. In an instant he is calculating the risks of breaking a procedure, a procedure he does not know, with the rewards to testing his serum. But subconsciously he knows he is well connected, from the intellectual class and with a fair share of privileges, and is finally totally Redeemable. "I'll be there in an hour."

Sung Pak Dong leads his Professor into the room where Hung Cho Kin lies in a filthy bundle on the floor. The Professor has never been in such a place, and never seen such a scene. "Sung, you did this? I cannot believe my student did this!"

"Not I, sir, but it is a class. A different class from ours at university. He is a peasant and maybe a slanderer. The serum can show us."

"Let's clean him first," says the Professor.

"Not inject him sir? Now, like this."

"You have changed Sung Pak Dong. Have you forgotten your humanity as a scientist? The serum will work best with the accused, not against him."

They haul Hung Cho Kin to the shower room, and start to spray him. He is not strong enough to wash himself, but only to move his head towards the water so he can drink. They let him drink. He slumps back on the floor. They direct the spray all over him. There is no soap, but the water going into the drain is filthy. After three minutes, Hung is strong enough to push himself onto his elbow. They turn off the shower. He looks up at them, and weakly asks who they are.

Professor Ju Flo Mong tells him they are his friends and have come to help. He looks at Sung Pak Dong, notices his uniform and cowers. Sung Pak Dong holds his left arm straight and wraps his belt around Hung Cho Kin's bicep. The professor takes a box from his pocket, and needle and syringe from the box and empties half of it into Hung Cho Kin's vein. Within seconds Hung Cho Kin has slumped back, a distant smile on his lips and look of bewilderment in his eyes.

They take him back to the interrogation room and seat him in Sergeant Ming's chair. He can barely balance to remain upright.

"You are Hung Cho Kin?" asks Sung Pak Dong.

"No," whispers Professor Ju Flo Mung, "not that way round." Then in normal voice at the prisoner.

"What is your name?"

"Hung Cho Kin."

"What is your class?"

"Peasant."

"What is your family?"

"One father alive, one mother dead. Two children."

"Where would you like to see them again?"

"In the apartment. All of us togeth….". But the prisoner has now faded, and losing all control falls straight off the chair before they have a chance to catch him.

"What now?" asks Sung Pak Dong anxiously

"We are in unknown territory. The mice never faded like this. Maybe more serum for more truth?" but his tone was more statement than question, and Sung Pak Dong would not have argued anyway. They lay Hung Cho Kin down flat and injected him again with the other half of the syringe.

At first the prisoner rallies and is propped up back in the chair. The Professor asks Sung Pak Dong to question him now.

"Your friend Im Jung Son told us about another denigrator, the worker Jo Myong Chat. Do you know him?"

"I know Im Jung Son, but not Jo Myong Chat. Have you asked me this before?"

"Yes, but we need to know for sure. To protect your family, to save your children. We only need to know your collaborator, if it is not Jo Myong Chat."

"My children. The truth. I know no Jo Myong Chat."

The Professor held up his hand to Sung Pak Dong. "We understand. We understand. Your collaborator is not Jo Myong Chat. But who is it? Please tell us, for the sake of the collaborator, and his family, and for your family too."

Hung Cho Kin leans forward a little, and smiles at the far wall. "But that's the point, there is no collaborator except myself. I am my own one you see, that is really the t…" and then he slumps back faded again. They hear steps beating quickly along the corridor, becoming louder as they approach. The steps stop outside the door. The handle turns softly, and the door is pushed open almost gently. In the frame they see Sergeant Ming.

"I heard you were here Sung Pak Dong, and with company," and looking at the clean and slumped Hung Cho Kin added "and with your experiment in full progress."

"Sir, I must introduce you to Professor Ju Flo Mung of the Great People's University Biology Department."

"I am Sergeant Ming of the State Security and Safety Agency." The Sergeant bowed his head abruptly, the professor followed suit less certainly and with his some distaste. "Did the dog confess?"

"He did confess, and confessed that he knows nothing."

"Professor, you are a scientist, am I right?"

"It is my profession."

"And I am an interrogator, that is my profession. From the prisoner's eyes I would say you have given him some medicine, am I right?"

"It is more than a medicine, it is a truth serum."

"Very well, but you cannot know if the serum emits the truth beyond the most banal examples, am I right?"

"Not for sure, but…"

"Exactly. I cannot see the point. My methods may be more traditional, but they work to my satisfaction. For instance you seem to say that the slanderer here is innocent, whereas all my experience, and it is my profession, tells me we have some way to go to prove this one way or another. Perhaps a little further experiment, Professor?"

"But he is unconscious."

"Not with him, with another anti-statist we arrested this morning, a black marketeer selling South Korean literature. We know from a snitch, a very proper and productive snitch with many privileges, that there is at least one other recipient of these publications than the name he has already offered, another snitch as it happens. Professor Ju, let us have a wager between us?"

"What wager?"

"If the black marketeer confesses to what we know to be the truth with your serum we will assume Hung Cho Kin is telling truth. If he does not confess, well then according to your scientific assumptions Hung Cho Kin is still lying. In that case I will return with Sung's class tomorrow morning and when we return we will torture him to confession or death; and if to death it will not be a quick process. If you have faith in your so-called serum, I am sure you will agree to the wager, Professor Ju."

"Well, yes," agreed Professor Ju Flo Mung uncertainly.

"And you, Officer Cadet Sung, do you agree, and witness the wager?"

"Yes, sir," said Sung Pak Dong more confidently.

"And you have your medicine with you, Professor Ju?"

"Yes, enough for one more session."

Sergeant Ming walks over to Hung Cho Kin, by now semi-conscious with eyes open as if staring into space. He takes his cattle prod from inside his trouser leg. Then he points it at Hung Cho Kin, then holds it between his eyes. "Don't worry," he says to the room, "it is not turned on. But I swear to the Great Leader's memory that if it has to be turned on again I will have the truth from you, you slandering swine." He puts the prod under Hung Cho Kin's chin, lifts up his head to face his own. "You better hope the Professor's medicine works well, or you'll be idiot dancing upside down until I wring a confession from you." Then turning to the others, "Follow me."

22

Every rut and ridge at Shanghai International Airport taxiways seemed to knock another rivet out of the old Air Koryo Ilyushin-62. Bo looked around his fellow travellers on Flight JS160 to Pyongyang and saw that all six foreigners on board had been given, unrequested, seats in the emergency exit row.

Bo sneezed, cursed even the tail end of this filthy cold that been with him since his first and only, not to mention woefully inadequate, attempt at Blaineism back in Tokyo, and thought back to the last three weeks organising his journey to see Lo Hi, to meet Kimiko, and who knows, to free Pi Jam. To North Korea one cannot simply arrive unannounced; in fact from Japan one cannot simply arrive at all. There needs to be a tour, the tours are called Peoples Tours, they start in Shanghai and so it was to Shanghai that Bo took his stinking cold. Up four flights of the noisiest, echoing, paint peeling stairwell Bo had seen since the stop over in Kowloon on the way for some not totally successful R&R en route for Tokyo nearly nine months ago.

The door had said People Tours, Bo knocked and entered to see two New Zealanders talking on the phone in Korean, surrounded by piles of official looking paperwork with seals and stamps and string binding.

"Yes mate," said the man, hand cupped over the phone.

"I want to visit North Korea, heard I need to see you," replied Bo.

"Take a seat. You got a visa?" Bo shook his head. "OK, first thing is we get you a visa. Why do you want to go?" He looked at the phone, shrugged, put it down and held out his hand to Bo. "Mike Reilly's the name, this is my old lady Cerise."

"Well, you know, I'm here, it's there. Curiosity I suppose, usual thing. I need to join a tour?"

"You certainly do. Nasty sounding cold you've got there mate. NK is the last place you want to take a cold," he laughed. "We have tours of cultural sights, language, museums that sort of thing, all very political those. Then there are sporting activities like gymnastics, mountain climbing, martial arts galore. They are soccer crazy, no end of those. Golfing has just started, still only eleven holes though. Juche tours, that's to study their political philosophy which basically means man stuffs nature, opposite of the Toa in a nutshell. Then you've got your health tours, you know mud slinging, hot and cold running spas, whipping in the sauna. There's a motorcycle tour later on. What's your bag?"

"Well I could go along with any of those, perhaps not the physical stuff. What's the next one?"

"Next up, that's the steam engine tour, leaving in a couple of weeks. We'd have to start on your visa now though. You know anything about steam engines?"

"Only a load of hot air." replied Bo, "Why, is anyone going to ask me?"

"Not if you go through the motions, look interested, or at least don't look too disinterested or they might get suspicious."

And so they had agreed. Bo filled in the visa application form as a train spotting tourist on a tour of Asia. Mike and Cerise shuffled papers around to include him in the Friendship and Freedom Steam Engine Appreciation Tour No. 7.

Now shaking vibrantly on the end of the runaway, Bo did not realise it, but a minute after he left the People Tours office, Mike Reilly picked up the phone again, and dialled a number in Tokyo.

"Snide."

"Harry, this is Mike in Shanghai. Your man Flowerdew-Pett is on his way."

"Details?"

"Steam Engine Tour 7. Leaves on Wednesday week, he'll be staying at the Glorious Lodge. I've requested Choo as the guide, said he did such a great train job last time. Shall I warn Choo he's coming anyway.?"

"Yeah, and I got another one for you, one of ours this time, can you get him on the same tour as Flower-de-dah—and Choo if you can swing it?"

"It's going to be tight Harry, numbers and timing. Who is he?"

"He's a SoKo, US citizen, Nark Am Dim, flyin' under the name of Paul Kane."

"Can you make him Canadian?"

"Sure. He'll be with you day after tomorrow, I'll e-mail his new passport details and photos over to you in an hour."

"You don't ask much," said Reilly, winking at Cerise.

"You're too good Mike," replied Snide, "stick it on the Company's bill."

"I already have," said Reilly, putting down the phone.

The plane lifted slowly, tentatively exploring its place in the skies. Now shaking through the clouds, Bo saw the Aeroflot signs crudely scratched off the seat belt clip, and the Air Koryo sticker already peeling off on top of it. He reached forward to the tray, undid the clip and half of it came out in his hand. He smelt the cigarette smoke from those around, saw the full ashtray, closed his eyes, was sharply jolted by another cloud and looked out to see the flexing wing. Bo wasn't worried, he had never feared flying, or speed of any kind, but looking around at everyone else he thought that maybe he should be.

Next door in the middle seat, and the aisle seat beyond, his fellow foreigners were becoming nervous, some with eyes shut, all gripping the armrests. Bo looked around the cabin, no-one apart from the other westerners seemed too concerned as the plane bumped again against the disturbed air. Bo thought about the return journey, maybe with two or three invisible people on board, and him likely to be one of them. The plane landed, shuddering onto the rough runway, and he saw through the grimy, misted window a perfectly formed concrete block, with no windows and no signs, and knew this must be Sosan International Airport and the thought that this was as far as he wanted to go.

Bo and his fellow train spotters had been ordered to stay behind as the others had left the plane, and were then escorted into a rattley old Soviet era minibus and taken to an even quieter part of the airport terminal. The blinds were pulled down so Bo could not take in much of an impression of the airport. The bus stopped suddenly and they were marched, politely, into a cavernous but empty hall with bare concrete walls except for two large posters of The Leaders, Great and Dear.

As warned in Shanghai, The Democratic People's Republic of Korea Customs, Importation and Tariffs Brigade went through all their bags by X-ray and hand, looking for telephoto lenses and video cameras, tape recorders and binoculars, mobile phones and local addresses. Bo looked at the dark grey uniforms and black caps with pronounced beaks, and at the men and women inside them determinedly, procedurally, checking and rechecking every item of luggage. Ominously Bo noticed that smiling did not seem to work as now they pulled apart his smart new clothes and recently thumbed train books, and packed them more meticulously than he had in Shanghai.

The Democratic People's Republic of Korea Immigration and Resettlement Brigade were quicker about their work but still thorough as every page of every passport was examined and the visa entry details for North Korea matched exactly with the ones on a hand written master list.

"Trains?" asked a handsome young girl with an enormous cap and three brass stars on her each lapel.

"Ah yes, trains," replied Bo, smilingly helpfully. "Iron horses. Puffing billies. Stephenson's rocket. "

"Why?"

"Not sure really. Lure of the distance. Romance. Murder. Escape. Destiny."

"One week." She looked up at him for the first time; he wasn't sure if it was a question, but answered it anyway.

"A lot can happen in one week."

"For you," she said and gave him back his passport. Bo took it, unsure of what she meant again. He joined the others, and when all had been questioned and cleared they were herded out into the terminal, and there they met Sammy Choo.

23

Chung Son Nop relaxes as best he can on the concrete floor of No. 16 District Police Cell. He has been in this mess before, selling black market products. You get a good beating, go to some re-indoctrination lessons, volunteer to snitch and then it's back to square one. Best was to tell them what they wanted, but as little as possible. Where you bought it, where you sold it. Snitch on your greediest suppliers and stingiest customers, and then get out quick. The upside is worth it: some comforts the cash can buy, some electric gadgets and some whisky, Japanese whiskey too.

The doors to the cells are not locked; there is no need as the whole basement is sealed, guarded, and bugged.

"Chung Son Nop!" a harsh voice shouts from the top of the stairs. That's me, he thinks, time to face the goons. He has already given them a name, the one he was caught with so that was easy, but he knows they will want a seller and a buyer. He already has these in mind. The buyer he knows to be a snitch too, so that is his private joke. Just the right amount of pleading, just the right amount of cowardice, always a good thing, makes the idiots feel superior. The beating will be bad. It's his third time caught. The most important is to stay Redeemable; but he's a good snitch too. He leaves the cell, climbs the stairs, is handled roughly at the top and thrown into an interrogation room.

There are three other men in the room. He recognises two of them immediately, and can see they recognise him too. The other man introduces himself: "I am Sergeant Ming of the SSSA." Sergeant Ming now has his full attention. The SSSA never debase themselves with black marketers. Who has snitched him? He is no spy, no danger to the state at all. These others? The older one in the suit is Professor Ju Flo Mung from the university, but the young soldier he cannot place just now. It's a face he has seen a few times, but where and when? An eye message pact is immediately in place between all three; none of them have seen him, nor he them, before. The boy, yes, he is the son of Sung Pi Jam, also from the university, and worse is his father is now in a spot of bother himself.

Sergeant Ming is pacing the room, looking at him from time to time. No-one else speaks, all are tense, all are waiting for the SSSA Sergeant to make the first move.

"You are a black marketer, vermin to me. I don't care if you live or die. But the doctor here, a Professor no less, wants to make you a lucky black marketer. Am I not right, Professor Ju?"

"Yes, Sergeant."

Chung Son Nop is certain Professor Ju Flo Mung is not a snitch, at least not at state security level. The sergeant is now close to him, talking directly to his face. He notices the bad breath, but dare not give that away. "You are to be subjected to an experiment, a medial experiment. The doctor will inject you, and I will ask you some questions. You are also to be a part of a wager. Am I not right there too, Officer Cadet Sung?" Before the young man, the boy, could answer, he asks "An experiment, a wager? What have I done?" and with lightning reaction Sergeant Ming slaps him hard across the face. His cheeks and temple explode and his ears ache and throb.

"Sergeant Ming!" Professor Ju Flo Mung stands up and walks over. "This is not necessary!" Then he sees the Professor undo a bag and take out a needle, syringe and tie. Within seconds he is being held by Sergeant Ming and injected by the Professor.

His world becomes cloudy, then his body feels heavy, very heavy in the chair, the pain from his face disappears. He is content, even enjoying their company. Now Sergeant Ming is asking him something. He tries to focus on the question, and answers:

"I work as a driver. From the worker class." Something inside tells him not to mention the university, where he works as that driver. He must not know Professor Ju Flo Mung, for both their sakes. Another question.

"I have a few times, but I mean no harm. I am loyal. The Great Leader and Dear Leader are my heroes, and all their speeches I have studied." Another question.

He can hear his answers perfectly, as if spoken by someone else, but some faculty within him is still advising extreme caution in the answers "No, there is no need, the state provides everything." Another question.

"I am weak willed, and greedy, but not an enemy of the motherland, that is why." Another question.

"These are magazines. Only magazines for shoppers. Colour pages of goods." Another question.

"Never, I would never sell those." He felt very dense now, could not rise even if he tried. Another question

"From Nan Gong Won in the Saturday Exchange," his mind fell, out of focus, on the sneering face and greedy mouth of his most hated supplier, but now the feeling of hatred was detached, even comical. Another question.

Again, from deep within a feeling is guiding him carefully to reveal only what is needed. And he feels happy about it, and tries not to smile, but now his mouth seems apart from his body. "No, it is only from him." Another question.

"The only other one was Lu Dho Chan, and he is a snitch too." The room was now revolving slowly around Sergeant Ming, and even as the words came out he regretted them. This was his private joke, to snitch a snitch, no-one else's business. Another question.

"How do I know? How do I know? Who knows how I know, but I know." He is feeling nauseous now, and wants to talk about black markets, not snitches, safer all round. But as he tries the words block themselves, and then his body is on the floor, fallen sideways by itself and gently landed on the floor. He looks up and sees the Professor, he wants to talk about all the drives they have done, all the good manners they have shared, but he sees a vision of the door opening and hears a new voice say:

"Sergeant Ming, the slanderer Hung Cho Kin."

"Yes?"

"He is dead sir."

Then he sees the door close, and all three men gather round him, and the Professor starts to fret, to agitate, is he crying? No, just fussing. "Don't worry Professor, we will drive again soon," a voice, his old voice, is saying, then he feels light, then he feels movement from himself, then he remembers the time playing with his brother in the snow, then the time the car was hit from behind, then the first radio he bought, and used and sold, then his mind completely left his body and was above them all in the room. There was a dead man on the floor, a young man and an old man knelt down around him, and one, a soldier, seemed as if he was smiling to himself, lost in thought, nodding slyly and looking through the window.

24

Nark Am Dim reckoned he had good reason to be nervous, and he reckoned he was nervous. On his first active mission for the Company, and all the training seemed to have been for some other theatre, far away. He didn't even pack a gun. The flight hadn't helped, horrible old Russian transport, everything falling to bits in front of him, plus a rough and bumpy ride, all over the sky. He had noticed the blonde Englishman he had been told to watch out for, on a parallel mission that his masters did not hold up much hope for. Give him a wide berth seemed to be the gist of his instructions. Now in the terminal, in the queue, he looked at his right hand, and the Canadian passport in it, saw them both shaking. He put the passport in his left pocket and his right hand in his belt, trying to look like he was always next in line for the immigration check. Unlike the others on the plane he could read the slogans under the giant posters around the hall: "Rivers and Mountains of the Country Changing More Beautifully under the Leadership of the Great General", "Let Us Exalt the Brilliance of Comrade Kim Il Sung's Idea on the Youth Movement and the Achievements Made under His Leadership", "My Warship Means My Beloved Land" and "We will Defend the Headquarters of Revolution with Our Lives". Of what sincerity or cynicism that lay behind them he did not quite know what to make.

"Next!" a voice from above and in front of him snapped.

He walked up to the sentry box, and could read Immigration and Resettlement below it. The officer sat three feet above him, with only a square foot cut into the front of the box to see his head, itself half hidden by an outsize, antique looking olive green and brass cap.

"You are Korean?" he asked in Korean whilst taking the passport.

"Ameri, er Canadian?" hurried Nark Am Dim.

"But you speak Korean?" the officer asked, again in Korean.

"Er, no, just a lucky guess," replied Nark in English.

"But you said you were American."

"Er, no, Canadian."

The officer looked at him unblinkingly for several seconds. To Nark they seemed like minutes. Then the officer looked back at his list, then back again at Nark. "Paul Kane."

"Er, sorry?"

"Paul Kane, it says your name is Paul Kane."

"Er, yes, Paul Kane," Nark could feel sweat on his back and under his arms. He tried smiling, but in return received a cold stare.

"Why you here?"

"Er, trains, yes, trains, I have joined the train tour."

"Which train tour?"

"Er, the one we are on."

"The Friendship and Freedom Steam Engine Appreciation Tour No. 3?"

"Er, yes that's it."

The officer put down the passport and the list, and peered down at him. "No, it's not. You are on the Friendship and Freedom Steam Engine Appreciation Tour No. 7."

"Er, sorry, a simple mistake."

The officer rose in his box, stepped down to Nark's level and ordered "Come with me!" Nark followed him into an office. He was told to sit and wait; he sat and waited. From inside a further office he could just overhear snatches of their conversation; confused about his nationality, confused about his name, confused about his tour. He was led in to meet a more senior officer, he ran through his credentials again, this time with more certainty if similar nervousness. The first officer returned with another, older man in a cheap suit. He suspected they all had cheap suits. This one had a label on his lapel Choo Sang Wa. So, this must be the Sammy Choo he had also been told about, the Company's man on the ground, except they weren't sure how much of a man on the ground he was, so use him sparingly and in emergencies only, and above all don't, do not, do not ever, blow his cover. For his sake.

The senior officer spoke: "This is your guide, Choo Sang Wa, known to Westerners as Sammy Choo." Nark and Choo nodded at each other. Then the officer spoke to Choo in Korean: "We are suspicious of this capitalist flunkey. Looks like one of us, says he is Canadian, but he's probably from the land of the loudmouthed hooligans. Choo Sang Wa, this so called Paul Kane is on your train tour, we don't have to tell you to keep him under observation. Report anything of a deviant nature."

Sammy Choo took him to the coach waiting outside. All the other tour group members were already on board, and some looking impatient. The blonde Englishman, Flower something or other Harry Snide had said he was called, at least smiled and moved over to make space for him and share the seat.

"Tough ride?" the Englishman had asked.

"Er, the plane or the officials?"

"Both, I suppose." Bo held out his hand, "hello, my name is Pett, Bo Pett."

Nark wondered if he'd got the right Flower guy that Harry Snide was talking about, "Er, Nark, er, sorry, Paul Kane."

Nark saw the Englishman Bo smile again, thought he seemed friendly enough, and Nark smiled back. The Englishman Bo said: "Oh well, that's all behind you now. Do you have a favourite type of iron horse?"

"Er, how's that?"

"Trains, I thought you Americans called them iron horses. In the Westerns, that sort of thing."

"Er, you think I'm American?"

"Well I did actually yes. You're Canadian?"

"Er, yes."

"Awfully sorry, I know how it narks you Canadians. But trains, what is your favourite type of train?"

"Er, I like all trains," replied Nark

"Me too," said the Englishman Bo. Then after a while he added "I believe they have proper puff puffs here."

"Er, eh?"

"You know puffing billies, as they were in the old days."

"Er, sorry, I'm still not there yet." Nark wished the conversation would end.

"Steam engines. Why we're here," the Englishman Bo said and laughed, then half to himself, "some of us more than others I should say," and smiled again at Nark. Nark could only manage a wan smile back.

The coach pulled up outside the Golden Lodge. Nark left the coach as fast as he could. First, the officer from hell, then their man Choo he had to pretend didn't exist, then this space cadet English guy. And he hadn't even started on the NoKos yet. Nark wished he was somewhere, anywhere else but there.

25

Sung Pak Dong is resting on his bed in the late afternoon in the hour between the cross country run and the evening lecture on 'fifties romantic comedy films, a favourite subject of the Dear Leader. The loudspeaker in the room crackles on, then is silent and then announces that "Officer Cadet Sung Pak Dong to report to Colonel Krop's' office; repeat order: Officer Cadet Sung Pak Dong to report to Colonel Krop's' office."

Sung Pak Dong leaps off his bed, sprints over to the office block, knocks, is entered and inside he finds Colonel Krop and Sergeant Ming. They are laughing and at ease, each sitting on the two chairs in the office. Colonel Krop, waves at Sung Pak Dong to be at ease too, and then to sit cross legged on the floor.

"So, young Officer Cadet, you are making good progress I hear."

"Thank you, sir; I am working hard to catch up."

"And Sergeant Ming tells me you have an interesting approach to discovering the truth. This is good. Sergeant Ming is younger than I, but we are both in some ways set on our paths. Young blood like you, new mind, new methods, the scientific approach to our work, this is good. Isn't it, Sergeant Ming?"

"Yes, sir."

"We've hit some in our time, haven't we Sergeant? You remember that fugitive smuggler in Wanang Province? Not much left of him, eh?" and they are both chuckling at the memory of the human wreckage.

"He confessed in the end, Sir, gave us four or five other names too, though."

"Five names he gave us Sergeant, five names. But it took two nights, and it was tiring work in that sweltering cell, and then three further weeks to discover that of the five only three existed and two of those could not have been involved. But by then he was dead. Now young Sung here, with his patriotic Professor and his jungle juice, we just tie them down, inject them, and sit back and wait. It's modern. Less satisfying at times, eh, Sergeant, but more modern. Now Sergeant Ming here has an idea. Sergeant, please explain."

There is a knock on the door, and Professor Ju Flo Mung enters. "Just a moment please Professor, while we finish talking with Officer Cadet Sung Pak Dong." The door closes.

Colonel Krop leans over and in a softer voice says: "Officer Cadet Sung, I don't need to tell you that you have a father in prison on the most serious charge of all. I am going to be frank with you because you can help your country and your Officers and your father and yourself. We have certain information about Sung Pi Jam from not one, but two, snitches. This is unusual because the information is detailed and the snitches do not work together, or even know that the other works for us secretly. At the moment we are checking out the information with our spies in the USA."

Sergeant Ming pours them both some water and sits back down alongside them.

"This is expensive," Colonel Krop continues, "the Americans will talk, but only for money, and a lot of money. Sergeant Ming thinks that if your father is injected, he will tell the truth and save us money and time and if is he is innocent we can turn the investigation onto the snitches. Something is transpiring here. Either your father is guilty or innocent. If he is guilty...well you have worked here long enough already to understand our sentiments towards traitors. If he is innocent, we must find out why the snitches have been informing, who put them up to it."

Sung Pak Dong is now standing, "But sir, you do not know what happened before. The two pris.."

"I know," said Colonel Krop, "Sergeant Ming here told me, of course. Two prisoners are dead. The Professor gave them too much whatever it is. Half the dose was not enough. All the dose was too much." With a shake of his head towards the door, he gestures Sergeant Ming to fetch Professor Ju Flo Mung.

Colonel Krop stands when Professor Ju Flo Ming enters and invites him to take a chair. Professor Ju Flo Ming is concerned. He has never had any contact with the security service. Two prisoners, at least nominally in his care, are dead.

"Officers, please, I can explain about this most unfortunate…"

"This most unfortunate, surely you mean these most unfortunate, Professor?"

"Yes, Colonel, you see we have only ever calculated on mice and rats. Were the prisoners important?"

"So-so. One was Redeemable and a good snitch, the other Irredeemable and innocent."

"But if he is innocent, how can he be Irredeemable?" asks the professor.

"These are just classifications, Professor, no need to worry. But the rats and mice, tell us about these."

"We were requested to keep them alive for other experiments, and that was the problem."

"So, if we arrange for you to have unlimited rats and mice, would that be better, or dogs, they are bigger, donkeys, what do you want?"

The Professor looks around and is reassured. The faces are friendly, helpful even. He had been worried about the dead prisoners, worried about an investigation which would set his experiments back. "Monkeys would be best."

"Monkeys?" said Sergeant Ming incredulously.

"No, Sergeant, that makes sense," says Colonel Krop, now standing and smiling at Officer Cadet Sung Pak Dong, Professor Ju Flo Mung and Sergeant Ming. "What kind of monkeys, how many monkeys?"

"Chimpanzees are our closest relatives. Or baboons nearer the right size."

"No, professor, chimpanzees you shall have." Colonel Krop is enjoying himself, a break from the routine. "How many chimpanzees do you need?"

"Well we need to experiment. We can find out how much the prisoners weighed. The first one looked weak, the…"

"Weak! He was nearly dead, lying scum!" interrupts Sergeant Ming.

"Except he wasn't."

"Wasn't what, Colonel?"

"Lying, Sergeant, lying. That's the whole point. So, Professor, you were saying, one was weak and one was strong.?"

"Yes, but we can weigh them, and then calculate how much serum I gave their body weights, then weigh the chimpanzees and start with slightly less. We will need one to die to prove the dosage. Another may die, but three should be sufficient."

"But they cannot talk, any more than your rats and mice. What's the point?" asks Sergeant Ming.

"The point is not to make them talk, of course not, but to establish dosage levels, you see…"

Colonel Krop interrupts. "Sergeant Ming, from our contacts in the underground, three healthy, male, middle aged chimpanzees, to be delivered to the Biology Department of the Great People's University, to be paid for by favours and privileges, untraceable, tradable privileges to please Sergeant Ming."

"Yes, sir."

26

"Hello, everybody, I am Choo Sang Wa, but everyone can call me Sammy Choo, your guide for the Friendship and Freedom Steam Engine Appreciation Tour No. 7." A small wiry man in his early sixties, Sammy Choo adjusted his outsize spectacles, and somehow looked them over, slowly. "I am sure you have read the guidelines that have been recommended. Please ask me if you want to do anything, anything at all. I will help but you must obey my guidelines. Please no photography. No local contact without my guideline. Now we go to the hotel, Glorious Lodge. Newest in Pyongyang. Tomorrow stay here Pyongyang, next day leave for Cheudding, see first steam train."

"Good name for a guide, Choo. Let's call him Choo Choo," said Bo when their mentor was out of hearing range loading the bus. None of the others seemed to hear either, except a short haired sour faced warrioress from Australia who turned round, gave him a filthy look and told him to "Shhh! You'll get us all in trouble!". Bo turned to his neighbour, the local looking guy he had noticed on the plane over and took to be a North Korean. Turned out he was a Canadian called Kane. They chatted amicably for the rest of the journey, although Bo thought he was rather vacant, socially uncomfortable, even a little simple.

The Golden Lodge was in fact so new that it still smelt of clean paint and industrial cleaners. The group met for a buffet lunch of steamed vegetables and barbecued meat of unproven origin, washed down with orange flavoured water. Afterward Choo stood up, pinged the glass rather unnecessarily and announced: "This afternoon you are free to walk around the city, but follow my guidelines about cameras and people. In other hotels there are shops. You can buy, only with Euros. At five we have slide show here in Conference Room about our trains. We have locomotives too, not just steam. You can come to this. We have dinner here in hotel, same as lunch seven o'clock, then bed, or room. Any questions?" There were many in mind, but none asked. "Good.

Don't forget the guidelines."

Bo closed the room door behind him. "This is it, Mr. Bo," he said to himself. "You are now about to be in the international espionage business. When you walk out of here. When you walk out of here, you walk out of everywhere." He had two hours before the slide show, his first absence, which he calculated would not cause a full alert, but may well cause a minor alarm. Two hours to find Kimiko at the Japan North Korea Trade Authority, hoping she was at work, and that he could go from there to the safety of her apartment and the reunion with Lo Hi.

Bo wrapped himself up, trying to dress inconspicuously; it was already cold enough in the early afternoon to justify full scarf and hat, and bright enough to slip on large sunglasses. He raised his collar, hunched over and walked off looking as inconspicuous as a six foot blonde Londoner can along empty streets and crowded windows ten thousand miles from home.

It was only four blocks from the Golden Lodge to the Japanese North Korean Trade Authority, and four blocks that Bo had learned off by heart from the Pyongyang street map bought in Shanghai so that he would not have to ask or even be seen looking at street signs or the tourist map. Bo walked straight up the steps to reception, gave a business card which he had had printed in Shanghai, and which had entered North Korea in his socks, introducing him as David McMichael, Empress Seas Tooling Company from Osaka, and asked for Kimiko Sato. He was invited to wait; he waited. The glass doors swing open.

"Yes? You ask Kimiko Sato?" a tallish thin mid twenties Japanese woman asked. Bo immediately recognised the similarity with Lo Hi; maybe a couple of years older but still sporting the same full mouth, short sharp hair, and mischievous eyes.

"You are Kimiko?" asked Bo rather unnecessarily.

"Yes, but who you are, why you ask for me?"

"Can we go somewhere quieter and I will explain," said Bo softly. They sat on a sofa, around the passageway from reception, with no one in sight. "I am Bo Pett, you know from Amnesty in Tokyo. I've come to help Lo Hi, and her father too if I can. But I've only got a couple of hours, less now, before I'm missed. Can we go to your flat?"

Kimiko looked around anxiously, thinking quickly. "Yes, yes of course, we must help her, help him," she replied softly. She motioned Bo to stay, and a minute later, walking rather obviously too slowly, and now talking rather obviously too loudly, she told him to come with her and see the exhibits, the exhibits in the Worldwide Appreciation Gift Museum.

Wearing an inconspicuous, heavy grey woollen overcoat, she led him through the streets. So, this was the young British MI6 agent, with the ingenious Amnesty International cover, to whom the JCIA had told her to steer Lo Hi, and whom they now had told her had swallowed the bait and would soon be with them, but with or without CIA backing they were not so sure. But, they had also told her, the real CIA were not far behind, apparently they were sending over a South Korean American to spy on her, at last that what she assumed they meant by a SoKoAm. She didn't think he'd be too hard to recognise, he would have to make a conscious effort to wear the rags this lot of zombies wore. They walked together quickly without rushing, and talking softly. Bo, excited that his mission had got off to such a bright start with her, explained his life since Lo Hi had burst into the AI office in Tokyo. She commiserated about his Amnesty office closing, and he did not like to ask too much about hers but then she told him her office was in her head and harder to close. He could not tell if Kimiko thought him crazy or romantic, or both, or neither, but she kept saying "I see, I see." in reply to Bo's story, and from time to time looking at him with a degree of concentration.

Bo estimated that he had an hour and a half to go before being missed as they climbed the concrete steps outside another identical block and entered through a first floor landing to her apartment block. The hallway was clean to the point of sterility, the doors identically spaced along the long corridor. At least it's warm thought Bo as Kimiko pointed to two doors opposite each other. "This one mine, that one Lo Hi," she pointed at both together, her expression anxious.

She rapped a code on Lo Hi's door. The door opened three inches on a chain stop. "Surprise!" said Kimiko as Lo Hi released the chain, opened the door and fell back slightly as Bo removed his dark glasses, hat and scarf. "What ho!" said Bo, wanting to hold and kiss her. But rather he offered his hand, she shook it in shock, remembering herself replied "Shabbu Sh'u!" and watched him as intensively as he watched her as she sat him down. "My God," she said at last. "And thank God too. But why? Why have you come?" Bo looked at her, and said "For you." Then he looked at the ground and said "and for me too." Kimiko had not taken her eyes off him since he had arrived.

27

"They smell disgusting," says Sung Pak Dong looking through the chicken wire top into the three tea chests.

"So would you," replies Professor Ju Flo Mung. "There's not much life in them either." He walks over and looks at each chimpanzee in turn. Each chimpanzee is slumped on the floor and leaning against the side of its tea chest; each is staring blankly, not even fear left in their eyes; each is lying in and covered in excrement. "What do we do with them now?"

From the glass panel in the laboratory door they can see but not hear an excited crowd of students. Word has spread; three apes from China are in the laboratory. Nobody knows why, and nobody dares ask why. Professor Ju Flo Mung walks over to the door, opens it and invites them in. He is proud of his increased importance, and the monkeys bear witness to that. The crowd gathers around the tops of the tea chests looking down, some are taunting the monkeys, some are holding their noses, some are grunting and scratching their armpits, some are tapping the sides of the chests with their feet, other giving them names. Amidst laughter and claps they settle on Old Bush, Young Bush and Ronald Reagan. The chimpanzees retreat further into themselves.

"OK, time to go now," whooshes Professor Ju Flo Mung, waving them out, "time to prepare the apes to their fate, well two to one fate, and one to another." And when they are alone Sung Pak Dong asks Professor Ju Flo Mung what they should do now.

"I don't know, except make them stronger, as strong as your father. Feed them, I suppose. We can keep them in their boxes, put bananas and water in there. Then weigh them and inject them after that." Professor Ju Flo Mung, a little impatiently, points out they have no bananas. Sung Pak Dong is despatched to the canteen to improvise. He returns with a pitcher of water, some bowls, bread rolls, tomatoes and lychees. At arms length, he folds back a corner of chicken wire and lets a bowl of water, tomato and lychee in. It spills onto the foul floor as the bread roll lands there too. The chimpanzee does not even notice.

"This is no good," announces Professor Ju Flo Mung, "we are going to have to take them out, feed them, wash them. It is a scientific experiment after all. We must simulate your father's condition. We will take them out, one by one, wash them in the sink there. But first we must clear the laboratory of everything they can break. Go and find some gloves and thick coats for our arms if they bite. Then we will feed them, or leave food for them overnight. Then tomorrow we will weigh them, and adjust the dosage to your father's weight as we agreed. Go and find other food, ask Colonel Krop for access to the UN store, maybe even some bananas."

When he returns with more food, better food and protective clothing, Sung Pak Dong finds the laboratory surfaces clear, all the chairs removed and the windows left just ajar enough to ease the smell but not enough for an escape. They prepare themselves. They open the first top, reach in and each holding an arm lift out the first monkey. The stench is even hurting their eyes. The chimpanzee is a dead weight, offering neither resistance nor defiance.

"Put it here," says Professor Ju Flo Mung lowering him into the sink. And get that empty box out of here." When Sung Pak Dong returns he turns on the tap. The monkey does not seem to notice the icy water being poured over him. They put the floor detergent onto their gloves and try to work a lather into the monkey's hair. They pour more water over him, and the filth rinses off him down the sink. They repeat the exercise. They judge the monkey to be clean; the smell is barely there now, and mixed with cleaning chemicals. "Try making it drink."

Sung Pak Dong fills a bowl and holds it up to the chimpanzee's mouth. He offers out his lips and sips gently. There is still no expression in his eyes. He drinks some more, then the bowl is empty. They refill it and put it next to the sink. For the first time the monkey moves on his own, and finishes the second bowl of water. They lift him out of the sink and put him, quite carefully, against a wall. He starts to look around with gentleness and curiosity.

The second chimpanzee is in worse condition, and collapses when they release their grip on him in the sink. They wash him more gently, even worry that the water is too cold. They put water to his lips, and with his first movement he sips from the bowl. He does not want more, but looks back at them warily, not with fear, but even with a wish of death in his eyes. They put the second chest outside, and place the chimpanzee against the wall too, with a bowl of water and some fruit alongside. They repeat the process with the third monkey. He seems to them livelier than the last one, but weaker than the first. They notice he is the only one to look around as they clean him, showing some interest in the new surroundings, and even to make a small noise.

They leave the food and more water out on the tables and floor of the laboratory, close the windows, leave on one small light and prepare to leave.

"Tomorrow, sir, what will we do?"

"We will weigh them and decide on their doses. But I have been thinking as we cleaned them. Our instruction was to kill the two weakest and keep the Alpha male for more experiments. We should share him with other departments; everyone wants to subject monkeys, especially chimpanzees, to their tests and theories. But why? Why not keep all three alive? We can give the first one a safe dose, then increase it slowly, and again, until it is near death. We can monitor its pulse easily enough, then add, say, five percent of the actual dose and declare it to be the death dose."

"Yes, sir. That would be good for everyone."

"Except the monkey," laughs Professor Ju Flo Mung. Sung Pak Dong joins in when he sees the joke. "Then we can repeat the dose by weight on the second one. If that one just lives too we know we have a theoretical and practical maximum that your father can be given. And we lower that some for a margin of error. And the third monkey is untouched. We can use him for whatever we like later."

"Yes, sir."

"But will Colonel Krop agree? He traded the monkeys for us to kill two, not keep all three alive."

"I'll have to report this to him, sir."

"I know, but if he understands we have three apes alive for experiments in, for instance, chemical warfare, he will accept the change I'm sure. Tell him this evening, and we start our experiments here in the morning."

"Yes, sir"

28

Last night Nark had felt rather pleased with himself. He had managed to outwit the Stalinists at the airport and was successfully ensconced at the Golden Lodge. He had met, but not bothered, Sammy Choo, and likewise had met, but steered clear of, the Englishman with the funny name. He was looking forward to his daily radio call back to Harry Snide in Tokyo at 2200. Daily, that was, if there was not, as he had discovered yesterday, a power cut just before 2200. He had taken the electric lead from his razor, and then his coat hanger/signal booster combo from his wardrobe, and had plugged them both into the Company's camera/radio gizmo. Then he had tuned into 1457 khz and waited among the crackles.

At exactly 2200 the crackles had become: "Blue this is red, over." Blue was Harry Snide, red was Nark Am Dim.

"Er- red reading fives. All OK here. But the day after tomorrow morning we leave Pyongyang. I hadn't realised, over."

"How is our Oriental ally, over?"

"Er, I walked towards that office today, was on my way when I saw her and the other one you mentioned walking the other way, so I followed them. He hasn't been seen here since, I guess he took off with the girl, over."

"Where they go, over?"

"Er, to a residential block, over."

"That'll be where they live. OK, good work, what about tomorrow, over?"

"Er, we're still in the city, that's what I was saying. Tomorrow I'll contact her, over."

"Well OK, if you're sure, you're the one on the ground, but listen, be careful, out," Harry Snide had put down his headset, thinking about what could go wrong with his CIA Nark Am Dim meeting their JCIA Kimiko Sato tomorrow; Nark Am Dim had put his radio/camera away thinking about what was going to go right when he met Sung Lo Hi tomorrow.

No mention was made at the Golden Lodge of the missing Bo

Pett the next morning, either they thought he was skipping breakfast or didn't want to think about one of the group doing a runner. Choo gave them their instructions: follow the guidelines, respect any Leadership statues or national flags, and enjoy yourself on your free morning walking around the city.

Nark Am Dim knew from the briefing that Sung Lo Hi worked as a translator for the Ministry of Repatriation, Unification and External Affairs, and after breakfast and dressed as formally as he could, he armed himself with a map and made the short walk over to the Ministry. The capital was empty as usual, he had almost gotten used to it already. The buildings were disproportionately grandiose, and looked as empty on the inside as the streets were on the outside. The Ministry of Repatriation, Unification and External Affairs was in pride of place on a square surrounded by concrete benches with a disused fountain in the middle. Outside, over the front elevation, hung a large banner: "Pyongyang Citizens Rally for 'General March for Military-first Revolution'" and over the main entrance another, smaller sign: "Central Committee of the Anti-Imperialist National Democratic Front".

Nark Am Dim paused outside for only a second. He had weighed up the odds, run through the risks, drawn up a list of upsides and downsides, and considered this to be a no-brainer. He did reflect at the time that he wasn't sure what no-brainer actually meant, but the exercise had finished with him feeling there was nothing much to lose as she would be crazy to grass him to the commies. He walked up to the desk, and said in perfect Korean: "Miss Sung Lo Hi, please, she is a translator."

The woman behind the desk had looked at him suspiciously. "We do not expect visitors. Have you the permission, the paperwork for the appointment?"

"Er, no paperwork, it's personal really."

"This is not a personal place, you really do need permission for a working appointment. In her lunchtime, you can see her outside," she jerked her head towards the square. "I will tell her you are waiting when she comes down for lunchtime."

He had been outside sitting in the square for only ten minutes when a voice behind alerted him in Korean. "Hello, I am Sung Lo

Hi, you are waiting for me?"

Nark Am Dim stood up and brushed his trouser seat down, "Er, I was waiting for you at lunch."

Sung Lo Hi giggled, "She's a friend, the dragon on the gate. She said you wanted to see me about something personal."

Nark Am Dim took a quick look around, and although outside, lowered his voice: "Er, look, I have come to help your father. They will find him guilty, you know that, and then you will have to go to prison with him. I guess I'm here to help you both. Do you know where he is now?"

Lo Hi looked around too, and lowered her voice to match: "Yes, he's at the People's Founding Prison, but who are you?"

Nark Am Dim motioned to her to sit down on the concrete slab were he had been. "Er, I am from a friendly government, one that wants you and your father to leave here. For a better life. A free life. We can arrange your escape, and once outside we will all have some leverage to help your father leave. Through the media we can mount a campaign. Your father will be safe here, and then we can arrange an exchange."

Lo Hi looked as uncomfortable as she felt. She thought for ten seconds then said: "It's a good idea, meet me back here at end of lunch, at 1245, OK?"

Nark Am Dim felt a sense of pride and rose and smiled: "Of course, it's the right thing, see you back here at 1245."

Lo Hi waited until he was out of sight, said a few words to her friend the dragon and walked as briskly and inconspicuously as she could straight to Kimiko's office. Lo Hi was breathless and anxious. Kimiko listened quietly, but knew immediately that this must be the new CIA man her masters had told her about. She went through the motions of asking Lo Hi more questions, and Lo Hi repeated everything again.

Kimiko took her to one side: "Lo Hi listen, this is important. Of course it is not the CIA, they would not do anything as stupid as that. This guy was Korean, even if well dressed, he must be an SSSA man in disguise testing your loyalty. You must go back to your office immediately and report him. They will be suspicious you have not turned him in already. Quick, go now, quick, Lo Hi."

Lo Hi had rushed back to her office and told her superior what had happened. That superior told another superior, who in turn told yet another superior. At 1245 Lo Hi walked over to her window, and looking down she saw four plain clothes men, presumably SSSA, surround the hapless and over dressed Korean and frog march him away. She thought of Kimiko, and how much she was going to thank her tonight. And Kimiko would not be without thanks to Lo Hi; the removal of the CIA interference was a positive development, and one she decided to make more positive by not reporting back to the JCIA, at least not just for now.

29

Professor Ju Flo Mung arrives at his laboratory door at eight o'clock prompt. He finds two students already looking in through the glass in the door. One of them reports that the monkeys look better today, and the other makes way for the Professor. Professor Ju Flo Mung orders him to find some scales from another laboratory, scales large enough to weigh the monkeys. He sees all the surfaces are clean of food, and the apes moving, two slowly around the room and the third preening himself by the sink.

He unlocks the door, walks in slowly, feeling unsure of his reception. They all stop what they are doing and watch him intensely, still at a safe distance. Professor Ju Flo Mung then ignores them, goes over to his cabinet and starts to prepare the truth serum dosages. He is just wondering where Sung Pak Dong was and senses an annoyance at his lateness when the door opens without a knock.

"Good morning Professor Ju." He looks around and sees Colonel Krop, followed by Sergeant Ming and Sung Pak Dong last, and now carrying the scales.

"Good morning, comrades. Ah, Sung I see you have the scales. I presume you have heard of our revised schedule for the chimpanzees, and we hope to have your permission."

Professor Ju Flo Mung had never seen Colonel Krop so well humoured. "An excellent idea, Professor. Why indeed kill any of them? Most useful."

"The doses are ready, so let's start. First we will weigh one, any preference Colonel?" The colonel looks at Sergeant Ming. "Sergeant Ming, the choice is yours." The sergeant looks amused too and points to the one on the sink, "It over there". They walk over slowly towards him, unsure of his reactions, but the chimpanzee stays still and does not resist as the three soldiers heave him down, weigh him and then hold him steady by the sink. Professor Ju Flo Mung adjusts the dosage to the weight, walks over and injects the chimpanzee in a leg vein. Within three seconds he has gone limp in their hands, then rolls back his head moments later, and then instantly collapses into the sink, stone dead.

"Congratulations Professor Ju Flo Mung. Six, seven maybe eight seconds!" Colonel Krop had an edge of irritation in his voice. Sung Pak Dong thinks it is because they have lost one of the monkeys, then realises it is because he has missed seeing the experiment, and has wasted his time.

"They maybe our closest animal relatives," says Professor Ju Flo Mung, "but they must have a very different physiognomy. I am sorry, comrades, but we have not studied this before. It is truly an experiment. This time we will give half the dose." He is back by his cabinet with his preparations. "Next monkey, please."

They notice now that the other two have moved away from them as far as possible, over to the far side of the room against the wall. They walk over. Colonel Krop is feeling less magnanimous about leaving the choice to others. He points as he walks to the one nearest the door. Suddenly surrounded by three soldiers, and still weak in mind and body, he does not resist. They haul the dead chimpanzee out of the sink, and chuck it in a pile in a corner. They repeat the injection process on the second monkey.

They stand around it dispassionately for a minute. "It's alive, and not too affected I would say," announces Professor Ju Flo Mung with some satisfaction. He looks closely at the monkey, feels the pulse. The eyes are open but steady, without expression, the breathing short, but also steady. "So, we know a dose of 3 millilitres per ten kilos of body weight is safe."

"Increase it," orders Colonel Krop, still less jovial than before.

"As you say, Colonel." Professor Ju Flo Mung prepares another millilitre, makes a note, and injects the chimpanzee again. He repeats his check, and declares a slight weakening of the vital functions.

"More!" instructs Colonel Krop. Professor Ju Flo Mung hesitates for a second, and then obeys. He prepares a further half millilitre. He checks the monkey again. "It is only just alive, Colonel. The pulse is so weak I must press hard to feel it, and that maybe too hard for it to take. You can see the eyes have closed. I would say it is barely alive, and certainly in a comatose condition."

"Very well, Professor, you have one dead ape and one

successful experiment."

The two senior soldiers prepare to leave. Sung Pak Dong asks for permission to stay, making notes for his special assignment. "Agreed!" says Colonel Krop. "Report to my office tomorrow morning after exercises and patriotic pronouncements. These experiments have a purpose, a paternal purpose, if you remember Officer Cadet Sung Pak Dong."

"Yes, sir."

As they walk towards the door, Sergeant Ming following Colonel Krop, Sung Pak Dong sees Sergeant Ming take out his cattle prod from inside his trouser leg, switch on the handle, and point it towards the third chimpanzee. As they walk past him for the door, Sergeant Ming glances behind him, sees Professor Ju Flo Mung is not looking, winks at Sung Pak Dong who is, and casually prods the electric stick at the chimpanzee's chest.

Instantly the monkey leaps up at Sergeant Ming, with wild eyes and flashing teeth, scratching and biting Ming's upper arms and shoulders. Sergeant Ming screams in surprise and pain, trying to shake the embracing monkey off him. He is no match for the sudden attack, and soon stumbles onto one knee, trying to cover his head. The chimpanzee won't let go, and soon the others see blood from the bites, and hear Sergeant Ming yelping for help. With a whirl of arms and facial movements, and a stream of screeches of aggression, the chimpanzee's attack continues, now biting Sergeant Ming's right hand, now scratching his face. There are smears of blood all over the floor. Then one loud pistol shot stops all the commotion as instantly as the cattle prod had started it. Professor Ju Flo Mung and Sung Pak Dong look in the direction of the shot, and see Colonel Krop, with a look of thunder, re-holster his pistol.

"Well done, Professor Ju Flo Mung, you now have your two dead monkeys as you first proposed. Officer Cadet Sung Pak Dong, help your Sergeant. Now!"

"Yes, sir"

30

Bo looked at his watch. "Look, time is short. I need to know now if this invisibility machine works or not. Can we crank it up and try?"

"I see work many times. Fun." Kimiko said from the kitchen.

"Yes, I'm sure," Bo chuckled, "but I need to know for sure. About turning back to visibility I mean. I read H.G.Wells in Shanghai. His was a one way street."

"OK, let's have a lesson." said Lo Hi, holding his wrist, her first touch he thought as she smiled and added "you tell me what you know while I set up the dynamos."

"Well, it's something like this." Bo thought back to the tiny hostel room in Shanghai, the trawl to find The Invisible Man which ended up in the City Educational Library, the few hours it had taken to read, the few extra hours it had taken to make notes and absorb the theory behind the disappearing. "I mean I'm not a student of molecular physics with an absorption in the delights of optical density like your father, but it seems that there could be a general theory, or formula, for pigments and refraction involving, I think it was, four dimensions, which could lower the refractive value of a substance to that of air."

"So far so good," said Lo Hi unboxing the first dynamo and putting it on the only table.

"Visibility, or not, just depends on the ability of a surface to absorb or reflect light, and that all depends on the actions of the ultimate source of seeing things or not, light. It's the same general concept as a stealth bomber, except that we are dealing with light waves rather than sound or radar waves. So if you look at whatever is in front of you, it seems to be what it seems to be because on a purely physical level it absorbs some of the light and reflects the rest.

"Then he says that a diamond box, for instance, would neither reflect nor absorb much of the light until that light caught it at specific, favourable angles when the light would be both reflected and refracted intensely, so there would be the appearance of a skeleton of light, where a glass box would not be so brilliantly visible as there would be less reflection and refraction. How am I doing?" asked Bo, sipping the green tea brought by Kimiko.

"Yes, yes, keep going," encouraged Lo Hi, now setting up the second dynamo.

"Well, he says that different densities of glass would perform quite differently from each other. In water, it could be made to disappear altogether, especially if you could adjust the density of the water to correlate with the density of the glass. Same as hydrogen and oxygen is invisible in the ether, given our normal densities. Anyway, back to glass, and when it is broken the splinters have far greater visibility than the original glass as there are now hundreds or thousands of surfaces rather than just six. But if you could put the pile of splinters carefully and exactly in water, and adjust the water density to suit, the splinters would become invisible because the splinters and water would have the same refractive index; the quality of light would not change as it passes from substance to substance."

Lo Hi was now preparing some jars of ointments that looked like aromatherapy. Bo remembered H.G.Wells describing the subtle smell of invisibility. "You even have the scent of evening primrose," he smiled again at her.

"Quick, keep talking."

"Right, where was I? Ah yes, OK. So, if you can make either glass or splinters invisible by resting them in a liquid medium of the same refractive index, it surely follows that you can make them also vanish by putting them in an ether medium of the same refractive index. The human body's individual components are pretty transparent anyway, being largely translucence surrounded by liquid surrounded by skin, like a glorified jelly fish. The breakthrough came when he found a way of lowering this refractive index by placing whatever it is between two radiating centres of ethereal vibration. And now I guess I'm looking at two radiating dynamos."

"That's right," said Lo Hi. "That's the theory my father took to Russia. Not the dynamos, he had to work all that out for himself."

"I hoped he worked out the next part, about returning back to normal too."

"He did", she said, "I'll show you."

Kimiko started rubbing his left hand, on the top and bottom, with the deep yellow solution. "What's that for?" Bo asked.

"To make you reappear. Smells beautiful too, no. It is extract of labyrinthium, the countermeasure to evening primrose." she smiled as she massaged.

Kimiko rested Bo's hand on a deep book, and Lo Hi started the dynamos. "After three minutes, whoosh!" she said. Nothing happened for a minute, while Bo stretched over to read his wrist watch now turned away from him. He reflected on the two friends, so alike at first sight, so different underneath: Kimiko was less patient, less innocent, more abrasive, harder, yet what Lo Hi was doing was much braver, the softness her strength. Exactly one minute to go. Then slowly, in front of his very eyes, his hand, up to the cuff covering his wrist, turned slowly mistier, then seemed to go out of focus, then became totally invisible.

"Something is wrong," said Lo Hi and glanced a worried look at Kimiko. "It is working too quickly. What can it be?" Kimiko shrugged and pulled a quizzical face. Lo Hi said "I hope it has not altered the change back."

"Hang on a second," said Bo. "How long is that going to take?"

"Three hours, we have set the invisibility process at three hours, for three minutes. For the ointment, we have blended it for one gram per hour. We will give you twelve hours for the escape, that should take twelve minutes, that's the maximum we can do, or have tried really," said Lo Hi.

"You mean you are going to send me back to the hotel with an invisible hand?"

"Can wear glove," said Kimiko caustically. "Cold outside."

"And that's another thing I'm worried about, the cold. I tried some Blaine training but just caught flu for three weeks."

"Now that is a problem," replied Lo.

"Big problem," agreed Kimiko warily.

Bo had more immediate concerns about rejoining Choo and the train spotters. The experiment which he had hoped would either work or not, an experiment which would make the go or not to go decision for him, had proved inconclusive. Horribly inconclusive. And then what if his hand remained all there or only half there? He thought he really should run for it, actually really must run for it, back to the hotel right now, play around with steam engines, go home, get married to Kelly Cuss, but he knew he wouldn't even before Lo Hi jumped up triumphantly.

"Of course! You are pale skinned. We are darker, a different pigment. My father has set the pigment sensor to our colour tone. I put on the labyrinthium for three hours."

"Well that's a step forward," said Bo, walking over to look hopefully at the console and dynamos. "Have you any idea how to adjust it?" he asked with some curiousity.

"None at all," said Lo Hi, looking at Kimiko who shrugged and laughed nervously at the same time.

Four hundred yards away, in the nearly fresh air of Golden Lodge, Choo and the train team were just gathering in the foyer for the slide show.

31

Walking down the fourth floor corridor to his family apartment in the Morning Calm block, on his first leave from Patriotic Duty in three months, Sung Pak Dong is remembering Colonel Krop's instructions and advice: your father has been accused and we need to know the truth of these accusations for his sake, his family's sake and his country's sake; your sister is close to him, they live together, or did before he was arrested; your sister is under suspicion of samizdat activities, and at best holds the Leadership equivocally; her best friend is a Japanese woman, distasteful in itself, whom we suspect could be a JCIA spy; your loyalties are to your families: your larger family should hold your larger loyalty, and your smaller family your lesser loyalty; she does not know about your secondment to the SSSA, thinking you are just doing your three years Patriotic Duty as a soldier, more efficient to keep it that way; you have a sound future of promotion and privileges, don't throw it away on sentimentality and feminine traits; remember your first duty is to the truth: you hope your father is innocent of course, he is your small family father after all, and your career will not be helped by such a negative association, but if he is guilty you are pleased that the motherland has one less traitor to US values and aggression.

He stands outside for a few seconds, composes himself, puts on a boyish smile, opens the door and embraces his sister. They sit opposite each other around the table. They talk about cousins, and uncles and aunts, about the weather, and about the soccer, and the latest gymnastic displays. They talk about their friends in the block, their friends in the town. They talk about prices, not critically even though they are rising, and about the news on the radio, the always-on radio. They talk about everything except their father, what she does in the night, and what he does in the day. Eventually it can be put off no more.

"And your job? How is your job?"

"I'm still at the university, still lecturing, still teaching English, still translating. And your Patriotic Duty, are you enjoying it?"

"It is hard. Everyday we must train. Train in the forests, in the dark. But I must do my duty, we must be prepared for the invasion."

"It is only two years, nine months more, every month is a month less."

"And for you, after the long days of work, do you have friends, people you meet?" He thinks she shifts her eyes away from him as she blinks.

She does. "No, not really, just friends at work, but we are tired and just want to go to our own homes. Father, you will have heard about Father of course."

Before Sung Pak Dong can reply, the door opens. The opener, a foreign woman, looking to be Japanese, sees him unexpectedly, starts to apologise and leave.

"No, stay Kimiko. This is my brother Pak Dong, and this is my neighbour Kimiko Sato. She knows about Father because she sees the foreign press. We were just talking about him. Any news today?"

Kimiko looks awkwardly, embarrassedly in the direction of Pak Dong. Lo Hi says, "Don't worry, he is my brother, everything said in here is safe. He is only doing his Patriotic Duty years."

"Well," says Kimiko, "there is a report in yesterday's *Newsweek*. It says Amnesty International is demanding a fair trial. The government here says he will get one, but of course we know he won't."

"Why not?" asks Sung Pak Dong.

"Well because they need to keep the other nuclear boffins in fear in case they really do take a look at the dollars. 'They pretend to spy and we pretend to catch them.'."

An audible silence now overcomes the room, and as the unspoken tension builds Kimiko rises, says her good byes and leaves.

"Do you believe that too?" asks Pak Dong.

"Believe what?"

Pak Dong is whispering now. "Believe that it is a pretence, that they know him to be innocent but they need him guilty to keep the loyalty of others."

"Brother, you are a young man, and many unpleasant things can happen in this world. Sometimes they must sacrifice one ant for the benefit of all the others ants. It is our bad luck that this ant is our father. Innocent or guilty is irrelevant; there must be a trial but it is just for show. You know he will die, don't you?"

"I must tell you something. An officer in my battalion found out that Father was Sung Pi Jam. He told me that they are working with a truth serum, and that it is foolproof. This officer said that they want our father to be free, and that if he would take some serum he will have to tell the truth and they will accept it." As he said the words his throat becomes dry and immediately he wishes he hadn't.

Lo Hi stands up, walks around the room a little distractedly. Then she remembers her brother's work at the Great People's University on serums. She says, "But you did work in serums at university, didn't you?" and immediately she wishes she hadn't.

Pak Dong blushes deeply. She notices, and hurries off to the stove to boil some tea water and hold some time. She wishes Kimiko had not come in. "Do you think he will accept?" he asks.

"Would you?"

"Yes, to clear my name and help my country."

"To help your country?"

"The country must know who is loyal. Of course we know he is loyal, but he must prove it. The serum will prove it."

"Does it work?"

He now stands up too, suddenly more animated. "Yes, it works. We...there have been trials."

In the kitchen Lo Hi is thinking, and thinking quickly. She brings back the tea.

"Well, that sounds wonderful, and a wonderful opportunity for him. Why don't you go back to your officer and tell him Pi Jam's family agree but would like to wait for about then days until his signs are more propitious. I am sure they will understand."

"Good, I better leave now, back to the barracks and the battalion." They embrace again, both wide eyed on each other's shoulder. He leaves, with what to her sounds like a click of the heel.

"Good bye little Brother, heh, now big Brother, take care of yourself."

"Yes, Sister."

32

They put his other hand between the dynamos, and Lo Hi told him they will take it out after four minutes. "Why four minutes?" asked Bo with a certain amount of interest.

"Because you are paler than the settings," she explained carefully, "so we put you in for longer."

"Well if I'm paler, surely I should be in there for less time?" Bo offered.

Lo Hi looked at Kimiko, Kimiko raised her eyebrows and looked at Bo as if to say he may have a point, and Lo Hi said "OK, we will try two minutes. We know that works. It is not so much the invisibility, but the re-visibility."

"No, three grams not work then," said Kimiko.

Lo Hi clicked her thumb. "You're right Kimiko, let's try two grams."

"It's been two minutes already," said Bo, slightly anxiously.

"Probably so," said Lo Hi, pulling his hand free. "Oh no, we forgot to change the ointment too,"

Bo, Lo Hi and Kimiko gathered around Bo's two invisible hands.

"So, when will my hands become visible again?"

"Left or right?" asked Kimiko.

"Either."

"Sometime soon," Lo Hi was trying to be comforting. "We will try something else."

"Hang on, we've already used both hands," said Bo.

"Foot, your foot," pointed Kimiko, "use a foot."

"Now we've only two more chances, you're not going to use any more appendages after that!" said Bo.

Lo Hi giggled, Kimiko said "What an appendage?"

"Ask Lo Hi," said Bo.

"Kamatso-chi," laughed Lo Hi and they both giggled and helped each other take off his right shoe and sock, and haul his leg and foot rather unceremoniously onto the table.

"Don't forget the foot massage," said Bo, nodding towards the jar of ointment.

Lo Hi flicked the switch, leant back and said, looking at her watch, "so, two minutes dynamo and two grams of the ointment."

Two minutes later the three of them stared at Bo's right foot, marvelling as it vanished before their eyes. "Now we just wait for two hours." Lo Hi and Kimiko clapped and laughed.

"As they say, it's too late to stop now," Bo said rather more pensively, thinking about Choo and the gang and the rumpus to be back at the Glorious Lodge.

33

Lo Hi, or parts of Lo Hi, had gone invisible a dozen or so times, and she now explained to Bo what it was like. Although she had only done it for her own, or for her father's, amusement, and only outside in the summer, she knew enough to tell him the ground rules.

"The strangest part is to be naked and unseen. No-one is staring at you, but also they cannot see you moving. Normally, you walk down a street, everyone adjusts themselves a little to make room for everyone else, but when they cannot see you they walk ahead. Always you have to move away. The worst is in a queue, sometimes they bump into you from behind. Then you think why wait in a queue? So you go to the front, and jump over the barrier or rush or squeeze through the door first. Never get in an elevator, even if empty! And remember you must have eyes in the back of your head, as they cannot see you to stop, not just in a queue but everywhere. Always you must look behind. For some minutes it is all fun, but with crowds then it is not so much fun. And animals, animals go mad. Dogs go really crazy."

"What about dirt, in the book picking up dirt was a big problem?" asked Bo.

"It is true," replied Lo Hi, "the only thing invisible is the body, so if you splash in a dirty puddle, then the stains walk around on their own. But here in Pyongyang the city is clean, no cars, no dirt. Your big problem will be snow, if it falls on you it looks like it walks around on its own. And footprints of course, in the snow."

"Doesn't sound like much fun."

"It is not, but it can be useful."

"For example?"

"For breaking in and out of prison, for example!" she replied and laughed.

Then they ran again through the plan for rescuing Pi Jam. Kimiko had a map, well a sketch, of the layout and his cell number and location from an ex-political prisoner recently secretly contacted by Kimiko on behalf of Amnesty. Cold was going to be the big problem. Since the failure of the Blaine programme, Bo had had no more preparation, only in fact incapacitation. Kimiko knew she could always borrow the Japanese North Korean Trade Authority car for the evening without suspicion, as long as she dropped the Director off on the way home and picked him up the next morning. Now she had to do it for the weekend, or at least for Saturday when the prison was at its busiest.

They would spend Friday night at Kimiko's as they knew it was bugged, and she and Lo Hi would have a rowdy girls' evening at home, Bo sworn to silence and hand signals as he would certainly be a wanted man by then. The invisibility apparatus would be in Kimiko's room as after breaking out they would be looking for Pi Jam in Lo Hi's apartment, and they would make Bo invisible at eleven that morning. At midday they would drive up as close as possible to the prison, and wait for one of the gate openings, Bo would sprint in through the open gates. He would be naked, and had to minimise the time between leaving the car and entering the prison. The prison would still be cold, it was part of the regime to keep the prisoners under-clothed and permanently needing warmth, but compared to outside, survivable for a short while. They knew the cell number and where the keys were kept in the guard room. He had to take the key off the rack and hold it in his hands to keep it from sight. He had to find a fire alarm station, break the glass to set off the alarms for a diversion.

"Another thing, don't cut yourself," warned Lo Hi.

"The blood is visible?"

"Visible and likely to cause panic. These are primitive people," she replied.

He had to go the cell, open it, convince a startled and probably sceptical Pi Jam to come with him. They hoped if seen in the corridor the guards would assume Pi Jam had been let out officially for a reason, and would anyway be more concerned tracking down the source of the fire alarm. They had to approach the guard room, and deal with whatever problems were there, maybe by violence, this too a first for Bo; violence that is not involving a playing field and well known set of rules. Then they had to unbolt the main gate, rush for the car, head back to

Kimiko's where the apparatus would now be waiting and primed to make Pi Jam invisible.

"No problemo, and while we're fine tuning, can we run through the country escape plan once more?" asked Bo. "How do we get out of the country, that's what has been on my mind? Kimiko mentioned about the Canadians, how does that work?"

Kimiko came and sat in front of him. "I explain before, but again no harm. Saturday night cocktail party Canadian Embassy. All of us Japan North Korean Trade Authority invited. You and Lo Hi father invisible. You will enter with me. Lo Hi stay here, say nothing happen. Party finish. Stay in Embassy, later CIA smuggle out."

"But how, how do they smuggle us out?" asked Bo.

"Best not know. I not know. Happen before. Money."

"Hey, look, my right hand is coming back."

And sure enough over the next moments, his hands and feet restored to his former glory, he sank back in the arm chair, laughing and showing off his hands and feet. Kimiko sat on the left side of the chair, Lo Hi on the right side, he had his arm around both their waists, they were stroking his hair, and he felt as exhilarated as he had when she first burst in to his office all those weeks ago.

Kimiko stretched and yawned. "For me, bed, we meet again tomorrow."

With all the excitement of invisibility and planning, Bo had not paid much attention to the sleeping arrangements, but in a flash of recognition of a promising development he realised that he and Lo Hi were to spend the night together, minimum in the same flat, maximum in the same bed. She smiled at him bashfully, and got up to go to the kitchen. He followed her in, put his hands on the sides of her waist and turned her slowly around to face him. She looked up, he bent down, and he kissed her first on her brow, then her nose and then her mouth. She lifted her hands around his neck, and rested her head against his shoulder. "Bo, we must talk." He held her away, smiled, drew her closer and kissed her again.

"Of course, let's sit and talk, let's talk for hours," Bo said. They sat side by side on the sofa, she nesting under his arm, he with his feet stretched out in front. She talked and talked, he listened. She was worried and excited about the escape plan, anxious for her father, more than grateful for Kimiko, could not believe why he came to find her, the risks he had taken up to now, the horrible risks he was about to take.

"Well, the fact is I have come here for you. From the moment you left the office, with me on the phone to La Cuss, I have not stopped thinking about you."

They kissed again, easier now, for longer, their fingers gently stroking each other's hair, then their necks and shoulders.

"Who is La Cuss?" Lo Hi pushed away sharply and asked.

"La Cuss is just my own name for the girl on the other end of the phone when you called," said Bo pulling her back closer.

"Her name is La?"

"No, her name is Kelly Cuss. La is French for "the", so the cuss, cuss is old English for curse, so la cuss becomes the curse. Franglais."

One brow creased, and she asked "But she is your fiancée in London? You don't love her, or is it settled by both your parents?"

"I did love her, I thought I loved her, I moved to Japan and realised that maybe I didn't love her, well at least not marriage love. I met you and now I know I don't love her," Bo kissed her again, she responded more fully, she pulled away again and asked, "You will marry her?"

"No." said Bo, only half convincing himself. They embraced again, and Bo thought of all the horrors of the wedding, and the worse ones to follow. Denial was the best path for now, especially for now.

They lay together, kissing, stroking, playing, giggling, happy.

Bo, now with his hand on her bare back, tried his trusted first finger and thumb bra opening move. Lo Hi laughed, muttered something about North Korean lingerie, and moving her left hand behind her back, undid it and then took his hand and placed it on her breast. He moved down, lifted her tee shirt and gently kissed her breasts, massaging her ribs and back.

She moaned with happiness, sighed and said, "I have a cuss too," she laughed. Oh crikes, Bo thought, just my luck.

"That's a shame," said Bo, undeterred, still arousing them both.

"Yes, his name is Kang Wan Do."

"Ah. You love him like I love La Cuss?" Bo looked at her, still holding her tightly.

"Less than that. My grandparents kind of arranged it. I know him, we have not kissed. Bo, I am virgin."

"Mmmm," said Bo, "you're beautiful. Me too."

"Beautiful?" she asked.

"No, a virgin," they giggled.

"You are lying," she laughed, "stop joking. You are the opposite of a virgin."

"It's true," said Bo.

They fell back into their embrace, slowly and silently moving together. Bo's thoughts were on making love, and his hand ventured down the back of her jeans. After a while, she took his head in both her hands and whispered near his ear.

"Bo, when we are both safe, in Shanghai or Tokyo then I will not be virgin with you. OK?"

"From now till then I won't be able to think of anything else, but in the meantime." He took her hand and placed it onto his trousers, and started moving it slowly up and down. He took his hand away and she continued until, groaning, he pulled her closer still and hugged her tightly.

Hours later, still deep in sleep, lying together, each slowly noticed knocking on the door, muffled yet urgent. Lo Hi stood up quickly, straightened her clothes, said "Coming, wait" to the door, ruffled the bed and then unlocked the latch. It was Kimiko, worried.

"What's happened?" asked Lo Hi.

"The prison plan, I cannot find ," Kimiko was breathless.

"But you had it last month in the....", said Lo Hi.

"I know, I search everywhere in apartment. Do you think I raided? But why take only that? Have much worse documents." Kimiko slumped down.

"They would not raid your flat, not with your Japanese trade connections, they would just bug it. Unless they knew about Amnesty? But then you would know by now, that is for sure. You take papers to and from work, maybe it's in your office" said Lo Hi.

"No, I never. Maybe I threw out by mistake if it was with other papers. That could happen. Anyway I can remember cell number, P109. I can also remember where it was on sketch." Kimiko drew it out again from memory, but still looked desperate, and the others joined in not knowing quite what this might mean: Kimiko thinking it was the end of the plan, Lo Hi worried about a raid, but fatalistic, and Bo trying to think what he should be worried about, so far unsuccessfully.

34

They went through Kimiko's flat space by space, using hand signals to communicate with Bo. Bo took the kitchen, Lo Hi the sitting room and Kimiko the bathroom. Every surface was searched, under every surface was searched, behind every surface was searched. The prison plan was simply not there.

Back in Lo Hi's apartment they could talk again. Lo Hi was sure the apartment had not been searched; they weren't particularly subtle in the searching and in fact liked you to know they had been there. Kimiko was certain she had not taken it to work. Bo drew the only conclusion; it had been spring cleaned, autumn cleaned in this case, by mistake.

The prison raid was scheduled for tomorrow afternoon and Kimiko felt terrible. She went to work, tasked with returning with the car. Lo Hi and Bo had breakfast, and spent the morning talking and kissing, talking and cuddling, talking about themselves and each other, about London and Pyongyang, about Amnesty International and the North Korean gulag, and her father and their fiancés, in fact about anything they could think of except tomorrow's mission.

"So, Lo Hi, what happened when you went to the US Embassy?" asked Bo.

"It was late when I arrived. In fact they were preparing to leave and asked me to call back the next day."

"And did you?"

"Not likely. Later that evening I was at Kimiko's when the phone rang. It was the Embassy, someone called Snide. I asked how they knew where I was, and he said the Japanese had told him. Which Japanese? He did not say. He asked me to meet him in the lobby of the Sago Hotel at eight."

"You went?"

"Yes."

"That would have been when I called round to find you," Bo remembered.

"You came to find me in Tokyo?"

"Of course. Pledging my undying love and devotion to the cause. So what happened at the Sago?"

"He knew about my father and wanted to help. But first he wanted to recruit me. It all seemed too, too...what's the word?"

"Spooky?"

"Sounds right. It is one thing being an internal rebel, but something else to be a US spy. Everyone would have been shot. Even Pak Dong probably."

"Who's he?"

"He is my brother, the one who is doing his Patriotic Duty, you say conscription. Anyway, I did not trust Snide. I agreed to come to his office mid-morning, but took the first plane to Beijing and then home."

Lo Hi noticed Kimiko looking hard at her, and from behind Bo's back she held up a finger to her lips; a reminder that they had agreed to say nothing to anyone about the recent local recruitment incident at Lo Hi's office.

"Look!" Kimiko gasped.

She had caught a glimpse of something out of the corner of an eye, and swung her arm towards the muted black and white television. A picture of Bo was on the screen. She rushed over and turned up the volume.

"That's my visa photograph. What are they saying?" asked Bo. Lo Hi waved him quiet, then turned the volume off when more scenes of the Dear Leader's daily doings appeared.

"That you have disappeared. That you are British, and therefore a running dog of US imperialism, probably a spy sent for counterrevolutionary subversion, it is every loyal comrade's duty to surrender you to the authorities."

"Lucky I'm invisible! Or soon will be."

"Who was your guide?" asked Lo Hi.

"Choo, I remember that because of the trains. Which came first Choo the man or Choo choo the train guide? Sammy I think he said too, Sammy Choo," replied Bo.

"Well he is a nervous man," said Lo Hi, "a worried man."

"Because I did a runner?" asked Bo.

"It's the system, it's not exactly designed this way, but it just

130

happens to be self policing because responsibility is passed down the line. Don't forget everyone is terrified of his immediate superior, that no-one is to be trusted and that snitches are everywhere."

"But it's hardly Sammy Choo's fault if I fall madly in love with a beautiful girl called Lo Hi, abandon my previous life, risk my immediate life and have no certain future life," said Bo, "if anyone is to blame it is one of the grinning Leaders who have created this paradise we are all supposed to be trying to get into."

"Well maybe in theory, but Sammy Choo will be worried about privileges." She explained how he had a trusted position. Here, where there was no real money, privileges were everything. His section leader, whose position was even more dependent on good behaviour down the line than Sammy Choo's, would have a few more privileges, hard won over many years of senseless obedience to a system that everyone knew to be corrupt and useless. And so on up the line. You run away, and everyone up the hierarchy blames those lower down for the problem even if they were really blameless, like our Sammy Choo. The higher up the more to lose proportionately, but at the lower levels these privileges mean not just a slightly better standard of living, but a whole level above that enjoyed by the "broad masses". So everyone felt the pinch, and so it was self policing. The same was true in the gulags. The boss delegated to the guards who delegated to lead prisoners, who did all the dirty work for fear of being thrown back into the abyss of normal life. The less work you did, the less unpleasant work you had to do, the more privileges you enjoyed, but those just above the survival line appreciated what they have to lose the most, so keeping the top cats in cream.

Outside it was just dark, and the door knocked, Kimiko's code knock. "Good news, very good news. First I have car until Monday, second I have local Director's own car—not Trade Authority car. Not only that, it's new Corolla." Bo looked lost, but Lo Hi explained. The official car would have special plates which would make it stand out; it would almost certainly not be stopped and searched, or even asked for papers and permits, but it might well be followed like most diplomatic plated cars were, and even if not followed, noted and reported by snitches. A local registered car, especially a new Japanese one, especially a new Japanese one with two young girls inside, well any of the police forces would presume they were the daughters of someone very well connected, too well connected to be stopped at all, and even the snitches would not bother to try to use it to win favours.

"At last good news, " said Lo Hi, as they took themselves and the apparatus and a now silent Bo next door to Kimiko's bugged but safe apartment for the evening and night, although Bo's thoughts were of the apartment as chastity belt rather than an alibi base; he couldn't help wondering, if not wandering, as he glimpsed them together in Kimiko's bedroom while he slept on the sofa, his legs uncomfortably over the arms.

35

"I am Colonel Krop of the SSSA. Do you know who we are?" he repeated the question.

Nark Am Dim did not answer. He had not answered any questions. Why should he incriminate himself? He was innocent until proved guilty, and the burden on them was to prove him so. The Canadians had a consulate; they would come and arrange for his release. It had been the same on the way here; in fact it had been the same ever since the four gooks arrested him in the square. Questions. They knew he spoke Korean, was Korean, which didn't help a classic first line of defence. More questions; still no answers. Then they had taken him here, to this Peoples Founding Prison, the same place that bitch had said her father was staying. Even on his way into the cell, opposite the guardhouse, more questions, still no answers. Now this Krop character, he looked like a brute, but he could swagger all he liked, Nark Am Dim is not going to incriminate himself. He did however speak for the first time.

"Er-I am an innocent Canadian tourist, and I demand to see my consul and a lawyer."

Colonel Krop smiled, and looked at his three colleagues, they smiled, Colonel Krop laughed and they laughed and then Colonel Krop laughed out loud, and they too laughed out loud. They all laughed for a while, then Colonel Krop walked behind his chair, leant down and barked: "So we think we are a clever little spy, do we? Think we are in Canada or wherever so-called safe it is a little Korean boy finds himself, do we? Think that spying is unimportant to a country at war, do we? We do know we are in country still at war, do we? That the Canadians helped the US imperialists sixty years ago and war still exists?" Colonel Krop's bark had become a shout.

"Er- you can stop shouting at me, I know my rights," Nark Am Dim protested, and from behind him he heard Colonel Krop shout "and I know my rights!" and just then his head exploded as a fierce slap to his right temple sent him flying across the room. The others laughed again. He looked up to see Colonel Krop take off his belt, double it up and then start beating him with it, over and over. He held his hands and arms up to protect his face, but then he felt a kick, then another to his stomach.

"Get up! Sit back down! I am in charge of the Sung Pi Jam case, and you contacted his daughter and told her you would release him. This we know. Now, how and why are my next questions, questions you will answer. Why do you want him in the West? How are you planning his escape? You cannot be here alone. This is the third question. Who are you, who are you with?"

Nark Am Dim did not answer, but shook his head in confusion, pain and defiance. Colonel Krop shouted to his comrades: "You make him feel at home now. I'm going to bring in Sung Pi Jam himself, see if he can help this little mystery." For the next three minutes Nark Am Dim was on the cold hard floor again hunched up, reeling under blows from boots and sticks. He heard the door open, felt his eyes open, heard Colonel Krop tell them to stop, and saw a middle aged man, bedraggled and unkempt but not harmed, standing by the door. He felt arms pulling him up and heard Colonel Krop telling him to stand to attention. He did his best to stand upright.

"So, some introductions. By the door we have an intellectual, a scientist, a past patriot with valuable knowledge of our state secrets who has been informed against, and is being investigated as has to happen, no more than that, and who has been a most co-operative suspect. And in the middle of the room, a Korean man, but not from either Koreas, from Canada, perhaps, who has arrived in our country pretending to be a tourist. This is a bad offence in itself. But he makes it worse. Not from his own initiative, but from the initiative of a foreign power, which we will establish soon, he contacts the daughter of our patriot scientist, herself a potential counter-revolutionary, and offers to export her and her father out of their homeland."

"Colonel Krop, sir, I have never seen this man, this is the first time. I know nothing, nothing of this plot."

"Sung Pi Jam, I am sure you are correct. A more stupid plot I have yet to discover. But you must admit it does not look good for you. Here we are, becoming more and more convinced you are the victim of an unworthy, malicious even, snitch, when along comes a foreign agent who wants to abduct you, and your daughter, to so-called safety. Why? We must ask ourselves, why?"

"Tell him, please tell him, I know nothing about this," Sung Pi Jam said to Nark Am Dim, "now they will think I was a traitor. Who is your government, why they are doing this?"

There was a knock on the door, and another SSSA man walks in with Nark Am Dim's suitcase. They opened it and scattered his belongings across the table. They picked up each piece in turn, examined it and made two piles, one for innocent items such as small clothes and the simpler washroom kit, and one for suspicious items, such as all electrical goods. Nark Am Dim tensed as they picked up the camera and took it to bits. It did not take long for them to all be huddled, excitedly, around it. Then he saw another agent unscrew his coat hanger, and fit the two together, with a look of triumph and menace in his direction.

"Oh dear!" said Colonel Krop sarcastically. "A spy. A spy who is out of contact. A spy who nobody knows has been arrested. A spy who nobody knows will disappear. After the information has been extracted of course. A spy who is on his own, alone in a small bad world, a spy with questions to answer."

"Sung Pi Jam."

"Yes, Colonel Krop."

"You too will have some questions to answer. So far we have been kind to you. Now the questions will need more precise answers. Take them both back to their cells. Prepare the interrogation room."

36

Bo woke up early, at first light, partly through discomfort, partly through excitement. Today was the day; he did not feel fear as such, but a certain apprehension of what could go wrong. No doubt he was helped by not knowing what exactly might go wrong, still less the consequences. He did not feel particularly brave, not in the way Lo Hi thought him brave to the point of heroism; a myth he had hardly tried to dispel. Her bravery he felt shining from her, less obviously equipped by personality than Kimiko, and totally unprotected by diplomatic consideration should things go wrong; Lo Hi was living every second as it happened, whereas Bo always sensed Kimiko had her mind on other things, things she kept to herself.

Bo heard the others stir in the bedroom next door, and nearly shouted out "Good morning", but putting his hand theatrically over his mouth, pushed their door open. "Bo!" they both remonstrated at the same time. Shhh, he remonstrated back with his finger on his mouth pointing vaguely to where a microphone might be in the ceiling. Sorry, they gestured as one. Cup of tea? he asked them silently, then left to make it. In the kitchen he had to listen to the piped government radio station which was always on in the all apartments. You could turn it down, but never off.

....confirming again that the Japanese imperialists are a fraud of international laws and a shamelessly heinous robber.

Dear Leader and Supreme Inspiration Kim Jong Il has energetically led the building of a great prosperous powerful nation, foiling the moves of the U.S. imperialist warmongers to isolate and stifle the DPRK, always knowing that Korean-style socialism is sure to triumph as long as there are his wise leadership and people united close around him.

The National Preparatory Committee of Democratic Congo sent its fraternal greetings to the Workers' Party of Korea referring to the *fact that Great Leader Kim Il Sung performed immortal feats by building and leading the Party and Dear Leader Kim Jong Il has turned the Workers' Party of Korea into an eternal party of Kim Il Sung and led the struggle to defend socialism and build a great and prosperous and powerful nation. The people of Democratic Congo extend firm solidarity to the Korean Workers' Party in its efforts to celebrate these shining labour achievements.*

A plot by Western reactionaries to smuggle a suspected traitor out of the country has been foiled by the exceptional vigilance of the State Safety and Security Agency. A Canadian mercenary, no doubt in the pocket of US counter revolutionary influences, has been arrested, and the Canadian Embassy closed until further notice in justified retaliation.

Lo Hi and Kimiko entered the kitchen. Everyone looked horrified, shocked. The escape route was closed. Kimiko waved them out into the corridor. They whispered. They had to carry on, and think about a new way out during the day. There was no option. It had never occurred to them that the idiot who came to see them was Canadian, and that by making Lo Hi look more patriotic they would put the whole plan in danger.

During breakfast they turned on the TV news, hoping to have an update on the Canadian Embassy and the Bo hunt. He noticed, slightly disgruntledly, that he had been downgraded. Lo Hi wanted to explain that was because what they saw then on television would be the last mention of him; from now on the search would be undercover so as to give the impression that the infallible security forces had already captured him. There was no more mention of the Embassy. The last item was the weather report, and Lo Hi and Kimiko exchanged worried looks. Bo motioned, what's up?

"Looks like a blizzard on the way Kimiko," said Lo Hi, gesturing to Bo that flakes would be on his shoulders and head.

"For how long?" asked Kimiko

"All day it says, they are asking comrades not to go out unnecessarily and to use the minimum power to keep warm indoors."

Kimiko came over to the table and wrote: car in basement, move to street if snow, car stuck. Back in 10 mins.

When she came back she wrote underneath: v. cold out! She gave a worried look in Bo's direction. Suddenly all the lights and TV went out.

"Power cut!" said Kimiko. They looked at each other, all instantly seizing on what this meant. It was only half an hour to go before the apparatus was due to be turned on and the invisibility process to commence. No power, no invisibility, no break out. Kimiko and Lo Hi and Bo each thought silently, from their own ideas of fate, that maybe this was just not meant to be, but no-one said anything, and just looked at each other and the room silently. "Not even cup tea." said Kimiko.

Bo looked through a magazine he could not understand, even the pictures seemed to be from another planet, Lo Hi went through the motions of reading a book, while Kimiko did some unnecessary housework. She wondered if the bug was down too, but dared not risk it. They had planned to leave at 1200, she thought, noticing the clock now said 1230 and the invisibility had not even started.

Then with a whir from the kitchen and a crackle from the TV the power came back on. Without a word they plugged in the machine, motioned to Bo to get ready, and out of a sense of modesty went in to the bedroom while he stripped, anointed himself with the labyrinthium and turned slowly between the dynamos for two minutes. He did not want to see himself disappearing, and besides needed to keep his eyelids closed, and when the machine turned off two minutes later he looked down and saw only straight through himself. He walked over to the bedroom, was about to knock, then realising they could not see him, and he could not talk to them, opened the door, reached over to Lo Hi and gently pulled her up from the bed and out into the corridor, gave her a surprise unseen kiss, wrapped himself up only in the coat and scarf he arrived in, pulled the hat down as far over the void as he could, and heard Kimiko collecting keys and coats and following close behind.

Once in the hallway, next to the staircase, a still comfortably clothed Bo said "Well I can't see anything else going wrong today," and lead them downstairs to the car. Kimiko and Lo Hi looked at each other and smiled discreetly.

37

In the car they made up for the enforced silence at Kimiko's, all chatting, albeit nervously, about the task ahead. They were late, but only by an hour, on a schedule they had put upon themselves and so concluded no harm was done. The prison should be busy all Saturday afternoon with various visitors, shift changes and deliveries.

Bo looked around from the back seat of the car. Apart from the head down walk from the Golden Lodge to Kimiko's apartment this was his first view of the city. Everywhere seemed to have been designed by the same person at the same time. His first impression was of emptiness, like a Saturday afternoon in a ghost town. The pavements were even emptier than the streets. Everywhere there were right angles, and all at the same right angles to each other. Instead of traffic lights there were raised daises for immaculately dressed blue uniformed traffic directors with no traffic to direct.

"It's so clean here," he said, "no litter anywhere."

"Because nothing to litter," said Kimiko plaintively.

They drove towards the Kim Il Sung Square, along enormously wide and empty boulevards. Lo-Hi pointed out some of the attractions, here the Grand People's Study House, there the Korean Central History Museum, on their left the Korean Revolutionary Museum, on their right the Korean Workers Party Monument.

"Ye Gods, what's the Arc de Triomphe doing here?" asked Bo in mock amazement.

"It does look familiar for sure, "said Lo Hi. "Actually, we are taught to be proud to let you know it is one metre larger in every direction."

"Bad luck on our French friends," said Bo.

They drove on up past the Immortal Tower, and headed out of town on the Podunamu Street towards the Three-Revolution Exhibition on the northern edge of the city. Far from deteriorating as most cities do as you leave the centre, Bo was impressed that Pyongyang stayed as pristine, if eerily quiet, all the way out of town.

"Oh oh, road block," said Kimiko as Lo Hi looked around from talking to Bo towards the front again. "and it's snowing."

Bo looked too and sure enough the first flakes were falling just as Kimiko slowed the car for the checkpoint. Bo saw three security ahead, two on the driver's side, and one on the passenger's side. There were two other cars ahead of them, enough time for him to whisk off the coat, scarf and hat and stuff them below Lo Hi's seat.

"Choolies," announced Lo Hi.

"Who are they?" asked Bo

"They are the Workers and Peasants Red Guard Paramilitaries," she replied, explaining the slang. "Idiots mostly, but better lie down."

"Why, they can't see me," said Bo quickly slipping off his overcoat.

"Bo! Not playing now." said Kimiko, winding her window down. He immediately felt the icy blast of air from outside.

They looked at Kimiko's and the car's papers, took them under a nearby ledge and began phoning or radioing.

"I thought that two smart girls in a new Japanese car was security proof," said Bo deadpan.

"Bo, shut up," said Kimiko anxiously.

The Choolies came back, handed Kimiko her papers, looked hard at Lo Hi, looked in the back of the car and saw nothing. They must have asked where the women were going, because Bo heard Kimiko mention the Victorious Fatherland Liberation War Museum on the map, which was both their pre-arranged alibi for check points and anyway right next door to their destination, the Party Founding Prison. The car moved off.

"For Christ's sake close that bloody window," stuttered Bo, "it's worse than freezing back here."

By now the snow was falling famously and they slowed the car on the upswept roads. What other traffic there was seemed to vanish too.

Atishoo! Sneezed Bo loudly in the back seat.

"Bless you!" said Lo Hi.

"For God sake you two," hissed Kimiko. "Bo not sneeze OK, just not sneeze. Sneeze without form not exist. OK?"

They drove on for six kilometres, but now at almost walking

pace, the wipers barely able to show a clear screen ahead. Bo wrapped himself up again in his coat. Kimiko, tense, was looking intently through the screen and feeling the car slip under them. Lo Hi was lost in thought, uncharacteristically silent. Outside it was getting more overcast as the snow fell more densely. By now there were a few private cars; two snow ploughs, some gritters and camouflaged trucks rambled down the wide boulevards. Some of the street lights came on. They turned the radio on, then off. Then Lo Hi said, "We are here." Bo felt a tightening in his stomach.

They turned the car towards the prison, parked behind a cart and turned off the lights, keeping only the engine on for the warmth and the wipers. The idle chatter stopped now. They all knew the plan. They would wait for an arrival at the gates. As the vehicle emptied and the occupants headed for the main gate they would drive up, Bo would open the blind side rear door, and run for the entrance just as the newcomers were passing through.

They did not have to wait long. From the gloom an official white car approached the entrance as if to go through the gate. But it stopped short, and three men in uniform got out and headed for the entrance. Kimiko engaged gear as it was pulling off.

"Wait," said Bo. "A crowd would be better, at least more than a few people, and we need to be closer, much closer. They would have been inside by the time we had pulled up."

Bo was nervous now, really for the first time, and with his nervousness came a sense of authority, an awareness of leadership. Kimiko and Lo Hi sensed it too, and seemed relieved to have Bo in command. He rejected the next three vehicles. By now it was getting darker. "Better," Bo said, "I guess the shift will change at five at the earliest. As long as we move by then. In fact, let's just wait for the shift to change," Bo said, realising none of them knew when this would be and wishing he had taken this all a bit more seriously before.

They waited. Various cars and vans came and went. It grew darker, they felt safer. Kimiko turned on the radio, Bo told her to turn it off. She did. At ten to six a large semi-camouflaged bus appeared, and from the rear tailgate a large troupe of guards jumped down into the fresh carpet of snow and headed off to the prison gates.

"This is it," said Bo, "get ready to go, keep the lights off till I'm out."

Lo Hi said, "Bo, don't forget to..."

"I know," he said, "sweep the flakes off my shoulders, feet and head. You two wait for me here, right back behind the cart. Good luck to us all, wouldn't you say?"

38

Bo opened the rear door on the pavement side so it could not be seen, stepped out and within three seconds felt intensely cold. Head down, with ears, feet and scalp already hurting achingly, he ran to join the new guard entering the building. Remember to stay at the back, he thought, be aware of being jostled unawares from behind. Bo was half aware of being a complete amateur and half aware of now having to be totally professional. He looked around, sprinting silently on the spot to try to keep some circulation, looking down to check his footprints, rubbing his ears hard, then horrified, noticed his exhaled breath hanging in the air. He tried to stop exhaling in one direction, looked behind again, and kept rubbing himself as quietly as he could, rubbing in some warmth and rubbing off some flakes.

In spite of the intense cold the new guards seemed in no particular hurry to get to work inside the building, but gradually one by one they entered through the gates, each showing his pass to a controller who checked each one like he had never seen pass or passholder before. Bo could take the pain no longer, and risking footprints and breath being seen, he rushed to the front of the line, and vaulted over the barrier behind the controller. In the noise and bustle no-one noticed him and he moved quickly inside. There was a large and warm looking glass fronted guard room just ahead on his left, but Bo knew he could not go in there, not just yet. He saw an open door opposite, and went into the room there, just to keep out of the draft. From there he could see the old shift putting on their outside clothes, and chatting to each other, preparing to leave with half the weekend ahead. He heard the main gate slam shut and felt the icy draught subside, leaving just plain cold air. Bo knew the first hurdle had been jumped, he was inside, cold but so far safe, unseen and definitely inside.

39

"What does she mean 'until his signs are more propitious?'" Colonel Krop's chest is puffed up, his voice angry with disbelief.

"It must be her belief in astrology, sir"

"I know what it must be, Officer Cadet Sung."

"Yes, sir"

"And I suppose you believe in this superstitious nonsense too?"

"No, sir."

"And I thought she was from the intellectual class."

"Yes, sir."

"Ten days?"

"That is what she asked for, sir."

Colonel Krop considers his options. Normally he would interrogate a suspect whenever he liked and his least consideration would be some supernatural mumbo jumbo about lining up some stupid planets. But he had agreed to these experiments with the serum, and if this nuclear physicist was innocent, and the story got out that he had ignored a family request, well this intellectual would have some connections and that could be trouble. And it's only ten days; and there's no hurry. Let him stew in prison. We can increase snitch activity on the daughter too, something he had been meaning to do for a long time.

"Very well, Officer Cadet Sung, we will wait for ten days. Dismissed!"

"Yes, sir."

Less than an hour later Professor Ju Flo Mung looks over to the sound of the knocks on the door "Enter!". It was young Officer Cadet Sung Pak Dong. "Ah, Sung, it is you."

"Yes, sir."

"And?"

"I have just come from Colonel Krop's office. The experiment with the intellectual Sung Pi Jam will take place in ten days."

"That's fine."

"But I am behind with the writing part of my special assignment on the truth serum. Can I write it here with you?"

"Alright."

"And maybe we can experiment with that ape again, it was four millilitres that we reckoned was the safe dose last time. I can take note of its vital signs, for the report."

Professor Ju Flo Mung took off his spectacles. "We established that it could take four millilitres once, not repeatedly. Let's say it dies, then it cannot be used again. Even if it doesn't die, its nervous system may be too compromised to be of value to the vivisectionists who have requested an early experiment. Are we not being a little selfish, young Officer Cadet?"

"Yes, sir, sorry sir."

"On the other hand, if it survived intact it would give us more confidence with the appropriate dosage with your father, in which case it would be a valuable experiment."

"No, sir, it is of more use to the collective as it is now, for more decisive future usage, then that is more important."

"I think it is better for us all, except of course your father."

"Yes sir, certainly sir."

40

Bo looked at the clock on the guard room wall: 17.55. He was shaking badly by now, almost uncontrollably and he knew he had to find warmth, and find warmth quickly for the next ten minutes or so while the new guards settled down. He started walking, then trotting down the corridor. He pushed open the first door on the left, and found darkness and more cold. Running now, he swivelled around as out of the corner of his eye he saw a symbol of a man, and next to the door a fire alarm box with a glass case. Must remember that, he thought. He pushed on the door, the light was on, and the room was warm. He skipped over to the radiator, touching it lightly with his right hand, then when it did not burn touched it again, then his other hand. He sat on it, put his feet up onto it and sat still, just sat still and waited for his body to warm up. The staff loo, he thought, I'm in the staff loo. Bo laughed quietly, saw a brand new swivelling hot air hand dryer, but decided against pushing his luck.

From the passageway he heard voices becoming louder, laughing voices, then the door kicked open and two guards in heavy uniformed overcoats went for the tin urinal. Bo tensed on the radiator, ready to move off quietly should they come close, but they zipped up, redressed and left as noisily as they had arrived. Bo, on his haunches on the radiator, looked down at his feet, imagined them now slightly pink again, moved his toes and thought about his next move. He remembered the fire alarm, finding that was a bit of luck. Must remember how I got here too, he thought.

41

A warmer Bo was waiting for the quieter moment when the guards had resigned themselves to their long night shift. He heard a commotion outside and saw the lavatory door open and close a bit with the change of air. Bo waited until he thought the new team would have settled, and by now he was feeling the radiator too hot to sit on, and so just leant against it with his palms, then his buttocks, back of legs, and over again. Bo straightened, noticed himself to be fully alert but calm, totally in the present, carefully opened the door, checked that no-one was around and set off for the guard room.

He opened the door, looked gingerly left and right, and ventured down the cold, hard empty corridor towards the main room sure that the keys would be there. The lights were few, high and bright and Bo thought about how his shadows would have looked under normal circumstances. He smelt a curious mixture of cleanliness and hardship, of an existence just above the minimum needed for tomorrow.

Now looking through the glass walls of the guardroom at an angle, Bo noticed the key racks on the far wall. They were organised side by side with Block names. Bo looked over to P, and saw the key for 109 hanging along with the others. He moved with his back to the wall to where he could look straight through the glass front into the guard room. There were ten of them, jackets off, kettle on the stove, some reading papers, some chatting. Just like anywhere, Bo thought, not from first hand experience, and then wondered about how to get them out of there so he could take the key.

Bo noticed the dog an instant before the dog noticed Bo. Lying on the floor, the well haired German Shepherd looked up, it's ear pricked up, its nose twitched. Bo stood completely still, knowing he could not be seen at all, or heard or smelt through the glass. But the dog now got up onto its haunches, and trailing its short lead, approached the glass looking directly at Bo. It barked once directly at him, and Bo sprinted back to the staff lavatory, hearing the frantic barking of the dog, by now in full cry, recede behind him.

He ran up to the fire alarm box, was about to break the glass with his fist when he thought about blood, and rushed into the Gents to look for an implement. He found a handle on the end of the cistern chain, wrenched it off, opened the door again. The dog was now in the corridor, mercifully with a guard holding it back on a tight chain, barking even more ferociously straight at him. Bo smashed the glass, the alarm siren started immediately, Bo ran back into the staff loo, opened a cubicle and silently shut the door behind him.

Outside he could hear the sound of running and shouting, of orders being given and the alarm bells echoing around the passages, and the approaching sound of the dog. The dog's barking reached a crescendo of fear and anger outside the door, then appeared to be dragged away by its shouting handler. When the passage outside seemed to have only the clanging sound of the bells, Bo opened the door, looked carefully outside and scampered back to the guard room. "You better be empty," he said to himself, as much for the comfort of his own voice as hopeful thinking.

42

Barefooted, in fact stark naked, silent and invisible, Bo looked to his right as he stopped in front of the big glass window. One guard left. Bastard, thought Bo. He walked over to the right of the glass and tapped on it three times. He saw the guard shout to enter without looking up thinking it must be the door. Who the hell's going to knock? thought Bo, as he tapped again, but louder. This time the guard looked up to where the sound came from and headed towards the door. As he opened it to look outside, Bo breathed in, a little melodramatically he thought later, and squeezed in the space behind the guard, who returned almost immediately. Now they were both inside; Bo felt warmer again, the guard looked more annoyed than puzzled, and sat back down with his newspaper.

Bo crept over to the key rack on the far wall, and took off the key for P109, threw it in the air and smiled as it disappeared back in his clasp. He walked back to the glass front, knocked on it again at the same place, now on his far left. The guard looked up, then looked back down and continued reading. Bo tried again, again louder, but the guard merely hunched his shoulders and continued absorbed in his newspaper. Bo then picked up a paperweight from the desk in front of him, walked over in front of the door, and then threw it at a set of files resting on a shelf. Direct hit, the files fell to the floor, the guard looked around, looked back, looked around again, slowly stood up and this time looking more puzzled than annoyed, walked to the back of the room. Bo opened the door, walked through and closed it again silently before the guard had even started to tidy up the mess.

43

Bo ran off down the corridors, thinking of Kimiko's remembered sketch. From a plan view Block P should be straight ahead and off to the left towards the end of this central corridor. Bo looked at the letters on the walls, placed like street names, but there seemed to be no logic in them. He passed C then K then F on his left. He stopped, looked to his right and saw R. Maybe higher letters are to the left, but he was sure P was to the left on the sketch. He walked on through the main corridor, hoping to stumble across P. But no P. On a hunch he turned left at T, and noticed R heading off left again at the first intersection. Promising, Bo thought, now colder again, and noticing his breath in the air. Must slow down, breathe normally.

Bo and the dog noticed each other for the second time at the same split second. It was at the far end of T, and immediately flew into a barking rage, nearly pulling its handler over as it rushed towards where Bo had been. Bo had already sprinted along R, and noticing another Gents symbol, had pushed open the door and wedged himself in an open cubicle, feet on one wall, his back and hands on the other, the key now in his mouth. He noticed the vile smell and his wet feet slipping. An alarm bell was just above the cubicles and the ringing was now loud enough to hurt and block out thought. Must be the prisoners' loos, he thought, unheated too. Outside he could hear the dog barking more loudly and straining on its leash, choking itself as it barked, the handler raising his voice to it in turn. Now outside the door, Bo heard the howling dog now beside itself, he heard the door swing open and the dog in full cry, barking and choking, then saw the handler pulling it back. The dog stopped in front of the cubicle, and looking directly at Bo started howling so ferociously its feet were leaving the ground. The handler let it forward bit by bit, until it was less than a metre from Bo's bottom, itself suspended a metre from the floor. The handler looked in nonplussed, unable to understand what had caught the dog's attention, but seeing nothing, had to use all his strength to pull it away. He turned and left, and as the door closed Bo heard the protesting howls retreating back down the corridor. Bo exhaled, eased first one leg and then the other down to the floor, instinctively checked his soles for dirt, and shaking with cold and fear walked towards the door. The corridor has to be warmer than this he thought, when his eye caught the letter P above the door. He was in the prisoners' showers in Block P.

44

Bo looked left and right, saw that 109 should be sequenced on the right, and walked deliberately towards where he thought it should be. He breathed out slowly and purposefully, seeing his breath, thinking of his goose bumps. What would his mother, or Kelly Cuss, say? What an absurd thought. For Christ's sake. Get a grip Bo. He arrived outside the door, opened his left hand to reveal the key, and with his right hand turned the lock. He pushed it slowly open so as not to alarm Pi Jam, checked to see there was an inside lock too, then closed it gently. He looked inside, the room was bright with a plain bulb that was too high to reach. There were two plain wooden bunks, one on top of the other. Both had a small and dirty blanket. The bottom bunk was empty, and on the top one lay a man with his face turned towards the wall, away from the light.

"Pi Jam! Pi Jam!" Bo whispered, shaking his shoulder. The man grunted, turned around and saw nothing, but Bo saw no-one he recognised even remotely from the family photos. "Who on earth are you?", gasped Bo. The man recoiled, sat upright on his left arm and started gibbering in Korean. Bo reached for his shirt, grabbed two handfuls at the front and started shaking him. "Sung Pi Jam, where is Sung Pi Jam?" he asked slowly, hoping against hope the wretch spoke even a little English. The man now started squirming in horror, crying more loudly. Bo put his hand over his mouth, waited till he had stopped squealing, took his hand down and wiped it disgustedly on the blanket. They looked at each other, or at least in each other's direction. Bo saw a pathetic little weasel faced man with greasy hair and yellow teeth. The man saw nothing.

"OK," said Bo softy, "nice and easy. Where—is—Sung—Pi—Jam?" Bo pointed to the empty bunk below.

"OK, OK," replied the wretch, and with one had made a turning sound, with the other held above his head waving his fingers. Looks like he's having a shower, Bo thought. "OK, I wait." Said Bo, pulling the blanket off him, and wrapping Pi Jam's around himself too. The man crawled on his haunches into the open corner of his bunk, his sneaky eyes following the blankets around the cell, his features becoming paler and more hallowed.

Bo and he both looked at the door as they heard the key turning. Two elderly men, both in prisoner uniform talked kindly to each other outside, and shook hands. The door closed, and immediately the wretch started jabbering incoherently. Pi Jam, folding his towel, searching for his blanket, seemed to pay no attention, but slowly and with eyes now bright started to smile. He looked around, saw two blankets behind the door. "Lo Hi?"

"No, not Lo Hi," said Bo. "I'm a friend, I have come to get you out of here."

"Yes, but who you?" rushed Pi Jam excitedly.

"We have company," said Bo, with a blanketed arm pointing at the wretch.

"He nothing. Snitch try confess me, stupid people," said Pi Jam. "How escape?"

"Well I got in, so I suppose I can get out. With you of course." said Bo.

"Not sure can."

"If you can what?"

"If I go and you. Prison strict. Controls. If catch, torture. Death. Long time. Cannot."

"But if you stay you're fucked anyway," Bo pleaded incomprehensively.

"What you mean?"

"I mean you must come with me."

"Please you go. I stay."

45

"I am going to nail that bitch." Colonel Krop is talking to himself, thinking about Sung Lo Hi and flicking through his index card of snitches. He has never met her, but everything he has heard about her makes him detest her. A typical spoiled member of the intellectual class, she has been given everything by the collective, and yet despises everything it holds dear: patriotism, Juche, the Leadership, the devotion of the masses, the admiration of the world. And for what? US style gangsters and adventurism, dog eat dog, at least here man eats dog. He often finds he thinks better when talking aloud to himself.

"The problem is we don't know anything suspicious, but it is all enough to make us suspicious. They call themselves the English Language Improvement Club. They hold all their meetings in English. Bad for snitching, as if on purpose, that's suspicious. They meet after study hours, each time in a different place, outside in the summer, in noisy public places in winter, so they cannot be bugged. We know who they are, but we don't know what they are saying. That's the problem, we don't know what they are thinking. It's practically snitch proof. They must be plotting something, otherwise why not meet in a class room? No, we need an English speaker who needs a privilege, who needs a favour, who owes us a favour, who owes us a favour, yes, who owes us a big favour!"

He stands up triumphantly and tells his switchboard to find him Professor Ju Flo Mung of the Pyongyang People's University. He paces the room in anticipation. The phone rings.

"Colonel Krop, is that you?" Colonel Krop can hear he is sounding anxious.

"Professor Ju, how is our monkey today?"

"The monkey is well thank you, well alive anyway. It is due for different levels of biological warfare exposure this afternoon."

"And chimpanzees are the best monkeys for the university?"

"They are Colonel Krop, they are the most like ourselves."

"So to have more chimpanzees would be helpful, especially if they came to your department first, and it would be unhelpful to ask the department to refund expenses on monkeys already lost?"

"Yes, Colonel Krop, on both counts, but why are you asking me?"

"Because I like to help the scientific intellectual class of course. I suppose your English language ability is well developed too?"

"I read it a lot, some every day, but seldom have a chance to speak it."

"So, Professor Ju, an enrolment in an organisation to help with your speaking would seem a good idea."

"Yes, Colonel Krop, if you suggest it."

"More chimpanzees and better use of English would make your life fuller then could we say?"

"Colonel Krop, I am sure you did not call just to make these suggestions?"

"No need to sound so nervous, Professor Ju! I am merely trying to help, and I hope in a small way you can help me, and your country of course."

"Colonel Krop, I am afraid I have never snitched if this is what you are asking. I have never been asked, I don't know what to do."

"No, not snitching, Professor Ju, you are an intellectual and we would not ask for that, but it would be helpful for the collective if you were to keep an eye on certain activities, and report anything that might be counter-revolutionary."

"What sort of activity?"

"I think by now you know the Sung family. Officer Pak Dong works for me, and he was your student and, shall we say, a serum enthusiast. This could bring great benefits to us all. Then you know about, maybe have met, his father Pi Jam, who will be taking the serum test soon to see if he is a traitor. There is also a sister, Lo Hi, she also works at the Pyongyang People's University, maybe you have met her?"

"Yes, I know her a little, a foreign language Professor and translator for Ministry of External Affairs. Surely they could tell you more about her than me?"

"We know about her, thank you Professor, even that she is an astrologist, but we don't know what she is thinking. Here is how you can help. She plots with the English Language Improvement

Club, based at the university. You know of them?"

"I have seen their notices, Colonel Krop."

"Then you can join it quite legitimately Professor Ju."

"And tell you what they are talking about?" "I think we understand each other Professor Ju. Of course Officer Cadet Pak Dong need not know about this."

"Of course not, Colonel Krop."

"Take a note of this number. 456 389. Call me soon, and I am sure we can look after each other, and the patriotic cause together."

"Yes, Colonel Krop."

46

In cell P109, Bo and Pi Jam stood talking next to the top bunk, to keep an eye on the wretch and to keep him frightened. Bo explained quickly, shouting close to Pi Jam above the noise of the alarm: "Lo Hi pretended to be Kimiko and found me in Tokyo, thought I could help. So did I, thought I could help that is. Never thought it would be so bloody cold. Never mind that now. Listen, your famous gadget is at Kimiko's. They are both outside in a car, we need to get you out of here, and out of this hell hole of a country too. Sorry Pi Jam, didn't mean that."

"Better PJ no Pi Jam. PJ, my American name."

"OK PJ, are you ready? I mean, you are up for this now, aren't you?"

"I not sure."

"Look, we don't have time to argue about this. You love your daughter. I love your daughter. If you go to the gulag she goes to the gulags too, yes?"

"Yes."

"Well let's cruise."

"You English?" asked Pi Jam. Bo thought he detected a certain degree of distaste.

"Quite possibly," said Bo, " but let's not worry about that now. What about Chumley here?"

Without waiting for a reply, Bo took a hard and invisible swing at his face. His head was thrown back, and blood oozed down from his nose. "Sorry about that", said Bo, hitting him hard again on the back of his head and tearing his shirt off, then pulling his trousers down too. No underpants, Bo noticed. Charming, he thought, sodding place. Bo pulled off a filthy rotting sock, scrunched it up and put it in the wretch's mouth. Then he tore a strip off the shirt, held out the shirt arm and tied it tightly, as tight as he could while the wretch squirmed in semi-consciousness. Bo heaved him upright, flung him to the floor and replaced him in the bottom bunk. With one trouser leg he tied the legs together, and with the other tied the body tightly to the end of the bottom bunk. With one last kick of his foot into the wretch's mouth, Bo looked across at a startled Pi Jam, gave him back his towel and both blankets, opened the door and said "after you, Claude." Bo thought PJ's look in return was decidedly old fashioned.

47

Bo slammed the door shut, gave it another tug to make sure.

"Where now?" asked PJ.

"Main entrance, it's busy there, the same way I got in."

PJ started running, turning sharp left then sharp right.

"Stop, wait!" hissed Bo. "Listen, don't run OK? You have to look like you are going for a shower. My breath shows in the air if I'm puffing. Now just walk like you are going to the shower. Don't you need an escort?"

"Should have trustee," said PJ. "What I say?"

"Just don't draw attention to yourself. Walk slowly, well normally. I'll go ahead, if there's a guard I'll whisper back something."

As Bo finished the fire alarm stopped, the silence more deafening for a few seconds than the alarm. Korean announcements echoed around the passages from loudspeakers.

"What's that?" whispered Bo from the next corner, signalling to come closer, then realising his signs could not be seen. "All clear."

"Nothing. Alarm finish."

They walked as calmly as possible through the labyrinthine passages, Bo going ahead to each corner, finding out from PJ which next direction to take, PJ pointing left and right, both walking quickly without rushing. Bo tried to remember the loos, and looking for other doors which might offer an escape. They had gone through several changes of direction, and by being aware of greater light and noise ahead Bo thought they must be nearing the main entrance. From there he knew he could find the staff lavatory again, the one with cubicles where he could warm up again and hide PJ while he tried to work out the escape.

Then a piercing whistle from behind stopped them both in mid step. Spinning round they both saw a guard shouting at PJ from the far end of the corridor. PJ walked slowly towards him, holding out his towel. They exchanged in Korean, the guard aggressive and shouting, PJ quiet and submissive. Nice body language thought Bo, noticing the guard calming down, pacified. Then Bo, a dozen paces behind and to the left of PJ, felt it all happen in slow motion. First the intense sensation in the nose and within a flash an uncontrollable and indiscreetly loud sneeze.

The guard turned back to look to from where the sound came, saw nothing, bellowed fear and hatred at PJ again, as if he had noticed a ghost, a spirit. He started yelling into his walkie talkie, signalling PJ to wait, while he backed away.

"Damn, sorry, couldn't help it," whispered Bo when the guard was out of earshot. "What's happening?"

"Say wait here. Look help. What now?"

"We run, that's what," said Bo. "There's a staff loo near the entrance, do you know it?"

"Loo?"

"Loo, lavatory, toilet, privy, WC, khasi, dunny, crapper, throne, shitter" gestured Bo.

"Ah. Follow," tried PJ without much confidence.

Behind they heard the shrill of a new whistle and a guard yelling. Then another whistle from a different direction, still behind them but closer. "Need hide quickly" said PJ no longer bothering to whisper, before Bo ran to the first guard and hit him directly and squarely on the chin with as much force as was still in him.

48

Now the loudspeakers blared again, echoing again, more urgently this time.

"What are they saying?" asked Bo.

"Guards to D and K corner, we there."

"We need another alarm." Bo said, "Look for another fire alarm box."

"Left—there," PJ pointed behind Bo to a red box on the wall. "I break glass. You bleed."

PJ slammed his elbow into the glass, the glass shattered and splinters fell on the floor, but no sound came from the alarm.

"They haven't reset it from before," Bo said.

"What now?"

"I don't know what now, how about a flood," said Bo.

"Flood?" pleaded PJ.

"Yes, PJ, water, too much water, water everywhere."

"Where?"

"I don't know, you live here, where is there a tap, a washroom. Think quickly."

"Laundry!" PJ ran ahead, turned left and flung open a door on the right. Bo followed him in and closed it. There were several low basins, mangles and hanging lines spread around the room. Bo plugged the basin nearest the door, turned both taps on, thought about the glory of hot water for a fleeting moment, stepped back and waited. There were alone in a warm room. The water quickly started to spill over onto the floor.

"What now?" asked PJ.

"Listen. We turn on all the taps. When the water gets into the floor outside you find a guard, raise the alarm. I'll stay in here with the door locked to delay them as long as possible. I can get out when they break down the door. Stay close to the door so I can find you, but if not... you know where the staff loo is, right?"

"Loo, yes."

"Guard's loo?"

"Guard loo, yes."

"OK, we meet there if anything goes wrong. With a bit of luck everything will be going wrong!"

"Huh?"

"Forget it," said Bo, " see you outside or in the guard loo. Get in a cubicle."

"Cubicle?"

"In loo, to hide, you'll see. Wait, where is it, the loo?"

"Go left. One, two, three, yes three passage right, no four passage right, loo on end."

PJ opened the door, carefully looking left and right, then jumped clear of the emerging puddle into the passage. Bo heard him shout for help. Now he felt a new problem, the hot water interlude was over and the water was now icy, and icy from both taps. The room was warm, but his feet were now freezing, and he let out six big unheard sneezes in a row, then sat on the top of what seemed like a large drying machine. He did not have long to wait. First the alarm sounded again, Bo smiled and dangled his feet, feeling warmer and then, with time to wait and a pause in the action, a small twinge of fear. He was almost pleased when he heard the first banging on the door, then shouts and more shouts from outside. He leapt down from his quiet moment on the machine, felt the cold pains in his feet and stood beside the door ready to rush out as they rushed in.

They charged the door, again and again, more and more desperately, and from the inside Bo could see the hinges buckle with each fresh heave. After six charges the door flew open, followed by the first guard who then fell on the flood as others came tumbling after him. Bo noticed the fresh rush of water leaving the laundry, and as confusion, slipping, shouting and pushing entered the room, he neatly sidestepped out of it.

49

Bo walked into the corridor, turned left and walked quickly, looking for the fourth turn right ahead, then noticed his feet were splashing and slowed down. More guards came past him. By now clear of the running water, Bo broke into a loping trot and as he did so his bare feet slipped on the tile floor and he crashed heavily to the ground, elbow first. "Bollocks!" he shouted. He looked up and saw the last two guards he had passed look around, staring nonplussed in his direction. The one nearest him shouted back, and was unholstering his pistol. Bo pushed himself up, and whilst still kneeling two more guards ran around the corner and before he could move they both went flying over him, themselves crashing heavily on the tile floor, and knocked him back down onto the hard floor too. The one with the gun shouted at the two on the ground, they all panicked and drew guns, looking around. Bo jumped clear and sprinted down the corridor, looking back to the chaos behind him. By now he had lost count of the passages off to the right, but noticed one that seemed to have more light at the end and headed running in that direction, no longer worried about his breath showing, or wet prints on the tiles. He noticed the pain in his right elbow and knee, heard the commotion behind him and his own noise around him, saw the lights at the entrance and almost ran straight past the Gents sign on the staff loo. He skidded to a halt, turned right and opened the door. Warmth, and a closed cubicle. He knelt on the floor, looked into the cubicle, saw PJ's ragged shoes and said "PJ, it's me." The door opened, and he squeezed, standing next to the hapless prisoner who looked even more distressed than when he last saw him. They stood together shaking; PJ from fear, Bo from cold—and a little fear too.

50

"Come on PJ," said Bo resting his hands on PJ's shoulders, talking loudly above the new loudspeaker commands, now sounding even more shrill and quick fire, "we are nearly out of here, but we've got to keep moving fast. With a bit of luck the guard room will be empty, we'll grab some coats, press some buttons and just ship out of here."

They walked the short distance to the guard room, and Bo noticed again the green release button by the main door and pushed PJ against the wall by the glass while he moved down the hall and peered inside. There was one guard, standing with his back to Bo, and lying head on feet on the floor the German Shepherd. Bo eased back to PJ and whispered: "There's one guard and that sodding dog in there. And lots of warm coats. I'll have to go in there and whack them. Back me up when you hear a lot of noise. OK?"

"OK."

Bo walked straight up to the door, flung it open. The dog was on its feet barking immediately, and the guard turned round, still on the phone, and looked startled at the open and empty door, the alarm now loud in the room and the dog furious. Bo walked straight up to the dog, clenched his fist and took as hard a swipe as he could directly onto its nose. It yelped and fell back. Bo walked over and kicked it with the full force of his right foot under its mouth. It fell back again, quiet now, yapping, looking for a hiding place. The guard drew his pistol and started shouting. Bo noticed PJ rushing into the door as the guard aimed his pistol at him. Bo leapt at the guard, pushed his gun away and hit him hard on the side of the face. The guard crouched and Bo picked him up by the lapels, held him against the wall and kneed him savagely in the balls. The guard collapsed as the dog put his head out from under the table, looking and sniffing around the room. From above him Bo slammed the telephone onto its head, apologised, and took two heavy overcoats and caps from the rack. They were heading for the door. "Wait!" Bo said, "take his boots."

"No time, go!" screamed PJ and before Bo could pull him back he had pressed the green button, pushed open the door and with collar turned up and cap in place walked out into the snowswept square and freedom, freedom for now. He looked around, and behind him saw a walking overcoat and cap mysteriously following up a few yards behind.

Bo saw the cart, ran with freezing feet he could no longer feel past PJ, and pulled him towards the car. The engine was running, the lights came on as the left rear door opened. Bo pushed PJ in.

51

"I have one more thing to do," said Bo. "Have the car outside the door in exactly three minutes."

"Wait, Bo," pleaded Lo Hi, but he had already shut the door, leaving the warm car behind and ran to the front gate, still wide open.

Inside the glass fronted office the guard was still doubled up in agony on the floor, and, Bo noticed to his horror, the dog lay dead, or at least unconscious on the floor. Bo grabbed the first twenty keys off the rack, and ran down the hall past the deafening sirens, now seeming suddenly much louder after the peace of the still air outside. Fumbling slightly, a figure in an overcoat and cap but without a head, hands or feet, went down the first corridor opening doors to his left and right, shouting to the men inside to leave. One minute he thought. As he turned to come back he noticed all the doors open but the corridor empty. Running back to the gate, he went inside three cells at random, with frantic sleeve signals urging them to leave and follow him out. No-one moved. Bo rushed to the main door, pressed the green button again, pushed it open and this time shut the door firmly behind him.

Outside the square was empty. No Kimiko, no car, not where it should be, by the entrance. He ran, slipping on the snow, to the cart, saw the car still there with its engine screaming and wheels spinning hopelessly. He pulled the rear door open, jumped onto the back seat and trod on PJ lying down behind the front seats. "I'm the one supposed to be invisible!" Bo announced at no-one in particular. "What's happened?"

"We stuck!" cried Kimiko. "Stuck in snow." And, Bo noticed, they were, and not in an ideal position.

52

Nark Am Dim looked up from his place on the cell floor. The five other prisoners looked up too. They had heard the sirens on and off, then heard all the shouting and the movement in the corridors. Nark Am Dim was sore all over, his battered arms and bruised legs hurt whenever he moved them, but he pulled himself up to walk towards the door and see if he could see anything outside through the peephole. Nothing there, but he felt better just moving, doing anything except sitting on the cold hard floor waiting for Colonel Krop to fetch him to what unknown horrors he could only imagine.

He was lowering himself down again when he heard more shouting, in English this time, then heard locks being turned, then heard his own cell lock moving and then the door pushed open. A sleeve of a jacket was waving. Nark Am Dim looked and looked again. A sleeve on its own, and a voice in English, he felt over himself to check his reality, but the door was open, wide open. He raised himself again, walked towards the door, through the door, looked down the passage toward where he had come in. No-one else was in the passage, he was the only one who had left the cell. He saw the clothing moving at the end of the passage. It walked up to a green button on the left, and then disappeared through the main entrance. Nark Am Dim followed, jogging in pain. He passed the glass front of the guardhouse on his right, looked in to see a guard writhing on the floor and a dead dog by the table. He pressed the green button, heard a click ahead and pushed the door open. He was immediately hit by the freeze outside, turned back to just catch the closing main gate in time, ran back into the guard room and slammed his foot into the face of the guard on the floor as hard as he could. Barely conscious, the guard offered no resistance as Nark Am Dim tore off his uniform, boots and holster. On the way out he grabbed an overcoat and heavy cap from the rail, then pressed the green button again and once more was outside and free, at least for now.

Nark Am Dim stood in the middle of the square, without bearings or plan. He saw the only car around, the one behind a cart. He was going to steal it, no better carjack it. He drew the revolver from the holster and pointed it at the car. As he walked closer he saw inside the Korean daughter bitch Lo Hi and the JCIA agent Kimiko Sato. He aimed at the JCIA driver and pulled the trigger; nothing happened, he knew instantly he had not undone the safety catch. He examined the gun, looking for the catch. Then he heard another vehicle, and saw it was a van driving into the square. He put up his hands to stop it. Seeing the uniform and gun, the driver obeyed. Nark Am Dim pulled open the passenger's door and ordered the driver to take him to the Golden Lodge. The van turned round completely and hesitantly left the square. Sammy Choo, Nark Am Dim told himself, had better come good now or he was in big trouble.

53

The twenty nubile fingers are working their way around the soft pudge of his back and buttocks. The Dear Leader of the Democratic People's Republic of Korea, The Sun of the 21st Century, the Guardian Deity of the Planet, the Sun of Socialism, the Ever-Victorious General, the Lode Star of the 21st Century, the Peerless Leader, the Great Chieftain, the Sun of Revolution, the Sun of Life, the Fatherly Leader of all Koreans, the Leading Light of the Universe, the All Knowing Guide to Eternal Happiness, the Supreme Vanquisher of Imperialism, the Great Upholder of the Juche principal, the Favoured Son of the Divine Inspiration Kim Il Song, the very same Kim Jong Il is just wondering if now would be the right time to turn over and give the order "Down!" and feel the moistness of four lips and two tongues pleasuring him further. No, he considers, more back massage for now, then a reconsideration, he turns himself over, smiles to himself and before he can give the command himself hears the question "Down, Your Supremeness?" "Down," he replies and settles back.

The yellow telephone rings. He holds out his hand. He can feel one of the mouths stop working and a receiver in his hand. He gestures to the mouth to resume. Bad news on the telephone, his visitor from the UN Food Programme has arrived for their meeting. He claps his hands twice for the mouths to hurry up. They oblige. He leaves the massage room, and arrives in his dressing chambers where the valets have laid out some suits for him to choose. He selects his latest dark blue broad pin stripe, just flown in from Savile Row, London, and black leather shoes with three inch heels and soles to add to his stunted stature. The valets help him dress and clear away the unwanted clothes. No-one speaks, and he walks into his salon where the court hair dresser prepares his bouffant carefully and completes the setting with American lacquer.

Fully prepared he takes the elevator down to the Grand

Reception Room where his visitor awaits. As he enters the room a footman announces him as "His Excellency and President of the Democratic People's Republic of Korea, Kim Jong Il."

His visitor stands and bows, and is introduced as "Mr. Winston Amin, Global Director of the United Nations Food Programme."

Kim Jong Il dismisses the attendants so that there is just himself and Winston Amin in the room.

"Mr. Amin, I hear that in Ghana you face the same problems we have here of drought and famine?"

"Exactly the same, Excellency, plus continued interference in our economy from the World Bank which encourages our internal distribution of aid by outsiders, less easy to control."

"I have been thinking about the Food-for-Oil programme your relations ran in Iraq with Saddam. Everyone benefited it seemed to me. I believe we can talk man-to-man about this."

"Of course, Excellency, there are many ways of working within the United Nations framework."

"Quite so. Now with Iraq, you, and your family, ran the Food-for-Oil. Very well. We have no oil, but we do have uranium, processed uranium, and we do need food. The droughts and famine you see."

"Excellency, the Food-for-Oil was officially sanctioned by the international community. Oil is oil, uranium is a very different matter, a most delicate issue."

"Delicate, yes, discreet, yes, but certain parties want to buy and certain parties want to sell."

"But, Excellency, not through the United Nations, that is too blatant, you must see. I am not saying we cannot help, but in more creative ways."

"Mr. Amin, we are both family men, trying to help our blood families and our fellow countrymen, our wider families. You have the advantage on me because you are an official person, working for an official family, the United Nations, but at heart our interests are the same."

"This is true, we must all help our families."

"In the best way we can, and however we can. The UN will give us food, this year forty thousand tonnes of cereals, and this is a gift."

"It is a gift from the UN, and therefore from the people of the world."

"Quite so. But there are costs of distributing and storage, and that is part of the food gift, as we have always done."

"It is, and this money is paid to your nominated account, if I remember to a Euro account in Singapore."

"Nothing there will change, you know the cash amount per tonne, and we repatriate from Singapore the needful. But I am thinking beyond that. Not part of the United Nations, I understand those sensitivities, but the principles of Food-for-Oil could be the same with our processed uranium. We can give your family and their collaborators licenses to sell our resources, and you in turn can arrange to buy certain surplus foods, which will again require certain distribution methods."

"With discretion, of course."

"Discretion is your concern. Information here is controlled, which is better than discretion. But we have the same ends. This afternoon at three o'clock our teams will meet to discuss details. Before then, as their leaders we will instruct them on the outcome, and they can manage the details. Are we agreed?"

""Excellency, I think we will both enjoy the coming period. Until three o'clock. Good bye."

54

"That's the guy from the tour!" said Bo leaning invisibly forward, looking at the man in the uniform waving a gun at them outside the prison. "Look out, get down he's going to shoot us!". A few moments later they heard another car stop and drive away. They all looked up carefully; he had gone.

"And that's the one who came to the office, it's the same guy," said Lo Hi excitedly.

"And he in cell they take me. What he do there?" asked PJ.

The CIA's finest, thought Kimiko, but she kept all that to herself.

"Something fishy going on with that guy", said Bo as he rubbed his hands, then his legs, then his feet, slowly heating up in the back of the car, still with engine revving and wheels spinning uselessly. PJ was still lying on the floor, with Bo's feet on this arms, Kimiko was behind the wheel and Lo Hi alongside her up front. "Right," Bo said, "you three are going to have to get out and push."

"But you strongest," whined Kimiko, "and it cold."

"Oh, really," said Bo, "I hadn't noticed. I can't push with bare feet on the snow, besides I'm the only one who knows how to drive."

"But I..." Kimiko started.

"Kimiko out, Lo Hi you too, come on PJ quick. You are going to push backwards first, get out to the front," said Bo, clambering over the front seat as the others left the car. He noticed it was now completely dark outside. He wound down the window, felt the icy air again and said "OK, push, come on, really push," as he slipped the clutch with easy throttle and the Toyota started inch by inch to move backwards. He ordered them to the back, urging them to hurry and push. He used second gear, turning the wheel slightly. Then backwards again, hurrying and harrying them through his open window until finally the car was out of its trap.

"Jump in, we're off," said Bo. As the doors were slamming the alarm stopped in the prison, but was followed immediately by a siren, and spot lights going on all around them. Bo drove away slowly, across the square in the recent tracks in the snow, until they were away from the prison and back on the main road into town. No-one spoke for a minute, then Lo Hi, suddenly squealing with delight, turned round in her seat and embraced her father behind her, then Kimiko started laughing and then Bo too joined in, shaking his head and smiling. "I don't want to say we've done it, but I think we've done it," he laughed. "Hey, listen we better get serious again." He pulled the car over. "Kimiko, you come back to drive, I'll get this coat off and lay it over PJ. PJ back on the floor. We'll look just like we did before, two rich girls out for a nice drive."

Bo told them the story of the great escape. Every now and then PJ would chime in from the floor in Korean, all to much appreciative oohing and aahing from the front seat. Bo felt warm again now, and rested across the back seat with his legs out. He twiddled his toes; sore but survivable. He could feel bruises coming up on his elbow and knee where he had fallen, and then told them that part of the escape again. Outside all was dark and empty, but the snow had stopped and what little traffic they saw was moving as slowly as they were.

"I am in no hurry to get back to the apartment," said Lo Hi.

"I am," said PJ from the floor. They all laughed.

"But we can talk here," said Kimiko, "Not in my rooms. Search yours when they find father gone."

"But I go invisible," said PJ.

"Dogs," said Bo. "I tell you those dogs can't see you, but that only seems to wind them up even more."

"We near there now," said Kimiko. "I park under if no snow, then we go up fire stairs."

55

They first saw the flashing blue lights reflected in the snow. They fell quiet, antennae now fully aware of trouble ahead. The lights were coming from the direction of their block, but not necessarily yet from their block. "Just drive normally," said Bo quietly from the back seat.

From underneath him PJ turned over and propped himself up. "Impossible for us. Take hours, checks."

They turned left at the junction, and three hundred metres ahead were two old Lada police cars with all lights flashing, parked at their entrance.

"We can go down ramp and up stairs same before." said Kimiko.

"No, could be a trap." Bo thought for a few seconds. "We'll drop Lo Hi off, and Lo Hi, you just walk in the front door as normal, maybe ask them what happening if you can. If they are after you, they are after us all. Is there another entrance, apart from this and fire stairs?

"Yes," said Lo Hi, "the service entrance for garbage at the other end of the garage."

"Good stuff," said Bo, "now when you get past the police go straight up to your room and wait for us. Just like you always would, not too fast, not too slow. We'll drive around and park and go in from there."

"And if I am arrested?" she asked quietly.

"We'll worry about that later, but in the meantime you know nothing." said Bo, even more quietly. "So here we go, two girls out for a drive, and one is just dropping the other off at the front door. Everything is completely normal. Down you go again PJ, tight on the floor." Bo pressed his overcoat down on top of PJ.

Kimiko stopped right outside. The police all looked at them, but warily as hassling two well connected girls with a new Japanese car might be embarrassing later. Lo Hi opened her door, the new cold air caught Bo by surprise, but Lo Hi was soon on her way up the steps. "Just drive away slowly, slowly enough to see she is safely inside."

The police parted as Lo Hi climbed the steps and opened the front door. She had decided not to ask them what they were doing. Bo leant back and told PJ he was right, it didn't look like it was for them. Inside the building, Lo Hi walked past the elevator, still out of use, and up the three flights, along the hall to her room. She unlocked the door, peered in suspiciously, but everything was completely as she had left it. Still in her coat, scarf and hat, she flopped down in the armchair and blew out a long low sigh.

56

Kimiko drove right around to the back of the block, down a long ramp and through the service entrance, and then through the ramps around to her apartment's parking bay. She turned off the engine, and they all sat still and quiet for half a minute. All seemed to be normal, no new sounds, no disturbances. They opened the doors, Bo put the guard's overcoat on again, then the cap and scarf. PJ unwound himself from the floor, straightened up his uniform, and the three walked calmly but fully alert to the fire stairs.

"I'll go up each flight, check it's OK," Bo said softly, "then call you up." Without shoes, his feet immediately felt the harsh cold again, but they made no sound as he climbed the first flight, and cleared them up. They gathered together at the landing. "OK, same again," said Bo, and they climbed the next flight, Bo going ahead, and bringing them up after him when he saw it was safe.

They were four steps short of home on the third floor when the door crashed open on the four floors upstairs. Suddenly the quiet of the stairwell was broken by hard boots, lots of them, clattering quickly down the concrete steps, and the sound of shouting and pain accompanying them.

Bo leapt up the last steps, pushed the door hard and pulled the others through. He tore off his overcoat, threw it at PJ who then ran off hard after Kimiko. Bo went back through the door, and now stood, invisible, guarding the third floor landing.

He saw them all at once. One policeman leading, then two more with a middle aged and slightly pasty, slightly bald man suspended between them, his feet bicycling madly off the steps. They were shouting at nothing in particular, and he was protesting in pain. Behind was the fourth policeman, a fat one who looked to be struggling to keep up, and all four were heading straight for where Bo stood on the landing. He squeezed back against the door, expecting them to rush past him, which they did, first the leader, then the three struggling with each other, then the fat one, all running down the stairs. As the fat one went past, and without even thinking about it, Bo kicked out his right foot hard, and tripped him. The tail ender went flying through the air into the back of the middle three, who in turn crashed in to the back of the leader. Bo looked down: all were spread-eagled on the bare concrete landing below, all clutching various arms, legs and heads in varying degrees of outright pain and discomfort, all shouting at each other. Bo looked and smiled, said 'Bastards!' to himself, and after they had resumed, much more cautiously and were out of sight, went back through the door, into the landing and saw Kimiko waiting for him by Lo Hi's door, and inside Bo saw three giggling, nervous, happy and excited conspirators. He started laughing with them, hugging Lo Hi and Kimiko, and even PJ.

"What was all that noise?" asked Lo Hi.

"Just the secret policeman's fall." Bo laughed to himself, and they all joined in cautiously out of respect.

57

Lo Hi's was warm, gloriously warm, and Bo sat on the floor next to the radiator, and noticed how they all found talking to him as though they could actually see him as totally natural.

"How long till they realise you've gone walkabout?" asked the thin air.

"When escape?" asked PJ, "Half hour?"

"About that."

"Check cells. Start Block A, then B. Maybe half hour more not see me. Maybe half hour more check record. They come here, so maximum here is one maybe one and half hour."

Lo Hi arrived with the tea. "We can always hide in Kimiko's, but not talk there."

"Let's get the move happening," said Bo, "we'll have the apparatus and all traces of it, anything related at all, next door. Lo Hi, gather up anything you want or need for the journey, but let's leave the place looking like you still live here. The Canadian Embassy's a no-go. Let's make plans while we can talk. Any ideas?"

PJ and Lo Hi were packing the devices and some books and bottles in a box and moving them next door. Lo Hi said "All I know is we need to be out of the country quickly."

"We have car," said Kimiko. "so we drive car now, think later."

Everything they wanted was now in Kimiko's, and Lo Hi took one last wistful look around her family home and quietly closed the door. In the corner table next door Kimiko had laid out and now plugged in the apparatus.

"Look away please." mouthed PJ taking off his clothes, and sitting on the chair between the devices, which in turn were humming busily to themselves. Only Bo looked, fascinated to see the same process that had transformed him earlier now working slowly but with inevitability on someone else.

"Shall I have a top up?" wrote Bo, and handed PJ a scrap of paper.

PJ wrote a question mark and handed it back.

Kimiko turned the television on loudly and put her finger to her lips. In the kitchen she turned the compulsory state radio station, the one you could never turn off, up to a higher volume. Still, Bo whispered: "Maybe a booster, a top up for another twelve hours would be a good idea."

The others gathered around the two invisible men, and guessing were Bo was, Lo Hi said it had never been done before, then turned to the empty space in the chair, and asked if it was safe.

PJ shrugged an unseen gesture, then realising no-one could see him just said that no-one had ever done it before.

"But no choice," finished Bo and feeling out for PJ gave him a slight nudge, "move over Rover, and let Bo-Bo take over,"

"What now?" PJ whispered harshly.

"Sorry, just switch it back on."

"You in middle?"

"I'm in the middle."

The machine whirred again, eight minutes and eight grams for Bo's twelve hours, and both PJ and Bo, from their different perspectives, thought to themselves about the consequences.

The introspection was broken by running boots in the passage, and loud knocks and shouts at Lo Hi's door opposite.

"Quick," said PJ, almost admiringly.

They turned off the lights and the television, turned down the radio and sat in the dark with only the apparatus going about its work. In the passage came the sound of a breaking door, then more shouts from inside the flat, and then a new sound, a dog's bark from the end of the passage.

"Oh God!" despaired Kimiko, no longer even whispering. "My passport, you take to Japan, it in there."

Next door, furniture was shifting, drawers and cupboards opening and closing, furniture and beds scraping across the floor.

"They in here soon," PJ didn't need to say.

Then as quickly as it started the ransacking stopped, the heavy boots ran away down the corridor and the door slammed shut. In Kimiko's they started to move towards the door, then heard a cough and movement from outside. Kimiko knelt down and looked under the door, then stood up, and put on a sidelight. "One police outside Lo Hi door. So outside my door too."

"We, you say, sleeping ducks?" asked PJ.

"Sitting ducks, PJ, sitting ducks," replied Bo without much enthusiasm.

58

Colonel Krop is frightened. Something is clearly wrong. He is speeding in the back of one of the presidential Mercedes, an occasion of great privileges about to be won or lost. They are heading straight for the Dear Leader's Glorious Autumn Palace, which in spite of its name was one of his smaller and less opulent dwellings. Worryingly, Colonel Krop remembers it also has the Dear Leader's private interrogation chamber in its basement, and is home to his own secret police, so secret they do not have a name or uniform, only the nickname Red Widows.

The car is rushed through the gates with a hurried salute and Colonel Krop beckoned upstairs to an ante-room. He is thinking too fast to absorb the magnificent works of art on the walls or notice how his feet sink into the luxurious piles underneath them. Downstairs he hears a small flurry of activity, and moments later the ante-room doors hurl open to reveal General Mung, his superior at the SSA.

"Colonel Krop, do you know why we are here?" the General asks stiffly.

"No, sir, I have just arrived myself."

A connecting door opens behind them and they are waved into the Dear Leader's office. He is dressed informally but still immaculately.

"Can the SSSA explain what has happened?!" the Dear Leader's face is livid as he shouts.

"Excellency, what in particular?" asks General Mung.

"You don't even know! Well, I'll tell you. The intellectual, the nuclear physicist Sung Pi Jam has escaped from the People's Founding Prison one hour ago. How can he escape?"

"We will investigate immediately, Excellency," says General Mung humbly.

"He did not escape on his own. Either the US imperialists or his family must be involved. Who are his family?"

"I know that, Excellency," says Colonel Krop with some relief.

His son is Pak Dong and he reports to me directly at the SSSA as an Officer Cadet, and we believe he will continue beyond Patriotic Duty. The daughter is Lo Hi, and we have just increased our snitch activity on her. She is a trouble maker, plots and probably slanders in English at the Pyongyang People's University."

"Well, at least you know something. And who is this foreigner," he walks over to pick up a piece of paper. "Kimiko Sato?"

"She is the neighbour of Sung Lo Hi, Excellency. Your Excellency is very well informed."

"It's because I don't have to rely on you idiots for my information! What have Sung Pi Jam's interrogations revealed?"

"They have not started yet. We are using a truth serum, and so far the trials have been most encouraging," replies Colonel Krop.

"If they are so encouraging why has he not been interrogated?"

Colonel Krop sees the trap but to lie to a well informed Dear Leader would be madness. General Mung can only look on, unable to help even if he knew all the facts. All he remembers is asking Colonel Krop to absorb Sung Pak Dong into his SSSA unit, partly to help in the Sung Pi Jam investigation. But, his antennae tell him, no need for that now.

"Her family asked for a delay of ten days, Excellency."

"So! There you have it, ten days in which they help him escape. And which family member asks for this?"

"The daughter asked the son and he asked me. I agreed because the serums are still being developed with apes and there did not seem much urgency."

"In that case you will interrogate both the son and daughter with the usual SSSA panache. The Pyongyang Regular Brigade Police are searching for the daughter now. You have the son in your barracks, you know what to do. I want that traitor back here now!" the Dear Leader is shouting again. "Get out both of you!"

General Mung and Colonel Krop are sitting in the back of the car. They have known each other since childhood, both as orphans under state care. Both want to talk but know they cannot in the car. Once in the SSSA compound, the walk quietly together in a courtyard.

"It is good work you had this Sung Lo Hi under surveillance.

How did the Dear Leader know about the Japanese woman?" asks General Mung.

"Not from us unfortunately. I presume the Red Widows. If this Officer Cadet is linked to the escape it will not be good for us," says Colonel Krop quietly.

"And your opinion?"

"My opinion is that although he may not yet be all for his big family, he would never help in the escape of his small family. General, he is still only a boy; even if you or I wanted to plan an escape we would find it impossible, so forget him being behind it, let alone that daughter, even with a Japanese woman. Especially with a Japanese woman. No we are looking at the Americans, the CIA it is certain."

"Even so, take this Officer Cadet with you in the search. At the slightest hint of collaboration with escape, even sympathy for his father, we must interrogate him forcefully for our own sakes."

"Agreed, General, it will be done thus."

59

"Why don't we all go invisible, just walk out?" Lo Hi asked.

Bo explained that, apart from anything else, they would all freeze to death, just like he nearly had half a dozen times, and it would be hard enough not being able to see two of us, let alone none of us. "No," he said, "we need to remove the police guy outside from the equation, and leg it before they work out where Kimiko lives. We have the element of surprise."

"And invisibility."

"Yes PJ and invisibility. Kimiko opens the door, distracts him a little, you and I whack him," Bo gestures.

"I not know fight," urged PJ.

"PJ, before meeting your cellmate an hour ago, I had never known fight either. You just hit him somewhere. Like cricket, well baseball. Come on, we really do have to make a move. Lo Hi, take something hard, a hammer maybe."

"What for?"

"To hit him with of course."

Kimiko apologised, there was no hammer, how about a saucepan? Bo thought a saucepan would be admirable in the circumstances, but a saucepan now if at all possible.

They lined up by the door. Lo Hi, with an iron wok in one hand and the door handle in the other, then Kimiko with the top buttons on her dress recently undone, then Bo and PJ, invisible to the world. Lo Hi opened the door, Kimiko walked up to the policeman and told him what a nice surprise it was to see him, he shrugged and smiled, Bo and PJ came round the corner and PJ said "He very big!".

The policeman turned to the unseen voice as Bo landed the first punch squarely on his jaw. It was like hitting a rock. Bo's fist hurt immediately and the policeman merely looked baffled and stroked his chin. Bo's right fist hurt too much to try again, so he now swung with his left fist, this time onto the man's temple, and this time there was a slight stagger back, but more from surprise than pain. "Get his feet PJ, upend him," Bo gestured again.

PJ grabbed his feet and pulled the ground from under him, just as the policeman pulled out his gun. Bo kicked at the gun as the policeman was falling, but he just gripped it tighter and now tried to fire the first shot, but in his surprise he left the catch on and the bullet destined for PJ stayed in his gun as Bo shouted "Lo Hi, wok him for Christ's sake!"

From the floor the policeman's legs were flaying, and as Lo Hi approached wok in hand he turned the gun to fire at her. Bo brought his right fist down with all his might between the policeman's legs; at last his attention was drawn away from his attackers as he doubled up moaning, legs now steady and under him. "Wok!" cried Bo, and Lo Hi reappeared, wok above her head, which she then brought down with a thunderous crash onto his head. He stopped moaning and lay breathing heavily on the floor.

"What have I done?" said Lo Hi.

"You've just winded him a little," said Bo hopefully, easing the gun from his grip, and taking off his boots, overcoat and hat. "Now let's hide him and scarper pronto. Tape, Kimiko, have we tape to shut him up?"

"Better than that," she said and came back with several pairs of knickers and a bandage and gagged him tightly. They tied his arms behind his back with a belt and his legs with a robe cord. Then they lifted him, by now a dead weight, into Lo Hi's clothes cupboard, shoved him in and locked the door. Then threw away the key.

60

Bo put on his new uniform, felt the welcome warmth of the boots, told PJ to put on his own warm clothes again from next door, and Kimiko and Lo Hi to take whatever they needed. He asked about her passport. "They have it. And I registered here. This address." Kimiko held up a briefcase. "This all I take."

From the cupboard they heard a new sound, a crackling radio. Then a few seconds later, the same sound, but now more loudly and urgently. With each lack of response from the cupboard the enquiries became more frenetic. "What do?" asked PJ.

"We need to get to the car as quickly and quietly as possible," said Bo, "this whole building will be on full alert very soon if it isn't already." Kimiko led them along the passage, rushing as quietly as possible, and down the fire stairs, back through the swing doors and over to her car. On the way she opened a large garbage trolley and buried the briefcase at the bottom of it. Four car doors slammed unintentionally; they all cringed at the noise they had made. Lo Hi sat in the passenger seat, and Bo and PJ lay flat on the back seat and floor. Kimiko started the engine, pulled away and steered back up the long service entrance ramp, and turned left sideways past the main entrance. Uniforms looked round and torch lights flashed onto the passing car, voices were raised from the front of the building, Kimiko kept her nerve and drove past them, almost serenely.

No-one spoke for several minutes, then first Bo and then PJ sat up in the back. "We need to get invisible again, so the car just has the two girls driving around," said Bo as he and PJ took off their uniforms and stuffed them under the seats in front of them.

PJ was the first to ask the question. "All bad. What now?"

"We have you out of prison, out of the apartment, you are invisible, now we just need to get you out of the country," Lo Hi replied encouragingly.

"We need plan," Kimiko looked over her shoulder to Bo's space.

"What are the options?" asked Bo, with PJ leaning forward onto the backs of the seats in front.

61

Lo Hi threw up some more questions and answers. The airport security was too tight. Although the invisible men could walk onto any plane, it would be far too cold getting onto it and anyway the next plane out would not be until tomorrow. No, Bo, there were no private airfields. Train? That would have to be via China, and there're as many spooks and feds on board as passengers, besides the Chinese were unpredictable, and anyway the invisibility would have worn off by then. A fishing boat was a possibility, if they could find one they would have to steal it, and the waters over to Japan could be bad at this time of year, but Japan was the place they should aim...

"Japan!" Kimiko struck the wheel. "By sea! Of course!"
"What?" They all wanted to know. "The Sanyo Moro leaves tonight! In office we do all paperwork."

"You mean you know the captain, the crew?" Bo leant forward onto her seat.

"No, but if arrive there we have chance."

"It's our best chance," said Lo HI

"It's our only chance," said Bo, "where is she, when does she sail?"

"From Wonsan, some time tonight."

"How far is that?" Bo asked

"Maybe one hundred kilometres," said Lo Hi. "There's a chance she won't sail till first light."

"Well, that's decided it for us, "said Bo, "Wonsan here we come."

"Wonsan here we come," echoed Kimiko.

62

After the evening meal, horse stew and bread, then semolina and sugar, the Officer Cadets clear up and prepare to leave for the lecture hall for the evening film. Although it is called evening film, it does not take place every evening. It is a treat and every cadet's favourite part of the day when it happens. To add excitement Sung Pak Dong and most of his cadre have not seen tonight's film "The Dear Leader Comrade Kim Il Song Gives Field Guidance to Work in Different Sectors".

They leave the dining room, and notice the blizzard that has just started. Sung Pak Dong races ahead, scoops up some snow to make a ball and throws it at the nearest cadet. This one in turn repays him and within thirty seconds all cadets are engaged in a full scale snow ball fight. The fight moves towards the lecture hall and when they can see the door through the blizzard they rush to it, brush the snow off their uniforms and noisily and excitedly take their seats.

This is the first winter's cold evening of the year and the lecture hall is still unheated. The projectionist turns on the machine and the reels turn. Some cadets shiver but they all stay attentive. The Great Leader is in a factory, sitting at a sewing machine, and now working at it. The comrades in the film are glowing. Now the cadets in the lecture hall are glowing. Then the Great Leader is at sea, then a flickering sequence shows another boat, a Japanese fishing boat, but it's a spy boat, and the Great Leader is encouraging the officers on his boat, a naval boat, to show no mercy to those who would undermine the progress made by the incumbent masses against tiger-like imperialist interventions.

The klaxon sounds. Not in the film, the klaxon is clear and real. None of them, and certainly not the projectionist is clear what to do. To turn off the Great Leader would be an insult, certainly a punishable insult. But the klaxon continues, and outside they can hear running, someone slipping and cursing. Someone turns on the ceiling light while the film continues. No-one is looking at the screen all the time now, but no other instructions are being given.

Outside some heavier running footsteps are heard. The door swings open. It is Sergeant Ming. The cadets all stand to attention while all now looking directly at the screen again. Sergeant Ming takes in the scene immediately and knows what they must do. The sound of the film can no longer be heard above the klaxon and commotion outside. "Be seated, watch the Great Leader!" he orders. Then he sits, but cannot help himself looking at the reel. He knows the film well too, and estimates half an hour still to play.

Then it stops. Everything stops: the film, the klaxon, the lights outside, even the commotion for a few seconds. Sergeant Ming wants to order them outside to join in the search. Someone has escaped from prison. But if the power comes on again soon, and sometimes it does, and the Great Leader is resumed to an empty audience, the insult would be unforgivable. They sit still, almost to attention, now noticing the cold again. Sergeant Ming knows he must seek permission for them to leave the lecture hall. He has to find out the extent of the power cut. He orders them to wait for his return. They sit still, all now shivering, silent and uncomplaining, in the blackened lecture hall. Outside they can hear muffled noise of people moving, and occasionally a shouted order. Everyone is keen to know what is happening. Someone has escaped from prison is all they know; Sergeant Ming arrives in the middle of the film; they presume he wants them to be part of the search for the fugitive.

The door opens again, led by a light beam. It is Sergeant Ming with a torch. "The power cut is unfortunate but may last some time." He shines the beam onto the projector and then its projectionist. "You may discontinue, with all regret and respect, the film concerning the exploits of the Great Leader. The rest of you follow me to your quarters."

Outside the blizzard has stopped but the air is even colder. Sergeant Ming walks ahead holding the beam. Around them all is quiet: they are the only soldiers now in the barracks. They enter the dormitory, and with only Sergeant Ming's torch for light automatically line up beside their beds. "Take all your winter uniforms, bedding and firearms. We are joining in a man hunt. A traitor has escaped from the People's Prison, about two hours ago, three hours ago now. Our unit is to report to Hard Labour Camp 27 at Nonking on the north east Chinese border and to patrol the border to the west of that. Sergeant Hong's unit has already left for there and will patrol to the east. Our transport is outside. Everyone is clear?" They all shout affirmation with a potent mixture of excitement and apprehension.

They collect their kit and jog in time behind Sergeant Ming to the courtyard. The military bus is waiting, engine on, headlights on, black fumes passing over the fresh snow. From the side of the square they see a jeep. Sergeant Ming calls them to attention. They stop jogging, two slip and recover and then stand still. Colonel Krop is already walking purposefully towards them.

"This will be your first active duty as a unit. You have been trained together and will work together." Sung Pak Dong thought about his trip to Camp 18 with the Christian bitch, then snapped back as Colonel Krop continues. "A traitor has escaped. It must have been planned by outside counterrevolutionary elements and he will be leaving the country. Part of your military duty is to protect our borders against those less fortunate from decadent societies wishing to enter, but tonight it is to stop one of these aggressors escaping. You will perform as a unit and bring back credit to the SSSA as will all the other units. You are the last to leave. Now board your bus!" he shouts at them. One by one they walk to the steps.

"Officer Cadet Sung Pak Dong!"

"Yes, sir"

"You will come with me!"

"Yes, sir." The others want to turn to look at him, but the training prevails and they all board the bus.

Sung Pak Dong is in the back of Colonel Krop's jeep with another man, uniformed. No-one speaks. Sung Pak Dong again remembers the trip to Camp 18 and wonders if there is a connection. Did he do a good job or a bad job? Before a further thought arises the jeep stops next to a helicopter. "Get in!" Colonel Krop orders.

Sung Pak Dong is more excited than nervous as the blades above start to whirl and the helicopter starts to vibrate. The four from the jeep are sitting facing each other as the noise and vibration increases alarmingly and the machine shakes itself off the ground.

"Sung!" shouts Colonel Krop leaning forward.

"Yes, sir!"

"Do you know why you are here with me and not with the unit heading to China?"

"No, sir!"

"It is because the traitor who has escaped is your father. And you and I are going to find him!"

"Yes, sir!"

"But he won't be heading for China, Sung!"

"No, sir!"

"He will be going where we are going. To Wonson!"

"Yes, sir."

"And why do I know that, Sung!"

"Why, sir?!"

"Because I have a nose for this sort of escapade, that's why!", he growls and trusts his hunch about the foreign woman's predicament and what he would have done in her place.

"Yes, sir!"

63

"Problems," said Lo Hi, "paperwork problems. We have no passports, no identity cards, no Permits to Travel, no documents for the car to leave Pyongyang."

"Roadblocks. Check points." added PJ.

They drove on in silence, each thinking about what lay ahead. PJ knew he had had his stake raised uncontrollably, and that his fate lay in Bo's leadership, Kimiko's nerve and his daughter's good fortune. Lo Hi looked over to Kimiko, pleased she was driving and being driven by some higher being, even a remote force that Lo Hi could not place; glanced over her shoulder and reflected that her father was the cause and Bo the effect of her determination, and felt none the worse for either. Kimiko knew she would have to front whatever was to come, but had faith in Lo Hi and needed to have faith in Bo, and hoped for the best from PJ. Bo was trying hard not to think, and almost succeeding. Lo Hi broke the trance. "The first check point will be to leave the city. We should have a Permit to Travel to enter the city, and another to leave it."

"How far away is that?" asked Bo.

"At the end of Cholong Road, about a kilometre or two, five minutes."

"Thing is Lo Hi", said Bo, "they can't see your father or me, but they can see you."

"So?"

"So we can't make you invisible, but we can make you hard to see, like hiding in the boot. If we are searched we've more or less had it anyway. We can cover you with these coats, will keep you warmer too.

"Kimiko, listen. You don't have your passport, but you do have your Foreigners Permit thing, you have a Japanese name and accent, you can show you work for a Japan North Korea Trade outfit, you do have a locally registered car, you are on the road to Wonsan, and there is one of your ships there. And they can see you are travelling alone. A smile and an air of confidence, and we'll breeze through."

"You not know this place," Kimiko replied, "but we must try," then turning to Lo Hi she said "You alright this, in boot?"

"Same as you, we need to do it and hope. We are nearly there, best to stop here and let me out."

Both front doors opened, Lo Hi opened a rear door to give her the uniforms and boots; a few seconds rush of icy air was enough to start PJ sneezing again and say "Sorry, sorry." Inside the car they heard the boot slam, and Lo Hi moving around behind them. Kimiko jumped back in, adjusted the driver's mirror, applied some make up from her bag, said some small prayer in Japanese, slipped the Corolla into first gear and drive off.

"Some radio I think," said Bo from behind her.

She reached forward and asked testily "any particular station? There are three to choose."

"Whatever a pretty young Japanese female executive on official business would listen to."

She punched in the classical music station, then changed it to the news programme. "Need to keep up to date," she said and settled down into her seat. Ahead in the distance they saw some lights. "That will be it."

They pulled up close to the red and white barrier. Inside the cabin one of the four police stood up and waved for her to go in. "Leave the engine on" said Bo. She ran inside.

The police stood up as she entered, and the one who waved said "Your Permit to Travel."

She replied in Korean. "There was not time to organise it. But here is my card and Foreigners Permit of Temporary Residence."

"Your passport?"

"Same with that, it's at the Immigration and Resettlement Brigade office being renewed. You can call them."

"They are closed."

"So they are. Anyway, you can see who I am."

"You cannot leave without a Permit to Travel. Your car papers?"

"No car papers."

From the car PJ and Bo could see her smile and flirt. Inside she said "Look, I really do not want to be driving alone to Wonsan on a freezing night, but I had a call from your Overseas and Foreign Trade and Investment Ministry an hour ago. There is some problem at the port with one of our ships. I am sorry that it is unusual, but your Ministry says I need to be in Wonsan straight away."

"But there are procedures."

"Yes, and there are emergencies."

"We cannot let you pass without permission."

"Well please get the permission. You have a phone."

One of them, reluctantly stood and went to a separate office in the back. Through the closed doors she could hear a conversation, a one sided telephone conversation. In the back of the car PJ sneezed again, and said "sorry, sorry" again. Inside Kimiko tried to look calmly at the notices on the wall.

The guard came back in and handed her back her Permit and business card. "You are lucky," he said. "You can go." replied, "and will there be other road checks?"

"Yes. Can you call them ahead and let them know, save me explaining everything again?"

"That is not our function."

"Thank you," Kimiko said on her way out, with her back to them smiling to the anxious car.

64

After some minutes Lo Hi was the first to speak. "I don't know if I can go through that again. It is terrifying in there in the dark and cold. What is worst is not knowing what is happening, I mean you all could have been arrested and I'm stuck in there forever."

"Horrible in check point too. I never so much nervous. I try be friend, but they look to me. They hate."

"Here too", said PJ in Korean. "All we can see is you in there, with no idea what you are saying, what they are asking, and Lo Hi what it must be like for you in the back of the car."

They tried to work out where the next road block would be. Wonsan itself lay in Kangwon Province, the border of which started just over halfway between Pyongyang and Wonsan port, so it was logical to assume that the check point would be on the border, about fifty kilometres away, nearly an hour away.

"Well, it may not have been much fun, but we did it, well you two did it, all PJ and I had to do was sit here and hope for the best. I can't believe the next police guys are going to be worse than those leaving Pyongyang. Who are they anyway?"

"Almost certainly the local traffic paramilitary, that will be something like the Kangwon Province Transportation Brigade," said Lo Hi.

"For heaven's sake, how many police forces are there?"

"Dozens," said Lo Hi. "Maybe no-one knows. There are even special police forces to watch the police forces, and special military police to watch the military police, and then special army units to watch the other army units. Then there are the political police to watch the politicians, except there aren't any politicians." Lo Hi explained more, about the different police forces and army brigades, and how to recognize them, how the Korean People's Army headbands gave away their intent—blue for intelligence, red for army, green for reserves, how the bell bottoms were always navy, dark blues always the Air Force and the light greys the Construction Brigade.

"No wonder you wanted to be invisible PJ," said Bo. "Tell me about the first time."

PJ recounted while Lo Hi translated "It was in Moscow. He had taken the notes from his experiments where H.G.Wells had finished. He did not need the book, he knew it backwards. He could obtain or make the electrical apparatus in the university there. He had not so many friends; all the other Koreans were too political or frightened to be too friendly in case of snitches. Anyway he was more fascinated by the whole process of invisibility. Just think about it, what an amazing dream to come true. How much good he could do for the world, for his family, for himself.

At first it did not work at all. He had a cat in his apartment, and it would spend hours dozing like all cats. He put one device one side of it and the other the other and nothing happened. He went back to the notes, tried different formulae, nothing worked. Then he thought to change the colour of the surface that the rays were touching, and that meant buying some oils, some coloured skins oils. Of course in those days in Russia you could hardly buy a loaf of bread, let alone coloured skins oils. But at the Chemistry department he could make some. They were suspicious, but he was a foreigner and told them it was a custom in his country. Eventually he had several different colour potions, but then the cat did not like being covered in oil, so he had to find another solution.

"From the Medical department he stole a frozen hand, and then would keep it in the icebox in the summer or on the ledge in winter. Eventually he found that with a very certain shade of very deep green the skin would become translucent. He just kept experimenting and eventually found the correct time and colour for the process to work. Then one day he put his own hand in there, and it worked on that too. He'll never forget the day, or the moment when it came back to visibility."

"So how many times have you done it completely?" asked Bo. Lo Hi replied "Dozens. He has never had any ill effects, but he has never used it like he had hoped for, as a force for good. It's really been just for fun."

"Up till now."

PJ looked towards Bo's space. "Yes, up till now. But we do

OK, no?"

"We're doing fine PJ, we're doing just fine. Mind you, you and I have got the easy part. We just sit here looking pretty. How much longer Lo Hi?"

"I was just thinking about that. We will see the lights first." Twenty minutes later, Kimiko was the first to notice them.

"Lights ahead. That will be it."

"OK everyone, piece of cake compared to the last bunch of Nazis," said Bo. "You'll be fine back there Lo Hi. Here, take these clothes again. Kimiko get into character, and through we go."

"It has to be easier than the last one," said Kimiko pulling over for Lo Hi to climb into the boot. She drove up to the barrier, next to a door with KWTP Kangwon Province Transportation Policeforce written above it, opened and closed the door the car, leaving the engine on for warmth, opened and closed the door of the check point, walked up to the desk and introduced herself and her urgent, official business.

65

Kimiko walked into the hut, smiled and said good evening. Behind the desk sat a middle aged woman, in an immaculate uniform adorned with medals. Two younger men, one still a raw teenager, sat on chairs around the desk, watching her every move as if on instruction. She did not return Kimiko's smile.

"Your business, madam?" she asked politely.

"I was hoping they would have called you from the Pyongyang city limit check"

"Why would they call me?"

"Ah, I have some urgent official business so maybe they would have already explained. Never mind, here's my card, you can see I'm from the Trade Authority and..."

"You are not from THE Trade Authority, you are from the Japan North Korea Trade Authority, and why would they have called me?"

"It doesn't matter, they clearly haven't so let me explain."

"Did they say they were going to call us here?"

"Not exactly, but I hoped they would, you see..."

"Well you can hope all you like. Pyongyang City Frontier Police have no regulation over us. We are the Kangwon Province Transportation Policeforce, that is a separate function altogether."

"Look, I'm sorry, I did not realise, as you can probably tell by my accent and my car I myself am a foreigner."

"Very well, but you should know we are a separate regulatory force. I know you are a foreigner, and suppose your car is registered to a foreigner too. Your passport and card papers then please."

"That's the point, you see I had to leave without my passport."

"And car's papers too I suppose?"

"Yes, that's why I was hoping they would let you know the special purpose of my journey."

"I have already explained that they cannot dictate to us, even if they had tried. And your Permit to Travel?"

"No, I don't have that either."

"So you arrive in Wonsan Province, a foreigner with no passport, in a car with no papers, and in our country with no Permit to Travel. And you want us to allow you to enter here?" she looked at the young men incredulously, and they both laughed and shook their heads. "Turn off your car engine, we will have to ask some higher authorities, if they are still at work. It's past office hours for them now. Maybe in the morning."

"You don't understand, there's one of our freighters in your port..."

"Your engine, you are wasting valuable resources. Maybe in Japan such waste is tolerated. If your country had not stolen all our resources, maybe we could be more generous."

Kimiko was thinking fast, but couldn't. She left the hut, opened the car door, said "we have problems" to the back seat, turned off the engine and walked back inside.

With a fresh blast of icy air and no more heat from the engine Bo cursed, "Just our luck, a sodding Jobsworth."

"What Jobsworth?" asked PJ forlornly, and sneezed,

"Bless you and stop sneezing. A Jobsworth is someone who won't let you do anything not preordained, with the words "It's more than my job's worth." Then remembering Lo Hi in the boot turned round and said in a load whisper "Lo Ho? Can you hear me? Knock if you can hear me?"

There were three taps from behind their seat.

"Kimiko has problems. And we're slowly freezing to death."

"How long, me too?"

"Don't talk. I don't know how long."

"Start engine?" asked PJ.

"We daren't," said Bo, "at least not until we are about to die and there's nothing left to lose."

Inside the hut Kimiko ran through her story. The freighter, the urgent call to attend, the absolute necessity of reaching it with urgent news before it sailed. The KPTP were unimpressed.

"What urgent news?"

The growing desperation let Kimiko rise to the occasion. "I am sorry, madam, but this is a matter of the utmost security and sensitivity. But if I'm not allowed to reach that freighter before she sails, you will have some very high level explaining to do."

"And if I let you through I will have even more high level explaining to do."

"Look, I can leave you my Foreigners Temporary Permit of Residence as security."

"So?"

"I will be driving back past here in a few hours, and I can collect it."

"I am not on duty in a few hours."

"But you can leave it for whoever is on duty, it's a deposit. I can leave money as a deposit."

"Are you bribing me? This is a most serious offence."

"No of course I am not bribing you. Relations between our countries are at a critical point, and this is an emergency."

"Very well, wait here. I will speak to my Colonel, see if he knows about it."

From inside the car Bo and PJ could see a light go on in a different room, and through the window they saw the woman on the telephone. "Shit or bust." said Bo.

"What?" said PJ.

"Never mind. For God's sake hurry up, we're dying out here." Bo and PJ were rubbing their invisible skins. "I hope this doesn't bring us back to life," said Bo. From the boot they felt shaking, unsure if it was from cold or fear, probably both.

They saw the woman put down the phone and the light turn off.

Inside the hut the woman said "My Colonel was at home. He is not pleased with this disturbance. He does not know anything about your circumstances, or your mission."

"Well he wouldn't; it's secret, that's the point."

"But he is a Colonel in the KPTP, it is most unusual."

"Did he say we could go?"

"We? You are not alone?"

"Sorry, yes you can see I'm alone, I meant me, the car, the job, everything."

"No, he did not say you could go."

Kimiko slumped back in her chair, now feeling desperate.

"He did say you could go if accompanied."

"Accompanied? By whom?"

"By an officer of the KPTP of course." She looked at the two men. You will take Yung Mo Lee here, on his first official business. Yung Mo Lee, you are to escort this...this foreign woman to the Port. You are to stay with her all the time, and immediately she is finished doing whatever it is she is claiming to be so important you will escort her right back here. Understood?"

The youth stood up straight and saluted. "Yes, comrade Captain."

"Good, and be quick. Now go, both of you."

From the car Bo saw them approach, told PJ to stop his chattering teeth and on no account to sneeze. He himself felt close to hypothermia, his body aching with cold blood and joints. Kimiko opened her door, the youth opened his door and she started the engine, and turned the radio on loudly.

"So" she said above the noise of the radio," you are my escort," and with that turned the heater on full blast and drove away through the dark black night and empty eerie countryside towards the port city.

66

Bo had noticed that like a well trained Japanese motorist Kimiko had fastened her seat belt, whereas the DTTP youth, quite probably on his maiden voyage, had not. After the first brush with warmer air he had stopped shivering, he felt in the dark for PJ, and pushed him gently but firmly onto the floor behind the front seats. Then he leant forward and tapped Kimiko gently on her left shoulder. She leaned back imperceptibly, and he whispered softly into her ear "Go faster and in ten seconds brake as hard as you can". Bo crouched behind her seat and waited. He could feel speed building and then felt himself and PJ being thrown hard into the seat back. Instantly there came a thud and cry from the passenger side. Bo sprung forward and grabbed the barely conscious youth, the blood from his face smeared visible on Bo's invisible arm.

"Everyone swap Lo Hi," said Bo, reaching into the youth's holster and taking his gun. PJ moaned and banged into Bo as he unwound. Kimiko was already out of the car, opening the boot. Bo followed from his side, felt the cold air and rushed to help bundle the youth into the boot. Lo Hi, a mass of coats, slammed her door shut and started cursing in shock, anger and relief in Korean.

They compared notes, bringing each other up to date, Kimiko's nightmare in the hut, PJ's conviction of dying from hypothermia, Bo's running through plans B to Z, and poor Lo Hi in the boot cold, dark and when the engine was off, desperate and abandoned.

But they were now back together, warm, amongst friends, with another hurdle behind them and a feeling of determination and unravelling fate binding them.

The sounds from the boot started softly at first, like thick dull thuds. Soft enough to ignore, but gradually too loud not to ignore. "What are we going to do with him?" asked PJ.

"Brake again?" suggested Kimiko.

"Not a bad idea," laughed Bo, "speed up a bit first and let us know."

Kimiko obliged down a slight hill then said, " Ready, five, four, three, two, one" and in spite of being ready in the back PJ and Bo crashed into seats in front of them. From behind a larger thud, then more groans. Lo Hi was even giggling again, "this could be fun."

"It is, but we do need to think what to do with him, he's only going to become more conscious. We don't want him yelling, screaming and bashing at the next roadblock."

"We cannot let him out and free, that is too dangerous," said Lo Hi.

"And cannot leave him there," said Kimiko.

After a few moments Lo Hi gasped." Bright idea!"

"Let's hear it," said Bo.

"Why don't I swap with him? They are expecting an escort, I'll be the escort."

"So we dress you up like him? Why not?"

"Bo, you have his gun, his ID will be on him somewhere."

"Well, he's too young to shave, looks like a girl, if you can pass yourself off as Kimiko you can pass yourself off as the KPTP Kid back there. Let's get him in the back between PJ and me, that'll shake him up too. Here's the gun."

"What do I do?"

"You could try pointing at him. Close range might be worth a try too."

Kimiko stopped the car. They were immediately confronted by the vast empty dark cold of the night, forgotten inside the cocoon they had been driving. Lo Hi and Kimiko walked round to the boot, opened it and pointed the gun at the terrified youth. Quaking, he got out and followed them round to the back door. Bo, as quickly as he could, jumped out, pushed the boy in next to PJ, and climbed back in tight beside him.

Pointing the pistol straight at his face, now already swollen and with dried blood wiped across it, Lo Hi told him to undress, and with shaking hands he started to undo his tunic. Then he felt first Bo's, then PJ's invisible hands pulling at his sleeves, felt their invisible forms squeezing against him, and started whimpering uncontrollably. With much squirming and cowering he was soon down to his underclothes.

"Look away please," announced Lo Hi from the front as she started to unbutton her clothes. Bo felt aware of PJ next to him putting his hands in front of his eyes, and feeling slightly caddish opened his wider to take a quick unseen peep. For the first time since arriving Bo's thoughts turned to Lo Hi and less noble deeds, and he quickly shut out the idea that this might be why he was in this mess in the first place.

Bo had to admit she looked surprisingly fetching dressed as a teenage storm trooper, the uniform was made to measure, and when she pulled her fingers up through her hair, and quickly put the cap on top she bore more than passing resemblance to the boy in the middle. She felt inside his pockets, and produced a thin wallet, but inside was his KPTP I/D. "Perfect. I am him," she said a little nervously.

"So we put him in back no clothes ?" asked Kimiko somewhat uncharitably.

"Firstly we need to wrap him up, tie him up to stop him banging around. What have we got?"

"One pair tights," said Lo Hi, holding up her recently discarded underwear from the floor. "One belt. We could tear off these sleeves and use them. The belts too, the belts from the overcoats."

Bo turned towards him. "Now a lot of boys would be very happy to be wrapped up in Lo Hi's lingerie, but you are going to be tied up tighter than most."

His arms and legs were knotted tightly by the belts, his mouth stuffed with his own underpants which were held in by Lo Hi's stockings, reinforced by her sleeves. "He not go now," said PJ.

"Except the boot," said Bo. "Come along now my friend," and the terrified boy was led back to his pit in the back of the car, and covered with the two thick coats.

They drove on through the night. Long empty roads passed through unlit empty villages, the road rose and fell through the dark, then there seemed to be a hill that rose and rose, and from the summit they saw distant yellow lights glowing behind lower hills. The port was now in sight, a large cold space away. A sense of nervousness returned at the thought of another roadblock and ensuing uncertainties. They rehearsed the most likely scenarios, none of which had a satisfactory outcome, or even the ring of likelihood attached to them.

At the bottom of the hill, just as one or two larger buildings suggested the city limits were nearing, torch beams moved in the night ahead of them. They slowed down at the familiar shape of a road check hut, and red and white barriers came out of the night.

"Here we go," said Kimiko as they approached. She wound down her window, and Lo Hi leant across to intercept them.

"From the KPTP. I am to escort this lady to the...."

"Yes, yes, we know all about you and the foreigner. Madame herself called! Go straight to the Port Entrance checkpoint."

"Thank you, thank you, " said Kimiko and Lo Hi together, a little too enthusiastically thought Bo uncharitably, but he too soon joined in the high spirits inside the little Corolla now bound on nervous energy and unknown fortunes straight for the Port.

67

Sammy Choo was worried, a little concerned, somewhat pre-occupied. The Friendship and Freedom Steam Engine Appreciation Tour No. 7's dinner table at the Golden Lodge was now two members short. The Englishman Beaumont-Pett had simply vanished, and a full scale alert and search was in operation. It happened from time to time; and most of the time the outcome was not too sinister: they became lost or thought they would have themselves a little adventure; one had even fallen in love. Shanghai had merely told him to keep an eye on Mr. Pett, he was on some kind of private wild goose chase for Sung Pi Jam and his daughter; but, Sammy reflected, difficult to keep an eye on him if he then vanishes. But the second one missing was more worrying, this Nark Am Dim cum Paul Kane was full-on CIA, not some kind of mercenary camp follower like himself, and for Sammy's own sake he was more than hoping the agent had not fallen into the wrong hands. Shanghai had only told him that he was checking on a Japanese woman from the Japan North Korea Trade Authority, and this too worried Sammy as anything to do with Japan and trade and Japanese residents was outside his usual sphere of influence, contacts and snitches.

Then Sammy heard a soft voice at his shoulder. "An urgent word with you now please." He looked around to see a Korean man in a prison guard's uniform. He instantly recognised Nark Am Dim, and hoped the others had not, and merely said in reply "Of course, right now. We will go to my apartment. Don't talk on the way, it's not far."

Behind Sammy's closed front door Nark Am Dim came straight to the point. "Sammy, I'm in big trouble. Tokyo said I could only contact you if I was in big trouble. I'm in big trouble. You've got to get me out of here."

"Slow down, Mr. Kane, slow down. What have you done?"

"It's better you don't know. I just need to get out of this particular country very quickly. What am I going to do?"

"Have you any hard money?"

"Nothing. There was about a thousand dollars in my case, but they've taken everything, my passport, clothes everything."

"Your passport is no good to you, and you have clothes, and a gun. I have some dollars, three thousand. And papers—you can take my identification."

"But I look nothing like you!" Nark Am Dim was becoming agitated.

"Stay calm. You have money, hard money that will buy you out of any problems. Start at fifty dollars. If anyone asks for more than one hundred, demand to see their supervisor. My tourist guide papers will get you anywhere without suspicion, you won't even need a Pyongyang Exit or Permit to Travel. Hold your finger over the i/d. You are Korean, you speak Korean, you will be wearing my clothes, and have my papers. You have a gun. You have dollars. You'll be on a night train on a busy route. You have a good chance."

"Night train, where to, Sammy?"

"To Wonsan Docks. That's the nearest port, it's busy, it's your best chance. The train will take you into the harbour centre. Look for fishing boats. Pick the one that is in the best condition, they'll be the greediest. Offer them all the money you have left. Head to Japan, you will be intercepted by a Japanese naval patrol boat, but the fishermen will know all about that."

Nark Am Dim paced nervously around the room, talking hurriedly to himself, running though the plan. Then he said: "It's not bad. It's my best chance. My only chance. But what about you? Your papers, clothes, the money?"

"Don't worry about me Mr. Kane. I will say you must have followed me back from the hotel. I did not suspect anything because all I saw was a prison guard. Then in the block you pulled a gun, marched me in here and mugged me. You took off your clothes, look here they are, and put on my clothes, then I recognised you as Mr. Kane from the tour. You demanded my papers at gunpoint. Then you tied me up, you better tie me up. Tomorrow when I am not at the hotel someone will come looking for me. I will be here. By then you will be at sea."

"And the money?"

"Don't worry, I have friends in Shanghai. Company friends. It's only money. Agents are more important. Now get changed quickly."

Nark Am Dim set to work, and minutes later emerged as Choo Sang Wa, Official Recognised Tourist Guide, rank Superintendent grade four, Pyongyang District, Democratic People's Republic of Korea.

"Not bad," said Sammy Choo, "but take my glasses too. They're strong, so just put them on at check points. Now tie me up. There's the big belt from the uniform, and use my belt too." Sammy Choo sat on a chair and Nark Am Dim tied him up, tighter and tighter still at Sammy's prompting.

"One more thing", said Sammy Choo. "hit me, hit me hard to knock me over." Nark Am Dim slapped his face, but Sammy Choo remained undamaged and upright, and said "Never mind, just push the chair over. Now go."

Sammy lay on the ground until he heard the corridor door slam shut. He shouted "Hin Li! All clear!" and his wife came through from the bedroom, and together they laughed, as she undid him in a matter of seconds. He stood to look out of the window, and with the lights off he saw Nark Am Dim cross the road heading for the train station. He walked over to the telephone and dialled the number of an old school friend. A voice answered "Mung Ny Gu."

"General, this is Choo Sang Wa."

"A-ha, greetings to the SSSA's favourite tour guide, and my good friend. This is little late for a social call, you must have some news."

"I have news, General." Choo Sung Wa told General Mung the plan. General Mung was pleased to say that Colonel Krop himself is on his way to Wonsan right now.

"And one other point General. The dollars on him are mine."

The General laughed. "Of course, Sang Wa, you will have them back. All of them too. Long live the Great Leader!"

"Long live the Great Leader!"

"Long live the Dear Leader!"

"Long live the Dear Leader!"

"Good bye, good work, Sang Wa."

"Good bye, General, good work is good pleasure."

68

There was only one road into Wonsan Port, and from it they could see the cranes in the skyline silhouetted by floodlights and followed the road to the entrance. The grey of the four metre high chain fencing with razor wire and its shadows matched the chill of the sky. At the entrance a guard pointed to a row of booths in front of them and asked them which one they wanted. They looked across the road and saw: Customs, Importation and Tariffs. Immigration and Resettlement. Tax and Duty Police. Korean Peoples Army. Tourist and Guidance Police. Transportation Policeforce. Construction Brigade.

"Any preference?" asked Kimiko.

"Lo Hi?" asked Bo.

"It's just luck. I bet the Tourist Police are busy! Let's try the Army, with luck they will all be conscripts on a night shift."

Lo Hi, head bowed against the chill, went into the Army hut, showed her new KPTP i/d, and ran through the Kimiko emergency state business/all official routine. From the car they could see inside, and saw salutes and smiles. Lo Hi left the hut and came back into the car.

"Well, we can go to the ship easily enough, but we have to have an Army escort," she said.

PJ said something dejectedly.

"Come on, father, we have come so far, we cannot fail now. I am making a good loyal government soldier. We have to succeed now."

They waited for ten minutes, and still there was no sign of the escort. Kimiko was hoping the boat was still there, Bo wanted to keep moving, and even Lo Hi was becoming impatient, and now she waved into the glass hut with palms upwards and shoulders shrugged. The guard inside her gave her a thumbs up, and tapped his watch and held up five fingers.

"Come on," said Kimiko, "I don't know when it sails, and we don't know how we are going to get on board surrounded by the

Army either."

From their left, from behind a car park of new Japanese cars, an old Russian era jeep arrived with canvas flapping and four soldiers inside.

The driver opened a sidescreen. "For the Sanyo Moro? Foreign VIP?"

"Yes please," said Lo Hi, and winding the window back up congratulated Kimiko on her new favoured VIP status. Bo told them all to look at every scene possible as a means of escape. The convoy of rackety old Russian jeep and svelte new Toyota Corolla headed directly across the square expanse of tarmac to the side of large dark blue freighter towering above them into the floodlights and shadows. "Sanyo Moro," announced the driver, pointing and showing his sergeant's stripes on his overcoat sleeve.

From the car they looked around: there was no gangway down the quay, but cranes loading and unloading containers just close by.

PJ sounded excited. "We jump on container?"

Bo was unimpressed. "No way, it's far too cold, much colder here than in Pyongyang. But keep thinking, we need a break."

Kimiko left them in the car with the engine running, and standing on the quay looked up at the deck and waved and shouted for attention.

"There's no point in doing that," said the sergeant "they cannot hear a thing. Try this," and he blew the jeep horn on and off, on and off. Still there was no sign of life on board, and the Sergeant motioned to Lo Hi in the passenger seat to do the same from the car, and so a solid Toyota sound mingled with the jeep's tinny intermittent beep to echo meaninglessly off the hull.

Bo looked over to the jeep and saw the soldiers all put their fingers in their ears, and the sergeant turned on his siren. After only a few seconds a Japanese seaman leant over the balustrade and waved.

The sergeant pointed at Kimiko, who left the car to make signals to come on board. The seaman signalled to stay there and wait. Kimiko rushed back into the Toyota, and the sergeant huddled back into the draughty jeep, and they both looked up to the deck for more signs of life.

PJ felt the knocks first. "Oh no, he wake again. Listen."

They all fell silent, Kimiko turned the heater fan off, and sure enough from the boot they could hear the muffled thuds of limbs banging on the bulkhead.

"Well at least they won't be able to hear him," said Kimiko, turning the heater back on. Inside the car they could not hear it any more either.

"The car will be moving though, we have to keep them away from it." said Bo, "Can you go and talk shop with them for a while?"

Without answering, Lo Hi left the Toyota and climbed into the back of the jeep, pushing one of the young conscripts to the middle.

"Boring foreigner," she said in a voice deeper than her own. "Just sits there, never talks. I bet it's more exciting here than at my Province border crossing."

"We try to keep everything in perfect control, true to the Dear Leader's wishes, comrade. Very little irregular happens here. We have comrades from the Immigration and Resettlement and the Customs Importation and Tariffs here, and the Tourist and Guidance Police too."

"We get most trouble from them," laughed the middle back seater and they all joined in.

"Come on," said the sergeant looking up at the ship, "it's cold out here."

"Sergeant," said the other back seater, "that foreigner's car keeps moving around."

"How do you mean 'moving around'?" he asked.

"Look at it, you'll see. There. From time to time."

They all looked and sure enough the back of the car was, from time to time, moving slightly on its springs.

"That's just the wind, and she left the engine on," said Lo Hi.

Lo Hi looked over to the car, and from the back sidescreen tried to indicate the danger with her eyes. The sergeant was the first out of the jeep, and walked around the car slowly and suspiciously.

"Trouble," Bo said from the back of the Toyota. "Kimiko, better get out and scream at the ship, we need a change of attention."

Kimiko immediately left the warmth of the car and standing well away from it waved and yelled again at the ship, but still no-one had returned.

"Is there something in the car?" asked the sergeant from the jeep's front seat.

"No," said Lo Hi, "just the two of us, the foreigner and me, her escort."

"Open the boot."

"She will have the keys."

"Madam," shouted the sergeant to Kimiko away on the quay, and making a key turning gesture repeated "open the boot."

69

Sung Pak Dong's first helicopter ride has been in the dark, but now he can sense the shaking increase as the machine descends, and he can see light and then lights below. Down there are cranes, some containers, a few ships. As they become lower he sees men looking up and moving away. He sees snow flurry under them and then they are landing in the centre of the docks. The machine starts to whine as the blades slow down. Colonel Krop nods to the door then to Sung Pak Dong. He opens it and they all scramble out. Outside it is cold again, icy cold and windy too.

Colonel Krop strides, then jogs, then strides again towards the huts. Closing in he sees they are manned by the major agencies: Customs—Importation and Tariffs, Immigration and Resettlement, Tax and Duty Police, Korean Peoples Army, Tourist and Guidance Police, Transportation Policeforce and the Construction Brigade. He walks straight through the Korean Peoples Army door without knocking. There is one soldier sitting by the electric heater bar. The soldier looks around with annoyance, sees the SSSA Colonel and his three followers and jumps to attention.

"Who's in charge here?!" demands Colonel Krop.

"Sergeant Kri, sir. They are all out on an exercise. Helping a Japanese VIP find her ship. Shall I call them?"

"VIP be damned! No, give me the radio." The soldiers points to the radio-telephone on the wall, and before he could start replying Colonel Krop seizes it. "Sergeant Kri this is Colonel Krop of the SSSA. Report back to your base immediately. How many men do you have? Over."

There is only static in reply. Colonel Krop tries again, this time talking more loudly into the telephone handset. Still more static. The soldier tells him there is a loose connecter and sometimes it does not work. They are waiting for the authorisation to repair or replace it.

"Which other units are here?" asks Colonel Krop slamming

back the headset.

"The Tourist and Guidance Police are next door, sir. The Tax and Duty Police will be here in the morning. Immigration and Resettlement too."

Colonel Krop storms out, runs next door and throws that door open too. Inside are four young men. Conscripts, Colonel Krop knows immediately. He curses again. "Anyone in charge here?"

One of them stands up, sees the SSSA uniform and mumbles in fear. Colonel Krop asserts himself immediately. He orders them to attention, orders Sung Pak Dong and the plain clothes comrades from the helicopter to join them and orders all of them to form a line.

"Right. This is simple. A traitor has escaped from prison in the capital and will be trying to leave the country. He is working with a Japanese woman, and she is here already. We will spread out as I instruct and radio to me if you see any foreigners. The traitor himself is middle aged, will probably have his daughter and the Japanese bitch with him. Take a radio each."

"Sir," the leader of the Tourist and Guidance Police replies, "we do not have radios, we are the Tourist and Guidance Police. We use whistles."

"Whistles?" Colonel Krop feet are off the floor.

"Just whistles, sir."

"Very well. We each take a whistle. I suppose when you blow into it some kind of sounds appears?"

"It does, sir, the correct whistle sound."

Colonel Krop takes them all outside and directs them to different points around the docks. He beckons Sung Pak Dong to come closer. "Officer Cadet Sung, you will patrol that area behind the new cars over there. You see where I mean?"

"Yes, sir, the parked cars behind the two blacks cranes."

"That's it. If you see your father, your sister, the Japanese whore—wait till I get my hands on her—or any foreigner, any number of foreigners, probably white foreigners, what will you do?"

"I will blow this whistle, sir."

"Yes, Officer Cadet Sung Pak Dong, I know you will blow your whistle. What else will you do, will you do before that?"

"I will identify them, sir."

"Between identifying them and blowing your whistle, Officer Cadet Sung Pak Dong, what will you do?"

"Sir?"

"Duty. You will do your duty." Colonel Krop is staring directly, closely at him.

"Yes, sir." Without being asked Sung Pak Dong clicks himself to attention. Colonel Krop looks at him again, nods and dismisses him. "Next, you!"

Sung Pak Dong jogs off into position. His breath hangs briefly near him with each step, then blows quickly away. The floodlights cast strange shadows around him. He sees some ice and skips around it. Behind him he can hear some shouts and some mechanical noises, and then a whine as the helicopter engine starts. He stops to look around. The rotors are turning faster, and now he cannot see them except as a blur. The snow around it is blown clear and slowly it lifts off. He sees two search lights below it, and instead of leaving as he expected it stays close to the ground, its lights patrolling the dockside. With a start he remembers his duty, and jogs to his position behind the parked cars.

70

Captain Kenishi Ono, master of the Sanyo Moro, leant over the guard rail and said—almost to himself but so that First Mate Moriki Makino could also hear—"What the hell is happening now?"

"Nothing is easy here Captain."

"It's a first class heap of shit, Makino-san, as we all know. Any idea who they are?"

"Never seen any of them, but she's bowing and waving like one of us."

"God preserve us, better get her up here. Lower the gangplank."

Captain Ono was not in the best frame of mind; it was true to say that of all the ports in all the world this one was his least favourite. In and out. Job done. Home. His directions to himself and his crew were clear enough. He did not mind corruption; he knew Lagos as well as Mumbai as well as Vladivostok. But here it was the pretence that annoyed him; the pretence of the socialist collectivists, and the reality of private greed. And it wasn't straightforward like everywhere else. Here the rules were simple enough on the surface: money may not change hands, unless it finds its way into one of their famous Leader's Singapore bank accounts, but anything else is more than welcome. No, it was the structure of it all, the strict hierarchy of gifts and the appropriateness for respective individuals. A Sony CD player was worth more or less nothing to a crane driver, yet everything to a cleaner. Work that one out.

As the gangplank landed on the quay the Captain and First Mate walked down and saluted the sergeant. Distracted from the car, the sergeant walked over the quay's edge to return the salute and meet the two seamen.

Kimiko extended her hand. "Captain, I am Kimiko Sato from the Japan North Korean Trade Authority in Pyongyang. This is my local escort, Private Yung Mo Lee. I need to discuss an urgent matter regarding your shipment. Can we please go inside somewhere warm and private?"

"By all means," the Captain agreed, and told Makino-san to take them to the bridge.

"But first, Captain," said the sergeant "we must ask the Japanese lady to let us inspect her car."

"Later, Sergeant, I'm sure that can wait. The lady's business does sound more important. And none of us wants to freeze to death while you search a car. If you please."

From inside the car Bo and PJ could only look and worry. The Sergeant was gesturing to the car, pointing to the boot, and then they saw Kimiko, followed by Lo Hi, the First Mate and then the Captain walk, practically run, up the gangplank. The Sergeant motioned one of his men towards the car.

"PJ, we need another one of our famous diversions, and quickly. We'll get out your side. Then we'll rush them. I'll push the head man into the water, then you just push in whoever you can. Ready? Alright, shoot."

They climbed out through the half open door, and Bo landed on PJ who had not moved away. Immediately the cold hit again, and Bo rushed as hard as he could at the sergeant, and sent him stumbling towards the edge. He landed heavily, looked up and around startled and amazed at what had happened, and Bo picked up both his legs and swung him over the edge with a little kick to help him on his way. Before anyone knew what had happened there as a loud splash and a desperate cry from the water. The other three guards gathered to peer over, and Bo helped two into the water, but PJ was less quick and had somehow managed to get caught in a wrestling match with the last soldier. Bo walked over and hit the soldier in the face. He fell backwards as much with surprise as force, but it only served to tighten his grip and as he began to fall off the quay Bo heard PJ scream for help as they were both falling in together.

Bo grabbed at where he thought PJ would be, but seemed to find only his torso. Frantically searching for something to grab onto, a limb, any limb, Bo found an arm and held it tightly and pulled it at the same time kicking at the soldier who had now recovered onto the quay. Bo threw PJ to one side, shouted at him to run up the gangway and hit and kicked the soldier as he was unholstering his pistol. Bo leapt behind him, and grabbing his collar in one hand and hair in the other, manhandled him over the side to join his colleagues in the filthy melted ice below.

Bo shouted at the gangway, hoping he could still be heard. "PJ, get on board. I'm going to lose the car," Bo sprinted back to the car, landed on the driver's seat, adjusted it backwards, put the heater on max and as slowly as he dared drove it to behind the rows of new imported Toyotas on the far side of the quay.

71

Now standing still, Sung Pak Dong really feels the deep cold, much colder even than in Pyongyang. It is so damp too, and soon he is shaking. He walks up and down the line of cars. Toyotas. Japanese, he reflects. Why Japanese? Maybe one day there will be Korean cars, unified Korean cars. He hates the Japanese, looks around, sees no-one is looking and kicks at a door. The door remains the same. He kicks again, harder, still no mark or impact. He notices the helicopter to his right, and stamps his feet against the cold and looks at it scouring the quayside.

The headlights from his left he does not see at first, but then they catch his eye and he turns towards them. They are heading straight at him now. He ducks down behind a car. He crouches behind another car, better placed. He looks through the side windows and sees the headlights shining straight at him. He lets out a small breath and squats down again, fumbling in his pocket for the whistle. The car has now stopped just two rows in front of his. He cannot find the whistle, feels in the other pocket, hears the door open and looks up. He is terribly cold, and shaking all over from cold and fear. He will rush the driver, pull him down and then blow the whistle. He stalks forward. The door is open now, he is standing right behind it, but no-one is leaving the car. He notices the car move upwards as if a weight was leaving it. He sees the door slam shut and a light inside go out. He hears a human sound, not in Korean, and sees footprints and hears breaths, both leaving to his far left. He has not been looking in that direction. He does now.

72

Leaping out from the car and running flat out back to the gangplank, Bo could see a commotion building below the ship. He sprinted hard for a minute, silently but with large puffs of breath hanging visible incongruously in the air, just in time to see the gangplank being raised and the first of a crowd gathering around the soldiers in the water. Without pausing he ran straight up the gangplank, leapt onto the end now a metre and rising slowly off the ground, hauled himself up across the biting cold steel as he heard sirens building behind him.

73

Sung Pak Dong sees to where he can hear the phantom moving, and by the sounds he thinks it is moving at the speed of running, he follows to the first row of parked cars, then stops. He is feeling for the whistle again. Then he sees Lo Hi on a gangplank of a ship, then he follows a line up the gangplank and sees his father. Both are waving towards the movement. The gangplank is rising. The gangplank gives a jerk downwards. They all disappear into the ship. Then he sees some Tourist and Guidance men, leaning over the side and pointing to the water. The whistle. He finds the whistle. He pulls it to his lips, but stops. It is too late.

Sung Pak Dong has seen everything and he has seen nothing. He can feel the tears start to sting his eyes. He is shaking now with cold, now he is still he notices his feet and ears are hurting, then the sobbing starts, and the shaking from the sobbing includes the shaking from the cold. He has failed in his duty; failed both his families. The helicopter is now approaching, he can hear the rotor noise increase and can see the spotlights approaching. Instinctively he stands up and looks to his right. He knows they cannot see him crying and see what he has seen. He knows to look the other way, away from shame and betrayal. Even the deep, deep cold is better than the reality of failure, of dishonour.

74

At the top of the gangplank Bo looked up at the stairs towards the bridge, leapt over a chain and charged onto the bridge room, bitterly cold, out of breath, with aching muscles and agonised frost bitten feet. He flung open the door, saw Kimiko and Lo Hi, heard PJ breathing as heavily as he was, and the crew looking in shock from them to the Captain and back again.

"What's this?," asked the Captain incredulously. "Invisible men?"

"Captain, we can explain, but later, we must go. We must go now," urged Kimiko.

"No excuse needed, and I wouldn't believe it anyway. Now I've seen everything, except here I haven't seen it. How many are there?"

"How many what?"

"Invisible men? Women? People?"

"Captain, we are two," said Bo. The actual proof of hearing sound come from an unseen mouth, an unseen body, stopped all the wonder. "We've got the Exit Permits, let's go," ordered the Captain. "All officers to your work. Makino-san, pretend to help get those fools out of the water, the rest of you prepare to leave. I want to leave here now. Now."

PJ was sneezing again, almost uncontrollably, and Lo Hi asked for blankets for her father.

"Of course, and more," said the captain, and into a telephone "Steward, to the bridge. With blankets. Two blankets. Four blankets."

When the Steward arrived the captain told him to leave the blankets on a chair and to prepare four guest cabins, and to report back when ready.

"The less they all know the better. Philippinos, all the crew except the officers, very superstitious. What is your name?"

"Sung Lo Hi, and somewhere there is my father, Sung Pi Jam. The other person is an Englishman, Beaumont Flowerdew-Pett."

The Captain saw the blankets leave the chair haphazardly and become wrapped around two invisible human forms. "And you are not really Miss Sato's escort I presume?"

"No, Captain, I am not. My father's life was in danger, as were all our lives."

"Will we see them some time?"

"In a few hours they will be visible. Now they must be warm."

"Naked out there, I would catch pneumonia."

"We may well have done so," said one of the forms. "Please let me introduce myself, Bo Pett. I look forward to shaking your hand later. If we are lucky maybe over breakfast, if that is not too presumptuous. And thank you for taking such good care of us. We did not know what to expect."

"Breakfast is nearly upon us, and it will be my honour, Mr. Pett. As for the welcome, I hate this God forsaken dump a much as anyone else. No disrespect Miss Sung. Ah the steward. Yes, Jimmy, which cabins are ready? Very well."

The steward left, they gathered themselves and the Captain showed them to their cabins on the deck below. "Come up whenever you are ready. We will breakfast at eight if you feel like joining us. Otherwise at your convenience. Oh, and congratulations on your brave escape, we look forward to hearing all about it later."

75

Nark Am Dim arrived at Wonsan Docks train station. Outside it was dark, dark and cold. Still aching from his beating he stood up to leave. The journey had been tense, but two security checks and a hundred dollars lighter and later, he had arrived. He walked onto the platform, wrapped Sammy Choo's overcoat tightly around himself, showed his ticket and left the station.

Without knowing where to go, where to find any fishing boats, he set off to find someone to show him where they might be. There was no-one around. No-one, the docks were completely empty; cold, misty, echoing and deserted. He saw some huts in the distance, and one with a light shining, now two with lights shining as he approached them. Now there, he read all the signs above the huts: Customs, Importation and Tariffs. Immigration and Resettlement. Tax and Duty Police. Korean Peoples Army. Tourist and Guidance Police. Transportation Policeforce. Construction Brigade. The lights that were on were in the Korean Peoples Army hut and the Tourist and Guidance police hut. Brilliant, thought Nark Am Dim, here's the Tourist Police just when you need a little guidance from them, guidance to find the fishing fleet.

He knocked on the door. No reply. He knocked again, more loudly, still no reply. He opened the door, inside an old electric fire was on, but the hut was empty. He walked down to the other lit hut, that of the Korean Peoples Army. More knocks, another opened door, and this time an agitated young conscript who told him the Tourist and Guidance Police were all out, out on an exercise by the quays. Where exactly? The conscript took him outside and pointed. In the distance Nark Am Dim could just make out a group of uniforms standing by the water, with a big ship moving off the quay behind them. He thanked the conscript and huddled again in the overcoat, hunched his shoulders and walked briskly towards them.

He arrived at the quayside. Six men were looking down in the water. In the water were four other men, screaming desperately. As he watched one of them disappeared below the surface, rose again briefly, then disappeared again, not to return. To his right two other men were working their way down a ladder, shouting at the men in the water to come to them. Then from his other side he saw three planks being thrown into the water. One of the men tried to swim towards a plank, but he too sank below the water, rose and sank back again without rising. Another man was swimming towards the ladder, thrashing desperately in the water towards the outstretched arms on the ladder.

"I want that ship stopped! Now! Where is the news about this ship's Exit Permit? Swim for the plank, man!"

In a freeze frame Nark Am Dim recognised the voice. Out of the corner of his eye Colonel Krop recognised the face. Colonel Krop rushed over to him and grabbed him clean off the ground.

"You! What do you know about this Japanese ship?!"

"Nothing Colonel, I am looking for a fishing boat." Nark Am Dim thought he had said something particularly stupid as soon as he said it.

"Fishing boat is it? Well the best place to find them is in the sea!"

"No, please don't!" but it was too late, Nark Am Dim was flying through the air and felt his lungs fill with icy water. He rose to the surface, splashing uncontrollably and shouting for help. Then he saw a bicycle arrive and a soldier jumping off it and running to Colonel Krop. Then he heard Colonel Krop laugh and say "Thank General Mung very much, but he seems to have given himself in already!" Colonel Krop then walked over to the edge and shouted down to him: "So, CIA it is. Very interesting. I suppose we better get you out, but you will wish we had left you in. Fetch him out! Get down that ladder again!"

76

Kimiko said good night to the others in the passageway, closed the door of her cabin, leant back on it, stayed there for several seconds, puffed out her cheeks, blew them out again, and then burst out laughing. She'd done it! Against all the odds, against these Korean government dogs, against this filthy climate, in spite of the bungling idiots at the CIA, against her parents' advice in the first place and everyone else in the whole wide world since then, she, she, Kimiko Sato, yes she had done it. She went over to the mirror and looked straight into it. Eye to eye, knowing to knowing, slowly she saw a smirk then a smile, a smile growing larger, then a brush of the hair off the forehead. I'm going to look great again, she thought, pulling off all her clothes and pulling over the shower curtain.

Scrubbing and shampooing and rinsing and drying every last bit of the filthy place off she knew she only had some random clean clothes garnered from the officers to wear. She spreads them out: funny mix, she thought, yellow tee-shirt, thick blue sweater, brown jeans and tennis shoes. Ah, yes, and underpants. Socks even. What a sight. Could work out OK though, better on TV.

She lay down on the bunk, propped up the pillow, took out the borrowed exercise book and ballpoint pen and started to make some notes, notes to herself:

"FOR MY EYES ONLY. KS"

Passport…none, no problem, bigger drama, more heroic.

Clothes…no problem, look like bigger adventurer in these. Men's clothes.

TV….I'll be the only Jp. speaker, so spokesperson. Radio too.

Career….yes please! CIA direct from now? JCIA double deal?? AI treble deal??? Mata Hara here we come. But needs covert. Maybe publicity better = politics???

Or AI, big start too there now, maybe head of Asia, upstage Greenpeace daring-do!!

Career politics? Money, bank a/cs everywhere, fame, 1st Jp. woman PM, me? why not?? Parents help with Liberals, univ. grad. Top spy. CV or what?

VERSUS

Career secret service w/JCIA? . Underground, danger, fun, <u>but</u> no money honey. Yes to more Bo, no to more commie dog. Maybe more…no

So politics. Call home, get TV cameras on dock. Picture with captain. "TOP SPY ABDUCTS NORTH KOREAN BOMB MAKER" saves world. Standing for election.

Talk shows, find booking agent. Book rights? Film rights. YES! This would make v.g. vvg film!

Others? PJ to USA, maybe I take him! Grt. CIA intro. Lo HI, stay in Jp. marry some K. hope very happy only decent one K. Bo=back to England, marry boring.

Me: fame + fortune, destiny of grt Jp. woman history

Kimiko felt her eyes now tired, and having written nothing more on the exercise book for ten minutes, laid it down, turned off the light, and dreaming of the phone call home summoning the TV crews tomorrow morning, drifted off into a mightily contented, deep, deep sleep, soporific with the smug certainty of success and celebrity ahead of her forever.

PJ said goodnight to the others in the passageway, closed the door firmly behind him, and lay exhausted, still wrapped in his blankets, on the bunk. He lifted the blankets and saw nothing, but not long to go until he returns to flesh. He prodded himself in the thigh, and felt his finger reassuringly nudge into his flesh. At least he was warm, finally warm.

What to make of it all? He was happy enough in the Power Plant laboratory, had a certain seniority, had a certain amount of respect, and suddenly ooof! his whole life had changed. But why? He had never betrayed anyone, would not know where to start. And the thought of dealing with the U.S. warmongers was ridiculous. He hated everything they stood for. Why him? He would never know, and that was all he would know. Someone had snitched, for whatever reason, he had seen it before. But somehow, someway, he had crossed the divide, the divide between seeming loyalty and seeming connivance, and a divide between citizen and non-citizen, life in a warm apartment in Pyongyang and life freezing, ill and worked to death in a hard labour camp.

He thought back to his time in Moscow, the golden days. There he had the world around him; his youth, his future, part of a great power, and inside that great power, one of the elite working for the benefit of the masses. Things were not perfect, but he had everything, everything he wanted. A car, his was one of the few. Not that he wanted it really, it just came. Then back to Pyongyang. Fewer privileges, but everything was so certain. We were all together, together in trying to build utopia, and together in the hardships too. The years of near starvation. The rations were small, but deserved, deserved together, and in old age they would still come even if you could not work because you had worked for the greater good when you could. The Great Leader was not just an inspiration, an example, but the reason of our striving together, to please him and to love his vision of how we could stand alone against the US imperialists. Then the famine and drought years, the Arduous March, how they had all pulled together, even the worker and peasant classes.

And now that is where he would have to go, the home of US hegemony, he knew that much already. He knew what would happen. He would be arrested on arrival, but kept on board and interrogated here first. Probably by the Japanese running dogs. He would tell them all he knew. Under torture he would reveal nothing because he could reveal nothing because he knew nothing and he knew nothing because he was a scientist who kept his nose clean and loved the Dear Leader as much as the Great Leader. Then he would be transferred to the USA, more questions, more torture, probably in Guantanemo Bay with all the other victims of US expansionism. But if he told them enough he could stay, and he knew he would have to stay because he could not go back. The door of certainties had closed behind him. Even if the Chinese radio was right and his country was years behind in technology, he could only tell them whatever he knew; they could laugh but he could stay. Stay to be unemployed, with no pension, no future, working illegally, controlled by the mafia, but he would have to stay and fend for himself, one of the millions left destitute by the state.

Ah, but Lo Hi, that was the future, why he must work at what he could, collaborate with the US desperadoes, for her future. If she was there he would look after her like a Chinese husband who stayed at home if he could not work properly. He leaned over, feeling slightly better, with slightly more purpose. Maybe Canada has fewer gangsters, that's what they say, certainly in power they would have fewer gangsters, and with these less ruffled thoughts and a less perplexed heart he fell into the deep sleep from which he would at least awake with his own visibility.

Bo said goodnight to the others in the passageway, kicked the door firmly behind him with what would have been his heel, unwound the blankets and fired up the shower. Without thinking about anything else he jumped in and scrubbed whatever he could feel for all he was worth. Finally clean and out of the scalding stream, he leant back and, smiling with amusement, remembered the water jumping mysteriously off an invisible shield, himself.

He didn't want to think, never had gone in for that sort of thing much, but as he lay naked in the warmth of the cabin, he switched off the light, and lay there, surprisingly awake, without distractions and thoughts could not help themselves to arise.

It had been quite a crack. God knows how he had got away with it. Slipping on the tiles in the prison. Jeez, still got the bruises. And that sodding dog, hope it's OK now. And that young twit in the back of the car. And that guy in Kimiko's cupboard.

And for what? The chance to jump into bed with Lo Hi? That would come, something to look forward to. He smiled. Bo, they always said your brain was somewhere else! No, there must have been more to it than that. When she came to him in Tokyo. The walk in the park. La Cuss. Oh cripes, La Cuss and all that wedding stuff back home. Settling down, more studying, practicing law. Maybe not. Could he not just stay in Japan? He'd have to make sure PJ was OK, and Lo Hi too. That's it, a postponement. If I tell them now the wedding must be delayed, they'd understand. Or would they? Probably not. All hell would break loose. But if he wasn't there, all hell breaks loose a long way away. He couldn't let them all down, all relying on him for the big day. But it's not the big day; it's the millions of little days after that. And no-one back home had heard from him for two weeks, at least he should call from the ship now.

But what if he stayed here? Lo Hi was clearly some kind of freedom fighter, maybe they could go back in again, in summer next time, and topple the whole stinking lot. A life of adventure. Maybe MI5 or 6 or whatever it was called. After all he'd proved himself. He could go anywhere, do anything, all for some kind of cause, freedom, that sort of stuff. Amnesty, human rights, all good news for him and good news for everyone. Bo wished he could stop thinking, that it would somehow all just work out for the best. An hour later the same movie kept repeating, the choices stark, the solution somehow outside him. Call Kelly, at least call Kelly. Then his thoughts turned to Lo Hi next door.

He sat up and reached for the light, and turning it on noticed himself. He was back as flesh and blood. He stood up in front of the mirror. All there, bruised but all there, all here. Not very graceful, bit of a wreck. He sat back down, put his head in his hands, and without knowing why, stood up, wrapped himself again in the two blankets, opened the door and walked out into the passageway.

Lo Hi said goodnight to the others in the passageway, turned the door handle quietly behind her and sat on the edge of the bed thinking. A shower, yes first a shower. Clean again, refreshed and happy, she put on the random clothes provided, set to work on her hair with the borrowed brush, and rested against the pillow.

It would be America, she felt sure of that. America, the great hope of all freedom fighters in Pyongyang. She would look after PJ there, be his manager. With his secrets they could make lots of money, he could be a celebrity, like she had seen on the smuggled videos. California, they would settle in California, have some help in the house, a big house, endless summers. All the years of under-ground meetings, the danger, the terrible fate she had delivered for her father, all behind her now, not just behind her, but gone forever like waking from a terrible nightmare and find instead life is a fantastic dream.

But Bo. Missing from my dream. If only he would be there too. But would he fit into life in California? What little he had said about America was all old world. She could see he would not be easy there, not at first. She would have to do the work, but if she could get him some modern clothes, shorts and tee shirts, a Hawaiian shirt! Maybe he could learn Spanish, she had heard that is useful. He could live the dream too if he were shown it. She could see him now, with a haircut, that would be the first thing, and he could learn to barbeque. What a host, and she the hostess, with free people everywhere, honest politicians, no secret police, no phone taps. They would be rich, free and famous. Children, but what about mixing races? Taboo at home, but she had heard they make the smartest children. Bo is so handsome and she could be pretty with Californian hair and beauticians.

Then she remembered. How could she have forgotten? He is engaged, married by December. But still her dreams returned of life with him there, a new Bo, and new father, a new her, a new, new life. Well maybe there are other Bos there, who knows. But he'll be married, cold in England like in Korea, the lost part of her dream come true. She was feeling drowsy now, her eyes just closing for sleep, when there were three short taps on the door. She rose on an elbow.

"Shabbu Sh'u!"

"What ho!"

She sprung out of bed, loocked quickly in the mirror, run her fingers through her hair, and opened the door. Bo's hand went around her waist, and his kiss went from her forehead to her cheeks to her mouth. They closed the door and turned off the lights. Bo's blankets fell to the floor, and they slowly lay on the bed together, for what was left of the night.

Epilogue

That Christmas Bo could not help thinking that Lo Hi had gone a little overboard. He knew that in America they went in for that sort of thing, schmaltzy and all, but heavens above here they were in San Diego, baking hot, and Lo Hi had no more idea about the birth of the infant Jesus than she had about St. Nikolaus and the rest of them. Still, it kept her happy, and enthusiastic, and boy, was she enthusiastic. A freelance translator by day, and housewife superstar by night, she had just started a company, her very first company as she kept reminding him, organising conferences for South Koreans in San Diego, and for Americans in Seoul.

Lo Hi had adopted America, and all it and she stood for, as well as the CIA had adopted PJ. It hadn't been a bad deal for any of them. Bo got his hands on Lo Hi, Lo Hi got her hands on America, and the Americans got their hands on PJ. Kimiko had visited them recently, in California as head of a Japanese cultural delegation, part of her new job as a member of the Diet. She said one day she would be Prime Minister, and they had all believed her.

No, it hadn't worked out too badly, but Bo was listless, had been for some time. It hadn't helped when his mother, the dreaded Miriam, phoned and dropped in to the conversation that Kelly Cuss was engaged to a Belgian doctor and they were both working for Medicins Sans Frontieres in Mali, doing a little good for the world, having an adventure, she added pointedly.

Then she had called again earlier that week, said Bo had received a letter from Her Majesty's Government marked Strictly Confidential. It looked important; should she open it? He supposed she should. She did. It was from the Foreign and Commonwealth Office. He had been invited to an interview, at his convenience at Vauxhall Cross. What's Vauxhall Cross? she had asked. Bo was about to reply MI6, but thought better of it. Don't know mother. Shall I forward you the letter? Yes please. It was the letter he was waiting for now. He thought he would attend, for Her Majesty's sake.